The Curtain of Hope

Steven Sanderson

Steven Sanderson

Steven Sanderson

To My Sister Mary

The Last and Loveliest Leaf on the Tree

Steven Sanderson

CONTENTS

Steven Sanderson

Steven Sanderson

ACKNOWLEDGMENTS

I have benefited from patient and sometimes sympathetic editor/readers throughout the long process of writing. Their comments have improved the result, if not my disposition. Foremost among these is my dear wife Rosalie, who has enough trouble with me, without putting up with the characters who have come to live with us. Conrad Bibens, Brian Rickenbacker, Kent Redford, Richard Fagen, Steve McCormick, and Rosemary Magee have all given good advice without offering to bear responsibility for the result. My dear cousin Shirley Skufca Hickman, a writer, teacher and lover of fine literature, has been a constant source of encouragement, inspiration and love.

Steven Sanderson

Hope, that comforter in danger! If one already has solid advantages to fall back upon, one can indulge in hope. It may do harm, but will not destroy one. But hope is by nature an expensive commodity, and those who are risking their all on one cast find out what it means only when they are already ruined; it never fails them in the period when such a knowledge would enable them to take precautions. Do not let this happen to you, you who are weak and whose fate depends on a single movement of the scale. And do not be like those people who, as so commonly happens, miss the chance of saving themselves in a human and practical way, and, when every clear and distinct hope has left them in their adversity, turn to what is blind and vague, to prophecies and oracles and such things which by encouraging hope lead men to ruin.

Thucydides, *The History of the Peloponnesian Wars*

Steven Sanderson

PROLOGUE

Great trouble requires but a small place. Even ordinary trouble seems great, if the place is small enough and the people willing. The seamlessness of gossip, the claustrophobia of homogeneous communities, the one-sidedness of Main Street, the invention of drama in lives bereft of it. Small town dullness is black powder in a keg, inert enough as separate elements, until combined and touched by fire.

Were Narcissus the patron saint of small places, he would have a great remit where people are prevented from seeing beyond their own image. Small town people, in a limbo neither rural nor urban, live with only fitful understanding of the connection between past and future. They struggle to understand the structuring forces that limit their prospects or the historical confines that circumscribe their lives. But somehow they hope that the future will be better than the past. In other words, they are like everyone.

The story that follows is an emulsion of trouble and hope in a small place. Nothing happens nowhere. Life requires a stage. Pincus, Georgia, a faded smudge seven miles south of the Savannah River and the South Carolina border — which are the same — provides the setting. Like all places, it has its own integrity, decorated with ordinary people, its social orbits vanishingly small, self-centered in the usual ways, and weighed down with daily life. With all the world a stage, places like Pincus are the smallest venues, barely visible stars in the sky, which fail to stand out against the firmament. Normally, Pincus escapes notice, despite the burdens of its protagonists, their slow sink into entropy, and the dull specificity of their stories. But stages and actors ought to align, and sometimes they don't. Place and people are twin sides of a mold. When the place and the people somehow mismatch, well, that's how a story unfolds.

If Pincus now barely twinkles, in its heyday, some long time ago, the site on which it eventually blossomed must have been *something*. *Something* in the sense that the other side of the moon must be: unknown to most of human experience, but alluring. A long time ago would be before Europeans arrived, when the Muskogee federation presided over a vast network of towns and trading posts, now all long gone. Pincus wasn't Pincus then, but something prior, unnamed but still a place with its people, violent and dynamic and completely elusive to the modern mind. The Amerindians who waded in the swamps, left footprints in the mud, fought and fell ill, concocted stories to explain away the dark, invented tools from rough nature, traded broadly with strangers, left middens of shells and trash, perhaps stared out from the barrier islands westward across the spartina-carpeted salt marsh to dream of their future. As we might have in their place. The substance of those dreams is lost to us. The fires they camped by, the places they rested, the game they hunted, all are gone. They are gone, too, as if they never lived.

In a story more familiar if little better known, Spanish and English explorers and colonists contributed plagues, war and conspiracy, along with their singular devotion to land speculation and theft. None of these was absent in the aboriginal world, but as a result of European arrival, the Old Indigenous World died. Guale and Coosa communities vanished. The Creek Indians fell under the burdens of British settlement and the pernicious effect of trade with Europe, followed by American expansion. Little remained from that epoch but the story told by the winners. Sonorous indigenous names remain today, but mean little: Ashepoo, Combahee, Edisto, Yamasee, Yamacraw, Ocmulgee, Oconee, Hitchiti. Tribal nations turned into the names of subdivisions, rivers, bridges and reservoirs. Legends vanished, too. The fabled beauties of the Oauquaphenogaw lake, who, according to William Bartram, gave sustenance to early traders, now lie under the Okefenokee Wildlife Refuge, unimagined by tourists and park managers, except around the campfire. Likewise, the mythical city of Cofitachequi, said to be the home of a generous and elegant queen – gone, along with every recognized native nation on the South Carolina coastal plain. The remains of the pre-European world were swallowed up by relentless ignorance, messianism and ambition, dispersed by tide and time, forced west by colonial war and American imposition. The battle for the coast erased the past, both in myth and history.

Pincus sits biophysically on this same Georgia coastal plain. Its lowland geography lay underwater millennia ago and soon enough in the geological calendar will likely submerge again, a forgettable place, alive for a brief time, marked by vestigial dune ridges covered in pine. River meanders of the Savannah, Ogeechee and Oconee feed cypress swamps that betray no direction or end, edged by red cedar gnarls sporting blue berries, birthed to flavor wild game. Hardwood hammocks of oak, hickory and Carolina ash appear where fire is infrequent and the drainage good. Weedy Yaupon holly offers its leaves for tea. Wiregrass and switch cane meadows bake in the sun, all supporting an extraordinary abundance of fauna and flora. To lovers of the piney woods, with its tall, slender, whispering loblollies and longleaf, its beautyberry, wax myrtle and dog fennel, this is God's country. To outsiders, it is a buggy swamp. To the buggy swamp, humans come and go, ignored by the woodpeckers, alligators and snakes.

In the 1730s, the seed of modern Pincus germinated as a little entrepot for the deerskin trade, connected to the innumerable settlements of the great native Mississippian commercial empire and the newly arrived Georgia colonists. At least that's how the colonists viewed it. Blessed by a little creek that debouched downstream into the Savannah River, Pincus became a mercantile confluence. It preceded the death of Oglethorpe, the rise of slavery and the burgeoning legal rum trade in Georgia. Then, landed property grew from the deerskin trade. Slavery, that most brutal commerce, begat more land grants and more economic wherewithal to expand into the hinterland. Slavery's second phase of expansion helped chase the aboriginals even further westward to the Chattahoochee and beyond, as had the infamous Indian Wars against the Creek nation.

After the Civil War, agricultural expansion and consolidation doomed poor Pincus Creek, but not the town. The little tributary was eaten by its progeny, swallowed up by farmland, drained for irrigation, dammed to create a stagnant little remnant called Pincus Lake, which provided homes for turtles, gators and fat-bellied catfish. On an old warped cedar pier sat a bait shop, next to a gravel boat ramp leading from fishing cabins.

Among the litter of this potted history, modern Pincus blossomed a second time, and in the flower of its youth failed to see the signs of future decay. After showing promise as a cotton and farm market town, the economy sagged in the post-World War II agricultural letdown. Few Pincans found work in the federal impoundments being built along the Savannah River, miles away. US Highways, 1, 17 and 301, along with their East-West cousins 78 and 66, connected a rural region on the slow side of 1950s prosperity. Then, Eisenhower, with his dream of a national highway network, turned the southern countryside into a featureless multi-lane raceway. Interstate Highway 95 had shown Pincus the ditch, without even an exit ramp of its own. Thanks to a president from Kansas, who should have known better, the geographers of progress had passed Pincus by.

Now, the little town was neither here nor there, a wizened

remnant of its long history. In fact, to passersby, and even to most of its residents, it was hard to tell what kept Pincus together, other than some old stories about a past no one truly knew; or the inertia of residents with nowhere to go, living lives that were almost but not quite finished; or milky-eyed old folks with no compelling reason either to live or to die. Pincus was the county seat of the stuck, the hiding and the hopeful. Too far from Statesboro to prosper from the university economy, not close enough to Savannah to be a bedroom community for the port, too removed from the Ogeechee or Savannah rivers to have high property values, too upland to be tidewater, too swampy to be called upland, and too chopped up into little parcels to make much of the agricultural economy. Scores of such little settlements memorialized the Southeastern countryside's history: trading posts, turpentine towns, railroad crossings, fish camps and cotton mills. Surrounded by worn out cotton and peanut patches, a little tobacco here and there, and the occasional senescent pecan orchard, Pincus was pretty near the border, kind of near the river, very near the interstate, within earshot of the railroad, and closest of all to extirpation.

In the 1950s, in what today's children might call Old Pincus, before things started to come apart, the old carved wood welcome sign at the town limits had invited all who came, at least if they were white. WELCOME TO PINCUS, GEORGIA, est. 1763. Population 3,256. Now, all that welcome stuff was standardized, since the state transportation department required a boring metal sign of green with a white border, which simply said PINCUS, GA, pop. 2610, eliminating the comma between the 2 and the 6, as if Pincus would have to improve, or at least regain its lost residents from the last sign to deserve a new one. The new sign seemed much more disposed to sprout .22-caliber bullet holes and had to be replaced every two or three years. Each replacement announced a smaller population, some

5

decades by a little, often by a lot.

The little town's business establishments were few and anemic, remnants of the closed cotton mill economy of the 1920s, which endured far beyond humanity or reason. The main street on 301 had been ambitiously named Broadway, pushing its little storefronts into the street like frayed cloth buttons on a vest. Turner's Hardware stood on a corner, with a big bay window to the south and handsome double doors onto the street. From Turner's, a person could see almost everything. Next door sat The Dog Ear bookstore, across the street the Laurel Oak Inn and a few others, helping hold court on Broadway, flanked by side streets with the post office, Georgia Department of Agriculture County Extension, a Cash for Titles loan shark franchise and a Homesafe insurance brokerage. Near the so-called lake a bait shop reopened, sporting minnows, crickets, live herring and artificial lures for local fishermen looking for panfish or bass. Agitated minnows waited their turn in schooled alignment, either to die in the tank or meet their end staring at the Styrofoam wall of a minnow bucket in a bass boat.

The rest of Broadway was feeble in body and soul. Dropcic's Texaco station and general store, with a cranky, racist Slavic owner, funny old modernist spaceman pumps and a red Dr. Pepper cooler in front; Van Perkins, a men's store nobody went to because it was overpriced and under stocked and Mr. Perkins (the Van was added because it was classy, he said) was a little too frisky with the measuring tape, especially on the inseam; Tommy Noble's Rexall Drug, where pharmacist Tommy was nicknamed Tomcat, delivering prescriptions and more to the ladies at home. Green's Seed and Feed was now more of a vendor of backyard nursery supplies than farm goods, since Mr. Green quit selling ammonia and fertilizer after the Oklahoma City bombing; a small Yamacraw Red Rooster IGA, owned by local burghers and constantly in theoretical peril of being bought by Piggly Wiggly or Winn-Dixie, neither of which seemed to be doing all that well on their own, without adding another millstone to their necklace; and the Pup 'n' Suds drive-in hot dog and burger joint, which in point of fact was more known for its fried dill pickles and Carolina barbecue sandwich. Jim John Shelton, the proprietor of the Pup 'n' Suds, used the vacant lot next to the drive-in to park used cars for sale alongside an old, aqua-colored teardrop camper he used as an office. Mainly, the trailer and the cars accumulated layers of rain-lacquered dust, pollen, road oil and diesel exhaust.

Despite its general torpor, Pincus did show little signs of change. The appearance of a sushi bar at Kroger's grocery and the expansion of the House of Mao Chinese restaurant on Bridger Street attested to the inexorable globalization of hearth and home and the slow homogenization of small town life. Never mind all the Katrina refugees who had been taken in by the Thankful Missionary Baptist Church on East West Street. These days, Pincus was pretty near a Tower of Babel, old folks said, with Asian, Mexican and Louisianan languages being spoken in the streets, as if everyone could understand them. People did not object to these strange comings and goings explicitly, but everyone was happy to lament how much things had changed. When the old folks said they didn't recognize Pincus any more, the reference was clearly to brown and different-talking people. People liked to wake up to the same world every day, as it did not require flexibility and demanded less understanding.

The skinny-ribbed side streets of Pincus lined up neatly, offering a couple more layers of urban depth and the thinnest possible justification for a zoning commission, aside from petty graft. A hopeful sign stood in front of a dilapidated Queen Anne Victorian announcing ANTIQUES & QUILTS, with no sign of activity to back it up. Another house hosted a flea market in its yard on Saturdays, junk lined up on card tables and blankets and the collapsed piano key front porch. The oldest house in town abutted a ramshackle stable periodically used for auto repairs. A tiny sea-green cinder block building with a tin roof promised fresh-skinned rabbits and farm-fresh eggs. Most of the rest of Pincus lay quiet, growing weeds, manufacturing rust and breeding mosquitoes.

Aside from the Laurel Oak, and its restaurant the Sunnyside Café, the steadiest business off Broadway was a Beauty Parlor and Nail Salon called LeDonna's, after the proprietor and spouse of Brother Parsons, minister of the Thankful Baptist Church. On the other side of the grass, as they say, was Plummer's Funeral Home, in turn serviced by Perpetual Blooms Florist. Doreen Wagner managed the flower shop and was demonstrably the only hippie vegan in Pincus. She wasn't really a hippie, since she was all of 24 years old and blithely unfamiliar with the 1960s, but she did have tattoos, a stud in her nose, and several wiry rings in her ears, which was sufficient to qualify for the hippie label.

Each of Pincus' businesses had its own story, stocked with *dramatis personae* whose ordinariness belied their character and singularity, Pincus' little human snowflakes, unique and evanescent, lined up dutifully in their roles, holding together a small town's social life with love, recrimination, regret and empty storefronts. The transitory nature of that life was not evident day to day, but only revealed itself through significant passages. Or so it appeared on a humid late spring morning, when the doors opened on Turner's Hardware under new ownership. Assuming a routine that had not changed in a generation, the proprietor thought he would fall into a scripted role. But all of Pincus and its denizens was poised to play an incremental part in collective change. The momentary mismatch of hopeful characters in a hopeless place created turbidity in a stagnant little world. A municipal leaf borne by the wind, Pincus was going to get up and move, but not because it meant to.

Steven Sanderson

Darkness covered everything,

Blacker than a hundred midnights

Down in a cypress swamp.

James Weldon Johnson, *The Creation*

CHAPTER I

A moonless black pall fell over Pincus on the evening of what came to be known as The Great Fire. The daytime air of June-almost-July had been thick with eye-watering bright heat that baked the pavement sticky. Fields of blond grass danced with dust in thermal puffs of wind. Dogs and old men dozed on porches, waiting for the evening to cool. Their ears twitched away the sand gnats. Then, all along the hem of darkness rushed a sky-wide purple of thunderstorms, east from Alabama across the Chattahoochee, tumbling over red clay valley and ridge, down the watershed past the piedmont to the coastal plain, lighting the horizon in warning. The wind rose to a hum. Pines swished in time. A choir of cabbage palms began to sway. Leaves whispered through the cypress swamp. Black gum branches rubbed moaning against each other in distress. The storm picked up pace. Microbursts flattened acres of palmetto. Water oaks came untethered from sandy soil, strewing giant hardwood barbells with root balls at one end and dying canopy at the other. Floods ran through the streets like the angel of death. Every inch of low ground became swamp. Porch dogs now trembled where they had lain asleep, wild birds fled to the hammocks, children ran to their parents' beds, and Pincus stood grim as a prisoner against the wall.

The storm chose to hurt the poor, who were least protected in their homes and unguarded by the modest resources Pincus martialed to help them. It was ever thus. The wrong side of town always flooded first and worst. Side roads with too little camber or drainage coursed with yellow clay slicks. Culverts jammed with debris, backing up filthy water into the street. Cars stalled in submerged declivities along the town's perimeter. Little frame shacks fairly lifted into the air with each new thunderclap. A hint of sulfur hung in the air. Satan himself was riding the storm.

In the noisy, wet dark, a homely strip of stores at the edge of town caught fire. Up in flames went a handful of vintage frame buildings lately revived after years of abandonment. No amount of rain could quench the blaze, which had the crackle and smell of fatwood in a fireplace. Among the stores was an old bait shop and gas station, converted a few years prior into headquarters for a charity called The Bread Basket. An enterprise of importance beyond its size, The Bread Basket was a food bank, counseling center and soup kitchen all in one. The front room cafeteria fed the hungry. Two small back offices offered quiet consultation behind ringed curtain rods. A side kitchen led to a walk-in cooler. The Bread Basket's acts of mercy sheltered behind weathered cedar clapboards, decorated with flaking painted reminders of the 1950s, cursing Earl Warren's Supreme Court and the United Nations and praising The Lord Jesus. Yes to God, no to tolerance, and never to One-Worldism. Interposition and Nullification, the defeated but unforgotten claims of the South. Welcome to Pincus, safe haven of disappointment. Lunch if you can spare the time.

At first, no one noticed the fire. The whole town had lost power, such outages being the stuff of life in the stormy lowlands. By the time the roof was discovered in flames, the building was half gone in curling asphalt shingles and curtains of fire waving out the windows. A diminutive Guatemalan manicurist finally noticed and came running out in plastic flats, from her little home tucked behind the street's weedy border. *"Incendio! Incendio!"* she shouted, waving her arms in agitation. No one could understand her Spanish cry of "Fire!" but no one was there to hear her raise the alarm in any language. The Bread Basket and its outbuildings burned to the ground, leaving only the walk-in refrigerator. Inside, the body of Oscar Thomas Turner, age 74, lay among the ruined vegetables, soaked from fire hoses that drenched the interior. A steady drip of water slapped his body as it lay on the floor. Thanks to his confinement, he remained unburned. In his shirt pocket was found a cheap paperboard journal he was known to keep, splotched and mostly illegible, save the occasional undamaged fragments of sentiment. His face was calm, though he had choked and gagged and gasped before losing his life.

Sister Angeline Bruce stood staring at the Whistler-gray and - black ruins, her wet eyes reflecting the strobes of emergency vehicles. As the rain eased, she watched her mentor and friend rolled on a gurney to the ambulance. He was muddy with wet ash, drained of color or life, trolleyed like furniture. The coroner would report the cause of death as heart failure, probably due to the stress of the fire and oxygen deprivation. His report would not say that Oscar had died of goodness, caught by the fire while replacing a finicky light fixture inside the walk-in. He must have been surprised by the heat and flame and kept the door closed tight, left a prisoner, alone with his thoughts until his death.

Crying and coughing in the wet breeze, Angeline saw her vocational hopes doused with fire hoses. Inside the charred ruins, swollen corpses of canned vegetables and ham lay bulging. Plastic canisters melted into warped sculptures. Sacks of sweet potatoes and onions, boxes of frozen meat, pork hocks and field peas, okra and collards all were lost to fire and water and mud and char. Worse, the walk-in refrigerator, the flattop grill, the deep fryer and chest freezer were also ruined. Any prospect of storing perishables for distribution to the needy was gone. The Bread Basket had cooked its last meal. Angeline's thoughts of Oscar made her personal mission feel somehow selfish, but her mind insisted on worrying over the future of her precious charity.

Into this small catastrophe drove Faris Turner, late into a long trip from the Midwest. Faris was a footloose man returning home, at the specific invitation of his old friend Henry Jeffords, who had written a letter inviting him to join in a grand new venture. Details were to be explained upon their reunion. Such a vague enticement would normally not move a man like Faris, but he had little reason to be anywhere these days, and home seemed a good enough choice. Maybe, he thought, he would be ready just to be home. He was tired of being anywhere else, and the imprint of Pincus was deep in his soul: the light, the humidity, the smell, the people, his childhood recollections. If he had any story to his life, it came from here. The ghosts of memory lined up along the roadside to greet him. He thought of home as it used to be, where people knew him and for the most part seemed to want him around. The memory of his childhood and the love of his parents lived here. Henry's invitation was the trigger for a long-delayed return. Faris wanted to belong, after a life of not belonging, and to remember what had not yet become, but surely would be, a forgettable life.

Faris may have demurred if he had known what he was driving into. The ambulance flying past him and interrupting his nostalgia conveyed the remains of his father. Startled by the ambulance's siren and frantic haste, he pulled onto the shoulder and then turned left into the downslope parking lot, passing the Apostolic Church of The Redeemer, with its convenience store sign. "Give the Devil an Inch and He'll Be Your Ruler." It could just as well have advertised "Nightcrawlers & Crickets, Minnow Buckets." The pastor responsible for the sign and the church was an ungenerous man drawn to a vengeful God, who would later give thanks for the divine mercy that spared the church. The fire also reminded him to replace the bulbs that had gone out on his church sign, which made it look cheap. The pastor's severe and bitter face showed him to be thankful, too, for the loss of The Bread Basket, which he considered an eyesore handing out undeserved rewards to the shiftless. Faris left the car running, as he was waved away by a fireman directing traffic with a flashlight. Then, he saw Angeline in silhouette. He jammed the car into Park and went to her. Several minutes of embrace and tears passed before he understood what Angeline was telling him about his father's death.

Strangely, it was Faris who comforted Angeline, holding tight to her with one arm, staring with her into smoke and mud. He touched her teary face with the tenderness of an old dog, and found it cold and rubbery with shock, tinged in venous blue, child-soft, shining intermittently in the lightning and headlights.

The manicurist stood weeping a few steps away in her wet plastic slippers, with no one to console her. She always wept when bad things happened to others, in a histrionic style that had several component parts. She usually began with a low mewing that built slowly to concertina wheezes and grand blubbering and snot, punctuated by occasional whinnies, until even the grief-stricken tried to cheer her up. Since her arrival in Pincus, the tiny Latina had wept a lot, and might have planned for more to come.

Faris led Angeline to his car and drove her home, accompanied by Henry's now diminished enticement, the wet beauty of his old girlfriend, a trunkful of recollection and the absurdity of his father's dying of fire in a refrigerator. As he loaded Angeline into the car, he moved his memories and hopes into the trunk – Faris, hoping, as he always had, that the agency of adulthood would allow him and his friends to act out their dreams; Faris, taking his place in a world unintelligible to him; Faris, Henry and Angeline, together again, as they were in childhood.

They had fallen in together as children, thanks to Mrs. Whitman's fifth grade class. A widow of late middle age, given to dressing in square-bodice navy blue organdy dresses that swooshed her into the classroom, Mrs. Whitman introduced them to modern poetry. She focused mainly on the moderns, beginning with Dickinson, and then Auden and Yeats, which filled their heads equally with dreams and dread and visions of beyond. Many years later, as an adult, Faris found himself chronically afflicted with dreams and dread, just as he had been in the fifth grade. He still reviewed each day for mistakes, now worrying about whether he talked too much or too little and whether he was welcome in the places he had been – a Southern boy outside the South, a thinker in a thoughtless world, a debater in a society that would not surrender to sweet reason, an idea man in a world of action figures. By now, he had recognized his daily penance as an intellectualized neurosis, deep enough in his psyche to require him to forgive himself every day before going to bed. In order to sleep, he had to peel the psychic toilet paper off his shoe and promise to be a better person the next day, a quest at which he routinely failed.

They were like him, Henry and Angeline. They worried about whether they were decent and whether they did any good in the world and whether the world could get maybe just a little better if they tried on its behalf. They fooled themselves routinely into thinking the answer was yes, that they knew what was good for the world, and that three disconnected solitaries from a withering small town could prescribe remedies for a world of over-connected adversaries and calamitous misfortune. It occurred to Faris, though, that they were not like him at all, not really. He worried that their kinship was unreal, an artifact of his own self-absorption, that they would doubt him, too, soon enough. His doubt of their fidelity persisted, raising feelings of guilt and anxiety.

They did love to read and talk. It was their currency, their popcorn and movies. Talking with them was a lot like the best of college, which was full of excesses, right down to the thinking: utopian socialism, existentialism, free love, human potential, whether Shelley's death was authentically portrayed in art, whether Camus' murderer Meursault was an amoral sociopath or an existential prophet. These were matters for the internal world and for the cosseted world of adolescents preparing for intellectual life in dormitories, not the world of human affairs. Nietzsche rightly would have included them in his category of spoiled idlers in the gardens of knowledge.

Henry was the most melodramatic. When he read as a boy that Coleridge was unable to breathe through his nose, Henry walked around for a week with his mouth open. Angeline and Faris loved him for it, and he knew it. Plus, he thought it made him look like a young William F. Buckley. Now, as adults, resisting all evidence, they still liked to argue and hadn't abandoned the cause of pure wondering. They still appreciated a beautiful word or feeling, and embraced life in their worried ways. As careworn as the next person, they had accomplished more than just enduring; they had not given up, at least yet. But they suspected that they had been rehearsing for a life in a world that didn't exist, walking toward a path they had never managed to find. And their worries had left them to remain alone. None had married or even sustained a long-term relationship. None of the three had circles of friends or networks of others like them. Unlike Faris — and this was the great difference — the other two had found clear identities, Henry a didact and Angeline a saint.

Sparks stirred in the dying embers of The Bread Basket, fighting their fate as Pincus would, following the flickers of false hope in an effort to create a new town. In the shadows of Faris' departure, downwind from smoke and fire and grief, stood a solitary young woman dressed in a black rain poncho, observing the scene impassively. Angeline's eyes turned curiously in her direction, as Faris walked her to the car. She looked familiar. The manicurist, still ignored and now finished with her symphony of weeping, wiped her nose on her sleeve and turned back to her home, sitting on the flank of a roadside attraction called Wild Animal Kingdom.

CHAPTER II

The clientele at LeDonna's Ebony Salon was overwhelmingly black, with a loyal cohort of mature church ladies who patronized the parlor for its conditioners, smoothers, and special oils, along with various confections to make one's hair distinctive. LeDonna would tell you that she knew what she was doing with African-American women's hair, and she knew the preferences of her ladies. She did attract a small but devoted set of younger women looking for sexy hair, whether for their social life or the checkout stations at Wal-Mart, where they worked. With all the comings and goings, LeDonna knew all the happenings in town, whether they were her business or not. And she was an irrepressible advice machine, spitting out wise counsel *ex cathedra* to anyone within earshot, usually waving a curling wand or styling comb for emphasis. She was a large woman, with a welcoming face and ample bosom and butt. Her advice on weight loss was to "wait 'til the brothers complain." Her husband Brother Parsons never did. Proud of her marital success, LeDonna's always advised the younger set was to look for a Do Right Man before they dropped their drawers. Do Right Men were rare in Pincus. Drawers got dropped anyway.

An alcove of the shop devoted to nail treatments was a festival, especially on Saturday mornings. The radio blared with the local R & B wake-up show, clinging to 1960s MoTown. Women came and went, hugging and laughing and talking over each other to get LeDonna's attention with the latest story about their man or their kids or what was going on with the world today. New or nearly new movie star scandals cried out from dated gossip magazines, crackly from being left too long in the sunny window seat.

LeDonna's was the pre-eminent nail salon for miles around, thanks to Carmita, a Guatemalan woman sitting long shifts on a short stool, painting whimsical patterns on women's hands and feet, and massaging and soaking muscles knotted up by years of repetitive work and inappropriate footwear. Selections from the artist's portfolio on artificial nails went for $10 hands or feet, or a combined $16 mani-pedi. Custom patterns carried an extra charge. Carmita also drew a white clientele. One swampy-smelling little country girl named Bella had I MISS U MAMA painted on her nails every Mother's Day. No one knew if MAMA was dead or just gone, but she most certainly had departed before she taught Bella to wash her hair.

Carmita's daily routine was simple and inflexible. She left home early for work at LeDonna's, where she made coffee before the shop opened and hoped for the occasional quiet conversation with her boss. It was her best time of day, not yet tired, not close to going home. After her long shift servicing the vanity of LeDonna's ladies, she returned home to cook, clean and rest in the measure possible. Her household was not at all restful, though. She was as likely to get a slap as a smile.

The night of The Great Fire, Carmita came home reeking of smoke from the charred ruins of The Bread Basket. She opened the carport door of the house next to WILD ANIMAL KINGDOM, a dust-covered, roadside attraction adorned with yard art flamingos, alligators, and whitewashed wagon wheels. Like beheaded enemies on an Ottoman roadway, dusty, unsold sock monkeys impaled on bamboo poles stood vigil over the decline and fall of US Highway 301. At night the monkeys lit up in a blue strobe each time bug zappers popped something big. The regular zzzt and spark of a moth, witnessed by the spectral sock monkeys hanging in the dark, kept even the mischievous teens of Pincus at a safe distance. Old Man Strother, who knew the spirit world, had advised them not to risk the hants of 301. Even the most irreverent listened.

This was Carmita's second try at returning home. She had arrived for the first time just as the fire began, already exhausted from having worked a double shift on her little cushioned piano stool, after which she confided her marital troubles to her boss. Normally, she could set aside her difficulties, committed as she was to painting nails. But she had special grief that day, even before the fire.

This diminutive and unassuming woman saw herself through the prism of art. Her fears and disappointments disappeared into the precision of her craft. Esperanza Carmen Santamaría de Arizpe, known to all as Carmita, was as famous as they came in Pincus. Her handiwork had even garnered a feature in the local newspaper, heavy on the pictures, with minimal conversation, in light of her limited English. The newspaper had provided an interpreter, which spiced up the feature dramatically. When Carmita simply allowed that she found peace in her work (*me encuentro tranquila pintando las uñas*), the interpreter told the reporter grandly that Carmita found solace and oneness with the universe through the microcosm of nail art. The piece was titled "Pincus' Own Digital Artist."

Whatever the exaggeration, Carmita was one of a kind in the nail business. She had once painted ten of the twelve days of Christmas on the hands of Clementine Scroggins, wife of the local Nazarene minister, secretly wishing that the old bat had two more fingers, which would have permitted seven geese a-laying and four calling birds, now sidelined for lack of digits. As it was, the manicure nearly caused divorce in the Scroggins household, as Rev. Scroggins was much more given to the Holy Spirit than idolatrous fingernails.

Mrs. Scroggins was said to have early onset dementia, which caused the minister to accuse LeDonna of exploitation of the intellectually disabled. But LeDonna stuck up for Carmita. Right out in public LeDonna said, "if that old white lady wanted to go early onset on us, she shoulda started a lot sooner. And she was always dumb as a bag of rocks, anyway. Nobody is going to make me ask my customers their religion or give them an IQ test. And besides, Old Scroggins was happy enough to let his wife cold call people to tell them about her personal messages from Jesus, the creepier the better. 'Don't Drink Alcohol,' drawing out each word in her spooky voice." LeDonna was just getting wound up when her teenage daughter Janita had the final word: "That old Scroggins, she just crazy, that's all," the girl said, with the mandatory palm-out flip of her hand. Case closed.

Given her Catholic background and the highly Protestant piety of Pincans, Carmita included in her portfolio the Stations of the Cross for Catholics, crucifixes for the Anglicans, and plain crosses and crowns of thorns for all the other Christians. Everybody loved a crown of thorns. Personally, Carmita was a partisan of the 12 Stations, though liturgical inflation had grown the number to 14 or even 15, more fingers than she could hope to encounter on anyone's hands and too few to allow a combination Via Dolorosa mani-pedi. Nary a hand went uncounted in Carmita's workday, but only old Miss Imogene Doyle had an extra finger, and it was a little boneless ginger root of a thing with a tiny nail barely worth painting. She knew from the Book of Samuel that a giant man had six fingers on each hand and six toes on each foot, but he was killed young by David's people. Did that wipe out the entire twelve-fingered gene pool from then on? She hoped his kind were not extinct, but surely they were an endangered species, as she had never seen one. And she had seen a lot of hands.

To avoid any controversy, Carmita's portfolio emphasized

holiday bows and ornaments in December, Easter eggs and bunnies in the spring, fireworks and flags on The Fourth, and witches and goblins for Halloween. She did the occasional menorah -- eight candles, the attendant light and a Star of David for the extra fingers. Pilgrims, turkeys and pumpkins were popular at Thanksgiving. She could do a turkey head on the thumb and use the feathers as fingers, just like in elementary school cutouts. Ten little Indians worked all right, but they lacked individual personalities and had no special occasion to recommend them. Pocahontas, Tomochichi, Geronimo, a couple more, then you run out. The same for ten lords a leaping. Telephone numbers were hot this year and conveniently required ten digits. Amy Richard, the hot little liquor store clerk, had her phone number suggestively printed on her nails every week. According to the boys, it worked just fine. Carmita had themed sets for Audubon and Garden Club, as well as a complete Elvis treatment (Rockabilly Elvis, Vegas Elvis, Army Elvis, Hawaii Elvis, Elvis and Priscilla, Fat Elvis, and so on, culminating in a thumbnail Graceland). Over the years she had created a handsome portfolio in a laminated ring binder, complete with a back section offering risqué choices popular for bachelorette parties but too embarrassing to show. She was always on the lookout for more options that added up to ten or twenty. Carmita was so accomplished that LeDonna had urged her to blog as a way of garnering more attention. Carmita knew nothing of blogs and in any case did not own a computer.

Carmita made good money, and LeDonna was that rare combination of boss and true friend. Carmita loved their coffees together in the morning before work and valued LeDonna's advice. Today had been a rare occasion, when Carmita doubted her commitment to her wedding vow and confessed to LeDonna how she hated her husband Jesús and the sinful thoughts that entered her head. She cried at the thought of her son and of what she might do to protect him from his father. She cried for herself, too, as she knew she would burn in hell if she reneged on her sacred promise to love her husband until the separation of death. And she cried in fear of yet another beating at home. LeDonna, ever the preacher's wife, consoled her and cursed the devil in Carmita's husband.

The very same husband, Jesús Santamaria, owned WILD ANIMAL KINGDOM, and worked at it as a man possessed. He barely heard her come through the front door, perched as he was next to a silky bantam chicken he was trying to teach how to play tic-tac-toe. Flannery O'Connor, he'd heard, once had a Cochin bantam that was famous for walking both forwards and backwards, and Jesús was well aware of its fame and of the money to be made from Chinatown attractions of chickens that played games. His own chickens swung on little swings in their coop and showed enough personality to make him think they had potential. He could have been nicknamed Wuz Gunner, Sheriff Hockett teased. He constantly said he "wuz gunner" make a fortune with this scheme or that. He was forever on the lookout for a quick jackpot.

Jesús was wrongly named for the Son of God, as he was an irreligious man. Yet, he found himself presiding over a church. Carmita worried about his immortal soul. Such a sinner, much less one named Jesús, should never tempt God in this way. Jesús' neighbors, who had known him for about 15 years, refused to call him by his name, which they pronounced Jesus, as in Christ. It made them feel blasphemous, so, instead, they called him Jay, or the Mexican, or nothing. Not that anyone talked to him, or that he was Mexican. Or that he cared, either way. He was solitary and mean, given only to his ambitions.

Born to an Air Force NCO and a Chicana motel maid working in Del Rio, Texas, Jesús was a casualty of itinerant military life. His father was a terrible drunk, whose alcoholism eventually ruined his family but barely rippled in his military career. He worked in a bench stock warehouse, ordering and distributing supplies, a job made harder by sobriety and clear thinking. Jesús' mother understood marriage to be a rough bargain whereby she traded a life of cleaning hot sheets motel rooms downtown for access to a base commissary and possibly a survivor's benefit from a military pension. Though he was utterly dissipated, the old man was not especially abusive, just dispensing the normal kind of abuse associated with someone drunk all the time and full of self-hatred. It wasn't as bad as it could have been, at least if you weren't his wife or son. In the course of his father's alcoholism, however, Jesús had paid a certain price in school, and of course he couldn't ever come home with friends.

Jesús did not expect either his mother or father to do their jobs of parenting. His father stood in the kitchen downing a couple of shots before pouring himself a sit-down drink. His mother knelt in the bedroom fingering her rosary like an abacus, counting sins and indulgences, leaving out the most obvious failing: to nurture her son. Jesús became more invisible, a nuisance at the margin. He stopped coming home altogether, except to pilfer small change and cigarettes. His parents hardly seemed to notice. He spent his youth in the streets or on airbases where his father was stationed. He had worked at the base chapel as a teenager, filing parishioner address cards and picking off a Sunday envelope or two for pocket money. With his years of bouncing around through odd jobs, he had become a competent mechanic, bartender and office assistant, none of which spoke to his sophomoric creative sensibilities, his nutty schemes, his restless spirit or his hope. He boxed in clubs for a time, during which he learned to spit, received innumerable blows that rearranged his nose, and took enough punishment to scar his thick brow. Jesús' exuberant qualities slowly fermented into a sour, inarticulate aspirational bitterness, as he became yet another soul denied its rightful place in a disinterested world.

Certain experiences had mixed well with his crazy schemes.

24

He had been mesmerized by local sideshow attractions on Okinawa, in which mongoose were pitted against venomous snakes. Habituated Rhesus macaques were typical of the wildlife markets he roamed in Naha, where one could buy rare soft-shelled turtles, songbirds, squirrel-like flying sugar gliders from Indonesia, parrots and macaws and all manner of reptiles and amphibians, from spitting cobras to rare Vietnamese salamanders. Since that time he had dreamt of having wild animals in captivity, first as an attraction and later as merchandise for the incredible boom among private US collectors. He affected the style of Marlon Perkins and Jack Hanna, wearing khakis and broad-brimmed campaign hats. He had even looked unsuccessfully for jobs in Florida, where every wide spot in the road seemed to have a menagerie, and where the Alligator Farm in St. Augustine had long set the standard for bizarre and successful small collections. These funny little farms had little need for outside labor, though, which he learned to see as a virtue when he set up his own personal Wild Animal Kingdom. He preferred to go it alone.

For a time, he had worked as a dog handler for a small plantation near Pincus, which released pen-raised quail and pheasant for its owners to shoot on winter weekends. It wasn't a true plantation, just an ersatz affair that turned a thousand acres of lowland pine forest into a recreational retreat for the biggest car dealer in the county. A garish Neo-plantation Big House sat among small outbuildings, housing equipment and bird dogs. Working with pointers and Brittany spaniels and a big, lazy golden retriever named Peggy Lee, Jesús had found a true vocation as an animal handler. He could easily train the dogs to work the quail courses without shock collars, hollering and false points. The animals were absolutely devoted to him, responding to his every yip and hey, as he steered them through the scrub pine. His owners liked his work. Guests at the plantation gave him generous tips, which he kept in a sock and counted each day, as earnestly as Père Grandet with his gold. On the side, he had a little business selling Boykin spaniel puppies out of a mill run by an acquaintance in North Carolina. Boykins were the rage among the genteel set, and Jesús saved buyers the trouble of asking questions about provenance or shipping or the breeding ethics of the vendor.

Walking up released birds for weekend shooters is not a great challenge, and too seasonal for a proper income. So, Jesús emptied his sock of tips and bought an odd property at the edge of town for $800 in back taxes. The parcel included a Pentecostal Church that had lost its pastor Clarence Mays to a pants-down controversy at the highway rest stop, so Jesús became sexton until another cleric could be found. No one ever applied. Adjacent was a golf driving range, which was Mr. Mays' original business, the church being a spontaneous development that followed his being visited by the Holy Spirit at a tent revival he had attended in the hopes of seducing Pearl Charton, the town's librarian and most durable virgin. The church did not thrive, and his approaches to Miss Pearl, as she was known, were spurned without even a smile. With the erstwhile reverend now discredited, Jesús' decided to combine the two parcels in a truly innovative business model in any town, but it depended on an abundance of golfers and unaffiliated evangelicals, neither in great supply in Northeast Georgia. However, things were turning up these days, thanks to the growing number of Mexican immigrant evangelicals, whose answer to many eternal questions was *"Jesús es la respuesta."*

Jesús slowly transformed the cinder block church annex into a roadside attraction with outdoor pens, adding a three-hole putt-putt course and a summer ice cream drive-in specializing in Latin-style *helados*, which made for better cash flow. The signage was appropriately ambiguous:

Jesus is the Answer/*Jesús es la respuesta*

in tandem on a sign board set near the church parking lot, and *Helados: Coco, Piña, Fresa, Chocolate, Vainilla, Dulce de Leche* above the adjacent entrance to WILD ANIMAL KINGDOM. Come and be saved, it beckoned, hit a few balls, have an ice cream, promenade with the family, see the animals. He attracted a lot of Latino families, who liked to parade around on weekends anyway. To ensure that his religious-minded constituents not confuse him with their pious Christian slogan, Jesús wore a tattered baseball cap, self-stenciled NOT THE ANSWER.

In addition to WILD ANIMAL KINGDOM, Jesús had a part-time juke joint in the woods that provided good income and a hedge against the seasonality of his main business. He also liked to drink in the company of others who were drinkers, so he figured he might as well make money off the proposition. Jesús worked hard and constantly, but he only worked for more cash, more liquor and more spitting.

The reluctant star of WILD ANIMAL KINGDOM was a superannuated shock-headed capuchin monkey Jesús had acquired privately from a guy he knew who was under indictment for illegally transporting white-tailed deer across state lines to South Carolina. Known as The Admiral, the monkey had been a performer all its life, first as a traveling companion to an abusive organ grinder, who sold the little guy to the wildlife trader after The Admiral bit a little girl for taunting him. The trader promptly put the monkey into service for the disabled father of his estranged wife to save money on home care. The Admiral was a terrific home care aide, but when the old man died, The Admiral found his way to Jesús and THE WILD ANIMAL KINGDOM. Jesús parlayed The Admiral's charisma into a seasonal gig as a regular in the Veterans' Day and Homecoming Parades, where he would dress in an admiral's outfit and march with a miniature flag. The Admiral was Jesús' most reliable annuity.

The Admiral was an uncanny intellect, so Jesús took a proprietor's interest in testing the range of the monkey's knowledge and learning power. The Admiral had a broad vocabulary. He mimicked and learned, used tools and improved his food by mixing it. His gaze was direct and deep. Jesús' thought the Admiral might eventually learn pronouns and temporal abstractions. Thus far, The Admiral could recognize several species of bird by name, but if Jesús called out "There goes another one," The Admiral went blank. Similarly, The Admiral didn't seem to care when Jesús talked about tomorrow, later in the day, or The Admiral's next birthday.

Owning a Shock-headed Admiral was its own caution. The organ grinder had kept him in a tiny box when The Admiral was not performing and tried to use him in skits based on Shock-headed Peter, a suite of German morality tales for children that inevitably ended badly for the children. The monkey's tonsure made him a natural for the part. The organ grinder was popular among parents for his use of fables to scare good behavior into their children, but, as his foil, The Admiral often ended up licking his wounds in his hot wooden casket. The Admiral became insanely claustrophobic and harbored a morbid fear of the German language. The wrong stimuli could provoke violent flashbacks and almost suicidal recklessness. No one had managed to cage him since he escaped the clutches of the organ grinder.

An unruly clutter of animals acted as supporting cast to The Admiral, led by a javelina named Chancho. He had been trapped accidentally by friends in Texas who made a tidy business catching feral hogs and selling them at a premium as wild boar meat. Young Chancho was captured in a hog trap, and a diminutive, well scarred but extraordinarily fierce pit bull named Jaylo joined him shortly thereafter. Jaylo grabbed Chancho by the cheek and threw it screaming to the ground. One of the boys hogtied the animal and, upon seeing that he was not a hog, gave him to Jesús as a curiosity.

Snaps, the Alligator snapping turtle, was understandably not part of the petting zoo, but for $1, visitors could watch Jesús feed him frogs at 11 a.m. Sundays. Snaps was a 125-pound monster of unknown age, harvested from a swamp near Pincus on a lucky fall day. He had since become the unofficial mayor of WILD ANIMAL KINGDOM, though he spent most of his time under water, waiting to surface when the next doomed frog dropped. Jesús employed Rubén to clear the water of algae, so that customers could see Snaps clearly. WILD ANIMAL KINGDOM initially advertised a standing prize of one hundred dollars to anyone who could dare remove Snaps from his pond. Then, one day a herpetologist from the Department of Natural Resources walked into the pond in waders, grabbed Snaps from the back by his shell and hoisted him expertly to the bank. Once released, Snaps fled to the bottom of the pond, the crowd roared, a scowling Jesús had forked over the reward, and the sign came down.

The rest of the animals were domestics, part of the petting zoo popular with children: a Nigerian dwarf goat, a miniature wild ass, a white rabbit whose leg-kick could make a kid cry, and a flock of silkie bantam chickens in various colors. Coin-operated feed dispensers turned a surprising and regular profit.

Jesús thought of his partner Carmita in much the same way as he did his animals, not without affection, but devoid of human consideration. He had called her Carnita, or little meat morsel, when he was wooing her. Now, years later, he scarcely bothered to show any affection or treat her as anything but a drudge. When she left, he gave her a to-do list; when she came home, he said nothing. At the end of the day, she was dying to rest her aching back, but began instead to fix his dinner. He expected it at the same hour every day. He had been known to backhand her without cause. Otherwise, she might as well have been a ghost.

Carmita was a homely woman, rich in devotion to God. That meant her awful marriage was locked in the cage of holy sacrament. He and she were complete opposites. His face cried out to be on a post office wall, hers on a tin of chocolate. He was strong and wiry, tall enough to affect a stooped walk. Carmita was square and dark, barely five feet tall. He rarely smiled and had to try not to scowl. Her full mouth, with a lonesome few bright teeth, offered a sweet and ever-present smile. Her chest and her belly were all one thing squashed together, and the span between her hips and her neck measured little more than a foot, torso stacked like a breadbox atop two bandy legs. Her only notable nod to style -- beyond her professionally necessary nails, which today were painted with the Ten Commandments in gold on a stone tablet grey background, --were her Jellies, tiny jujubes shaped into slippers. She affected her own style by mixing pairs, one aqua the other magenta. Her hair parted in the middle, coffee skin tone separating the rich black plaits of hair, she possessed a sturdy countenance, soulful eyes, rich color and prodigious endurance.

He cared for her, Jesús did, to the extent he cared about anything. That didn't stop him from beating her. Not hard, he would say, nothing that left a mark, maybe just a black eye or bruise on her arm now and then. His unpredictable rages caused him to pinch or smack her, but never with a closed fist. He did not need to beat her much before things changed for good. Carmita flinched when his hand went up casually. She walked a wide swath around him when he was drinking, which was pretty much every day after midday. His guilt turned to bile, her fear to hate. Behind her great efforts to avoid getting hit lay fantasies of escape and revenge, mashed flat by hopelessness and fear of her religion. Days without violence went by unrecorded, while every slap was marked down in the ledger. Carmita became evidence of the abuser's sin, accreting to the permanent shadow on his soul. In the night, Jesús would suddenly moan "Ay, no!" in semiconscious reflection on his mean temper and abusive ways. She dreamt of stabbing him; he dreamt of being stabbed. But they stayed together. God insisted, she said.

It wasn't the so much the beatings that made Carmita hate Jesús, or the fact that he made her dance with a small python in his matinee stage shows. He badgered her into it, but allowed her to wear a phony tourist Mayan mask to hide her identity. Given her stature and jelly shoes, no one was fooled, but most pretended otherwise out of sympathy. A modest person, she was humiliated to tears on Tuesdays and Thursday afternoons at 3:15.

No, Jesús' mortal sin in her eyes was his treatment of their son Rubén, a strong, handsome boy, now out of high school and working part time for Yamacraw County Animal Control and for the Sunnyside Café, where he hoped to be a line cook. He had always been an odd child, physically chiseled but mentally cryptic and suspiciously tenderhearted. He was intelligent enough but struggled to connect or to speak. People in town cruelly and erroneously called him retard. The school nurse suggested autism spectrum disorder, which to Carmita and Rubén only confirmed the public diagnosis of retard. The one happy aspect of his youth was the opportunity to tend to the animals of WILD ANIMAL KINGDOM, with which he had a special bond. He was so adept in gaining the confidence of the animals that he was able to hold Prickles, the North American porcupine, in his arms, as if it were a cat.

Everyone knew Rubén as Dizzy Pickles and called him Dizzy, Diz or Pickles, never Rubén. He had been nobly named Rubén for one of Jacob's sons in the Bible. But he had become a pickle, instead, thanks to a searing episode of his youth. As a boy, his struggle to read and to speak in any public setting set him up for abuse. He never managed to insinuate himself without stumbling into a group or a joke or a game. In Sunday School, where he usually stayed totally still in hopes of disappearing, the teacher required him to take a turn reading from the New Testament Gospel of St. John. At first, it went well. "And looking upon Jesus as he walked, he said, Behold the Lamb of God!" But, then, he froze. The text read, "And the two disciples heard him speak, and they followed Jesus." Rubén had no idea what a disciple was, much less how to say it. Recalling his mother's efforts to help his reading with a book of phonics drills, he sweated and stuttered and picked at his thumb, until the silence smothered him. In desperation, he managed to sound out, "And the two dizzy pickles heard him speak, and they followed Jesus." Not really such a bad try for a little boy, but Rubén knew it made no sense. He cringed, awaiting the blow, which came soon enough. A moment of silent confusion gave way to hoots from his peers and calls of "dizzy pickles!"

"Jesus wasn't followed by no dizzy pickles, you retard!"

Despite the teacher's sympathy, somewhat limited by her desire to teach only perfect children, Rubén's mistake became the sole subject of that day and a durable insult every day of his life thereafter, wrapped up in laughter and taunts from people no smarter than he. Even those who did not recognize it as an insult called him Dizzy Pickles. It was now his nickname, and it would be at least until he and everyone he knew and everyone they knew were dead. He actually thought of that prospect, not in a Columbine sort of way, but as a fantasy that would result in his being left in peace. Maybe if there truly were Rapture at The End of Days, a world of the remaining few could exist in which cruelty had no place and where he never made a reading mistake. He never considered that God would lift him to heaven. Maybe such a world would have to involve mass suicide, and not await The Rapture. He would be spared, only because no one would think to offer him the Kool-Aid.

When Jesús heard the dizzy pickle story, he joined in the

merciless fun, showing no kindness even for his own child, as he had been shown none by his father. He treated Rubén as a servant, growling orders to get him a beer or clean his shoes or muck out the cages at WILD ANIMAL KINGDOM. Jesús let no opportunity to humiliate Rubén pass by. "Diz, you fucking retard pickle, get me the remote," was the kind of routine order that flattened Rubén and added a layer of murderous venom to Carmita's heart. Yet, they stayed, Carmita and Rubén, because they could not envision what else to do.

Rubén loathed Jesús for his own sake, but especially for his mother's. His was the bottomless filial love of an only child, left otherwise alone in a friendless life. He could not speak easily or join in normal social life, but he could count on the most elemental of human qualities: he could judge. Rubén divided the world into those who were good to his mother and those who should vanish from the Earth. Jesús led the list of vanishers. Rubén imagined Jesús dead from any number of horrible accidents: gored by Chancho, lit up in flames from the old, rusty gas grill, beaten to death by one of his juke joint customers, choking to death on his food. Rubén feared that Jesús' death or disappearance would be his mother's only chance to escape, and the source of his own liberation. But he had no idea how to act on his patricidal thoughts. His will was like his speech, paralyzed when needed. He suffered for his mother. He needed to act against evil as he saw it, but could not. He hated himself for his weakness, his lousy fit with the world, his lack of self-defense, but most of all his inability to kill his father.

Except for his nightmares about Carmita, Jesús was spared any concern that he might be poisoned, stabbed, run over or shot by the simple virtue of not being aware of other people's feelings. He was dull to everything but control and continued treating people like animals, whose value to him was measured by their performance and their potential to help him. When Jesús periodically caught Rubén staring with black-eyed hatred at him, he never tumbled to the malice. He just saw retard.

CHAPTER III

Dark thoughts pressed against Faris Turner's neck, making it ache as he paced the cemetery before his father's interment. Pushing aside his exhaustion – he had only dozed intermittently since his arrival in town three days ago – he thumbed his father's journal again and again. Amid the water-damaged script, he could only make out a few words, which made little sense.

The....RUTH....born to die.
Everything....mournful....subject....said, b....mar....grave....The
final....life....like one....gait diff....anoth....no....fail at
dyin....you....no direc....f deat....veryon....dies, and no one fails
at.....ant to leave a ma....a place, hole in the ground

He wondered if the old man had been ill, or just morose. His father and his friends were funny old ducks, who promised to come back from the other side to tell survivors what it was like. No one ever did. His father had been uncomfortably matter-of-fact about his own mortality. Of course, he would die. Who didn't? The ruined journal entry was not surprising in its apparent choice of theme, but in its sad tone. But what did it mean? And who was Ruth?

The venue for Faris' rumination was the Yamacraw County Cemetery and Columbarium, about a mile from the center of town. With arched iron gate, it presented itself not as a humble country bone yard, but as a soulful sanctuary, a monument to life. Beneath the arch, visitors and new residents approached the graveyard through a simple cattle guard, and then passed along a winding commons rudely mown without attention to the overgrown collar along the tumbledown chicken wire fence. Old hardwoods offered graveside shade, as weedy myrtles lined up eager at the fence. Inside, the dead lay sorted unceremoniously by date of arrival, democratically filing into a plot matrix with all the charm of a bingo card. Section E, Row 1, Plot 3: Mrs. Ruth Biggers; Section A, Row 5, Plot 9: Rev. Clement Fordyce. The economies of gravediggers' work dictated that the flat spots near the front filled up first. Now, in the second century of the cemetery's history, only sloped plots toward the back remained, where the field drained slowly to a shallow cypress bottom. New plots lay separated by rain-eroded yellow clay and gravel paths. A rusty backhoe sat mainly out of sight next to a frame shed, hidden by weedy bluestem and switchgrass. A single, grizzled hickory served as the cemetery's hub, pushing away contemptuously at older graves with its roots.

Coffins and concrete vaults attested to the survivors' dread of future entombment and walled up their kin against natural decay. Plastic flowers and patched graveside tents lent the air of a hobo's picnic. The cemetery had a rule against plastic flowers but no one with the gall to enforce it. The canopies usefully protected mourners from the sun or rain or snow, even though snow was so rare as to tempt the very dead out of their graves for a look. Stone carvers chiseled obligatory remembrances of dates and sentiments on granite greeting cards. *Beloved Wife and Mother, Taken Before His Time, In our Hearts Forever, Wearing Wings in Heaven, A Blessed Child of God, In the Bosom of The Lord.* Newspaper death notices and funeral cards, too, sought to soften death's harsh blow with language of the Beyond. Hardly anyone just died; they passed away or made their transition or gained their promotion or rejoined their beloved or won their reward in heaven. The majority, it seems, were invited to join Jesus in celestial paradise. Absent was any report of the town's sinners roasting in hell. Saint or sinner, at the transcendent moment, the dying were inevitably surrounded by loving family, precluding any escape attempt.

The earth ignored it all, while swelling and shrinking with temperature, moisture and season. Hillocks heaved up under hickory roots. Unvaulted coffins collapsed into themselves. Sedge overgrew the graves. In time, headstones bent with the rhythmic uplift and subsidence of the land. Year by year, the cemetery's maw of crooked stone teeth slowly chewed up the dead. New graves mounded up in protest against overcrowding. Some of the dead, like the legendary town drunk Vernon Fuqua, never settled down into the dirt. Everyone else gradually flattened out, but Vernon was a pain even in death; his grave's big belly of dirt stood in cirrhotic testament to his taste for the grape.

No Hyacinthus here, giving birth to beautiful flowers from his blood; just dandelions and jimson weed, ragweed and crabgrass, maybe the occasional exuberance of a sweet gum sapling, reaching up to the sun where it was not wanted. April was not the cruelest month, after all; all months were equally cruel, receiving the newly dead, spurning remembrance, however long it might take.

Rambling along the defiladed graves, Faris was moved and slightly ashamed. He had no use for the weepy sop of funerals. In his mind, such high ceremonials hid our disregard for the dead, replacing genuine grief with stylized social gatherings, no better than a senior prom. Japanese Buddhists appealed more, with ritualized Obon Festival expressions of gratitude to their ancestors and the tradition of death poems as testament to life.

Earlier that morning, Oscar Turner's funeral had been held in a church he never attended, filled with friends whose love for him was deeper than he had dreamt and greater than they ever allowed while he was alive. Loving the dead, after all, is cost-free, whereas the living can be expensive. The venue was predictably Methodist, in the land of John Wesley. Sitting on a green manicured lawn in the middle of town, the church was built in a style that said Southern Functional – part town hall, part house of worship, vaccinated against beauty by weak Protestant imagination and a small construction budget. Inside, the whitewashed walls and oak pews sat atop clay-colored tile, a holy space consecrated to antiseptic Christian circumspection. It ministered to the whole community when called upon, but without excess.

The service was as memorable as the honoree. Reverend Chester Ridley, the rock-ribbed mediocrity who served as pastor, thought himself better than his congregants, who in turn thought of him as a closet Anglican. In the service of his ministerial arrogance, he spent much time alone. He was all mannerism, prone to arching his neck with his nose in the air, grimacing as he began a service, a great Methodist tortoise of indeterminate age and endless thick folds of skin lapping over his white collar. The movement of his lava lamp of neck flesh mesmerized his parishioners far more than did his sermons. Children worried that it had a life of its own and would come at night to make them pay for their little sins. Still, Old Ridley took his vocation seriously and tried to impart sacred lessons to his flock. In Oscar's service, the old chelonian humbug played an unsatisfyingly reduced role of emcee, since Oscar Turner never worshiped under Rev. Ridley's guidance, or anywhere else.

More than fifty people attended, the newspaper said, ladies in pastel straw hats and print dresses, men in a jumble of work clothes and Sunday suits. They came to be with each other and to show themselves and others their regard for Oscar and their right to a piece of him. They also hoped to show through their presence and remembrances that they were important figures in the newly past lives of the dead. And Rev. Ridley's neck was always worth the price of admission.

Now he stood in the apse, behind the bier, rocking on the balls of his feet as the attendants slowly entered and sat down. With practiced timing, he slowly stepped back into the altar, which elevated him by two steps above the congregation. Faithful to the ritual, Ridley coughed up the usual stuff, which in Pincus was less severe and theological than childish, religious understanding *qua* Sunday school coloring book. "Oscar Thomas Turner was promoted earlier this week, having earned his angel's wings after a earthly lifetime of goodness," of which the reverend showed he knew nothing. "As all of you know better than I, Oscar was beloved amongst men, and I say that by way of including the ladies, too. Countless were his good works, and I'm sure we'll all hear wonderful and heartfelt stories about him at the reception after interment. Remember him and his family in your prayers, and remember, too, that we'll all be together on the other side someday, as Oscar is now. Our life on earth is but a day, when measured against all eternity. I'm sure all of you must envy him, for who among us would wish Oscar to linger here in this vale of tears, when he is instead celebrating with his Heavenly Father and a host of angels?"

It grated on Faris that the preacher spoke familiarly of his father, whom he barely knew from buying light bulbs at Turner's. And of course, everyone in the room would have preferred that Oscar linger a bit longer, instead of heading to the other side. But, Faris supposed, this was a man of the cloth, and therefore limited in his thinking to the phrases of the clergy and the rudimentary theological palate of the town's faithful. Unable to resist, Reverend Ridley finished his introduction with the unhelpful observation that "God does not have an egg timer in Heaven to tell him when we're done. We are all called according to our time, inscrutable to all but the divine. Remember, too, that the ecumenist monk Thomas Merton also died accidentally, in his case electrocution, stepping from his bath on a visit to Bangkok." Faris was too tired to try to see clearly through the muddy logic of institutionalized religion and the apparent effort to associate accidental death with virtue and holiness. Instead, he sat in the hard-backed pew, bent forward to relieve his aching back, hands clasped and elbows on his knees. His fatigue looked to others as grieving prayer.

The reverend's odd words of comfort intercalated with a recorded medley of gospel music and spirituals, which Oscar had loved shamelessly, singing out in the hardware store alongside Mahalia Jackson, "I Been 'Buked and Scorned," an old white southerner singing songs of oppression and faith in God. At exactly the right moments in the service, with the congregants being dragged into the mysteries of celestial egg timers, a recording of The Blind Boys of Alabama sang out "Everybody's going somewhere," and then Mahalia pleaded, "If only I could hear my mother pray again."

The memory of Oscar comically singing these old songs moved the attendees to take up Oscar's story as their own, interrupting Old Ridley's formulaic plan for the funeral. It began with an unlikely spear carrier in the person of Tim Little, a middle-aged cotton farmer dressed in an old white shirt and his father's vintage hand painted tie. From time to time, he had worked on Oscar's car while not cleaning toilets and pumping gas in the winter months at Dropcic's Texaco. "Y'all folks please excuse me for standing up. You, too, preacher. But I just want to say that Mr. Oscar was good to me when my wife was sick," going on to relate in halting fashion every man's story of worry and loss. Tommy Noble, the concupiscent druggist, was next. Tommy had recently been laid up in the hospital after a car wreck, and when he got out, the morning coffee crew at the Sunnyside warned each other to break out the chastity belts. Everyone laughed, some harder than necessary. Staring now at his black tassel loafers, he remembered aloud, in a low voice better suited to prayer. "Oscar helped me when my daughter moved in with another girl, and I didn't know what to think. It was just beyond me. You know what I mean. I didn't understand the attraction. Oscar just asked me if I loved my daughter, and of course I did, and I do. 'Then,' he said, 'it's simple. Just keep to loving her. Focus on that.' And that sounded right, so I did. And he was right, and I don't care if she is a lisenby." He looked around for approbation; finding none, he sat down. Others told stories of borrowing twenty dollars, needing a ride to Savannah, finding the right gift, filling out a government form. Old Ridley blushed, as he charged five dollars and a week's notice to fill out forms for the illiterate. A beautiful, nervous young girl by the name of Fuchsia Tremaine remembered how Mr. Oscar had given her bus fare to visit her mother in the hospital in Statesboro and would not hear of repayment. And on it went for quite a while, until the church fell quiet again, except for the groaning of pews and muffled sounds from outside. Congregants tired of sitting still, sad for their loss, crying over their own dead, grateful for the good words, and satisfied collectively that Oscar had been honored. And enough was enough. Angeline Bruce rose, using her beatific voice to invoke St. Hildegard of Bingen, announcing that Oscar's life had been elevated "like a feather on the breath of God." To no surprise, Old Man Strother, a fixture at funerals, chimed in. He rarely spoke, but often sang. On the occasion of Oscar's farewell, he began humming a mournful tune no one had ever heard, a wordless melody that must have been written by a lonely dog. Strother mesmerized the little throng, wearing his topcoat and jersey work gloves, despite the heat of the season. Emmett Chesney from the Live Oak Inn provided the coda, by describing Oscar as a hopeful man, a person who hoped to be a friend and hoped to see a brighter day and hoped to serve people in his workplace. He signed his Christmas cards, Emmett remembered, "High Hopes from Turner's."

The recessional was disorderly. As often as people entered and left rows of pews, they seemed never to figure out the etiquette, so false starts and awkward smiles and the uncertainty of a four-way traffic stop slowed the exit from church. Outside in the morning sun, Oscar's friends smiled and looked around at each other, moist-eyed but agreeing that he'd had a great sendoff. Many wished he had been there to enjoy it as they had. Making their way from the church to the cemetery procession, they were followed by The Chuck Wagon Gang's voices, singing "Some fine morning, when this life is over, I'll fly away. To a home on God's celestial shore, I'll fly away."

Faris had chosen not to ride from the church to the cemetery in the deathly slow funeral procession, preferring to go on ahead in his own silence. He walked from his car to the graveside in roundabout fashion, as if to delay the inevitable. He scuffed at the cemetery's dirt ramble, dirtying his dress shoes, walking alongside his mother's ghost, thinking back as a little boy to his father's efforts to make his weaknesses go away. When Faris ran last in the third grade 50-yard dash, his father swore he ran as fast as anyone in town, but just stayed in the same place too long. And about Faris' over-large head, a perennial subject of teasing at school, his father said that Lenin's head was so large that he fell over as a child, his tiny neck no match for the great orb. It made Faris a youthful Leninist, though he understood nothing of what the Russian Revolution had done. His father's soothing anecdotes always ended with a big hand smoothing Faris' hair and caressing his child-soft cheek.

To Faris, his father was a great man, abandoned by divorcing parents after World War II, serving in the army as a young man, making his little business and family work, denying himself every amenity so that his wife and children could have more. He worked at every small job as if it were life's greatest task, hiding his fears and pain, lest he worry his family, and dying alone in a walk-in refrigerator, working for free. He's the one who should have lain in one of the cemetery's few great crypts, if that's the measure of a life. Instead, as Faris would say at graveside, his father was an ordinary man, a man who was born and lived in a time before men thought of themselves instead of everyone else, a man willing to die in wartime and lucky enough not to have been cast into one. His father was unpretentious in every way, unashamed of the holes in the elbows of his one Donegal tweed jacket, his single pair of oversize thrift shop grey wool slacks taken up so that the rear puckered two pockets into one, forming a delta wing on his butt. His father showed no concern for how he looked, but how he behaved. His integrity had buoyed him through life, even as the zeitgeist relegated virtue to pious eccentricity. Exhibit sympathy toward others, reflect on your shortcomings and try to do better. Forgive yourself and try again tomorrow. If life were measured by how a man lived, Mr. Turner had been a great man, which Faris knew the rest of the world thought was eyewash.

Faris wandered slowly now, Aeneas seeking a gateway to the underworld, yearning to visit the spirit of his father, not to bury his corpse. Postponing the ritual at his parents' graves, Faris stopped at an old stone, painted with chalky bird droppings and bright ochre lichens.

Kathryn Ann Weismuller

b. November 1, 1848 d. October 31, 1872

A Grave, Too Cold and Damp, for a Soul so Warm and True

An encapsulated life, stripped of blood and bone and breath, reduced to treacle. No record of what she looked like, how she laughed – a geisha's titter, or a barmaid's snort? Who would know if she could read and write or whether she cared to? Was she among the few in her time who died with all her teeth? What were her parents' feelings for her, did they knew of the revolutions in Europe the year she was born, did it rain the night she was conceived, did they secretly wish for a boy? Maybe she had a lover who tried to collapse into the grave after her, or maybe she was never loved. No one even knows who chose the fragment from Goldsmith etched on her stone. She may have made the flakiest biscuits or silkiest custards in town. No matter. The prayers, the crying, the generous remembrances, the imprecations of fire and brimstone, the momentary community at graveside staring into the ditch – all these aromatics that were to waft up again this morning in Oscar Turner's interment – have, for the forgotten Kathryn Ann Weissmuller, dissipated in decades of time. As she grew more remote from the present, the distance between her and the first human generations in ancient bogs and bone pits diminished, as if her death announced a long walk backward in time toward her Ur-brethren and away from her contemporaries. Curiosity about old Kathryn Ann Weissmuller these days was limited to Faris' noting that she had arrived and departed around the commemoration of All Souls Day.

Faris walked on, past a ridiculously large neoclassical family vault imposing itself in a rudely monumentalist way, shading nearby graves of lesser volume.

John Krieg, Born April 8, 1904 - Died August 30, 1969

Graceful angels perched atop a crypt more at home in Buenos Aires or Rome, or perhaps in Vienna, entombing a lesser Hapsburg. The stone angels beatifically extended their hands to trilling stone songbirds. The angels' wings hung relaxed, lithic muscles atrophied after years of not having to fly. Krieg owned the furniture store and movie theater, so he bought a tomb fit for

Mussolini. Was this an act of an accomplished burgher, satisfied with life, or a confession of longing for more, the last act of a man who felt he should have been better noticed – a bourgeois Willy Loman? He cheated his customers and stole from his partner. Neither his wife – sick to death from his "wanderings" – nor anyone else cared to join him in the capacious vault. His last mistress might have thought the crypt a step up from the dogtrot where she lived all her life or the barely-marked grave downslope, but no one invited her. Of Krieg's six children, only one appeared at his funeral, the rest ignoring or hating him. The faithful one died of drink, the rest didn't matter. If they were still alive, they were also still gone, which was as good as dead.

John Krieg suffered greatly in his last years, as his stroke-damaged mind spent more time in the spirit world. No one knows whether he knew of Mickey Mantle's retirement, or the moon landing or anything else in the year he died, alone. With time, though, the crypt made him look like a pillar of the community, so maybe the investment was worth it. "And a great sinner lyeth here under the Sycamore," thought Marianne Moore. Except there was no Sycamore here, and Krieg wasn't great, so didn't deserve even a fragment of a fine poem. A more appropriate thought might have been "Just trash ennobled by the crypt."

In the shaded lee of Krieg's vault lay a family plot, squared off by pavers dark as dust.

Gerald Prendergast

July 4, 1948 to June 10, 2000

Mary Ellen Prendergast

January 1, 1950 to April 6, 1980

Steven Sanderson

Geraldine Prendergast

May 22, 1970 to April 6, 1980

Nadia Prendergast

December 23, 1979 to April 6, 1980

They're all piled in together now, as they were in the moment of their death, killed in a single-car accident with Gerald at the wheel. He just fell asleep, pitching his brood into a flooded ditch. Surviving the wreck that ended his family, he managed to die on the same patch of road two decades later. He visited his mother the last afternoon of his life, talked to her about his baby daughter Nadia, named for hope. His mother cleaved to that last visit, convinced he knew his fate. It comforted her somehow. The gravesite is unattended, and the marker minimal, memorializing only the penury of an upholsterer who worked out of his garage.

In his slow procession, Faris, like every other visitor, failed to commune with the silent souls on the other side of the grass. Once, they were characters living unremarkable lives, in their ordinariness still able to move others to anger, laughter or love. Now, like his parents, they just lay silent, fragmentary narratives shorn of their personalities, fixtures in someone else's life. My brother this, or my aunt that, or little Bertie something else. Oh, wasn't it a shame, he died so young, she didn't ever marry, they had no children, she suffered so, his widow was alone so long. Lived clichés, secular litanies spoken over coffee or after church by acquaintances and friends and some who just liked to talk.

By the time the graveside blessing for his father began, Faris' head was ashimmer with disconnected thoughts, like bacteria on a slide, perpetual movement without apparent meaning. His head throbbed and his feet hurt. He was desperate for cold water, a wet cloth on his neck, a place to lie down. He had lost track of his mother's spirit, which had somehow wandered away. Now, no one stood between him and the void, with its ferrous smell of wet dust. No one, that is, but Old Ridley, craning his neck as he looked down his nose at the coffin and mumbled a prayer. With a handful of graveside dirt in his hand, Faris looked past the interment toward a drink to fortify his return to the world of the living. The clods sounded a brutal drumbeat on the casket top. At least the dead were past reflection.

Steven Sanderson

I have committed the worst sin of all
That a man can commit. I have not been
Happy. Let the glaciers of oblivion
Drag me and mercilessly let me fall.
My parents bred and bore me for a higher
Faith in the human game of nights and days;
For earth, for air, for water, and for fire.
I let them down. I wasn't happy. My ways
Have not fulfilled their youthful hope.

Jorge Luis Borges, *Remorse*.

CHAPTER IV

Pincus, with all its shortcomings, was still a place – a specific place, a proper place, a place with a story. Even more, it was a place in the South, which had fancied itself different in the tiresome regionalism of America. With the rest of the Old South, the public paid homage to The Cause, rural life, chivalry and the past. Pincus did not welcome non-Southerners who threatened to dilute its sense of place, or, worse, force them to defend what made this part of the world in any way special. Southern exceptionalism, now on the run from global homogenization, was intellectually muddled but obsessively cherished in Pincus. Also cherished was a strange literary vocation, thanks partly to the almost Russian romanticism of the South, and to the efforts of one man and the enthusiasm of ordinary people for the art of the word. Perhaps that idiosyncratic openness also provided space for an extraordinary experiment in classical democracy. Or perhaps it was just one contrivance following another, irrelevant to everyday life in the little town, but bent on reshaping its prospects. Like secession had been.

Faris could see most of Pincus through the skinny blinds covering the twin front doors of Turner's Hardware. The old store was the unlikely wellspring of Pincus' renaissance-to-be, a museum of dead technologies and antiquated ways of work. If pride of place had any meaning, Oscar Turner's old place of business took up the best spot in the middle of a short block near the traffic light on Broadway.

The little frame-front store listed a bit to the side, along the front line of the old downtown. Behind paired oak and beveled glass doors and a tinkle bell herald for each arrival, six fluorescent fixtures split the long narrow room, shedding the light of a morgue. Each ballast buzzed in its own way, creating a tremor of life above the usually empty store. The occasional patrons suffered the white noise, which smothered their urge to shop and curdled their good humor. Turner's subliminally irritating lights would not raise the dead to anger, but it would surely make them cranky.

Beyond Turner's front door blinds, across Broadway, sat the Laurel Oak Inn, in possession of practically all the charm Pincus could muster. It had been born in the 1950s as a little 15-room motor hotel, as such things used to be called in the heyday of motorized tourist travel after World War II. Travelers might stop in pleasant little Pincus for an overnight on their way from Maryland to Florida, finding the Laurel Oak a welcome end-of-day surprise. Guests found a warm place to rest in a funny little village, possessed of all the old Georgia folk traditions of sylphs, singing trees and root doctors, in addition to the complement of ordinary people calling themselves normal.

The Laurel Oak may have been a dowager, but she took care of herself. She sported a fresh pastel mint exterior with darker green and bright white trim, a signature shade oak in the coquina parking lot and a willow thriving in a poorly-drained patch of tiny lawn in front of Reception. Whitewashed stones lined the walk to the office screen door. Sedge peeked from every crevice. A flickering cursive neon sign unhelpfully announced NO/VACANCY to seasonal pilgrims. Underneath the light bulb, moths made love to a faux sun, and summer cicadas sang until people practically lost their minds and prayed for winter. Muddy when wet, dusty when dry, the footpath to the Laurel Oak's Sunnyside Café drew new customers, old friends and sand gnats.

According to Old Man Strother, the town oracle, ambassador to funerals and resident eccentric, the oak tree in front of the motel sang at night, possessed as it was of magical powers. Sometimes he could be found there around dusk, humming along, Pincus' own druid. To appearances he was no Apollo, but he often stood still before his Daphne, now a landmark Laurel oak in a little town, her heart beating beneath the bark and her uncombed tresses parading as leaves. No one would know about Strother's commune with the tree, because no one knows these kinds of things anymore. In days not all that long past, though, when Strother was a child, the people of Georgia were much more closely tied to antiquity through myth and folklore and belief in the spirits of the natural world. Now, Strother alone represented the history of regional conjurers. He was their solitary consul and interlocutor to the Other Side.

The Laurel Oak promised a clean room, crisp cotton sheets cooled by air conditioners, private baths, cable TV and pretty near the best buffet imaginable at night. Over the grill at its Sunnyside Café stood a yellow sign with red script that promised honestly, "Better Food Than You Eat at Home." The morning coffee was hot, and co-owner Ethel Chesney was a short-order breakfast cook nonpareil. Her husband Emmett cured his own venison jerky, which stood in twists in a two-gallon jar in the front of the diner. His pulled pork was the proud foundation of Ethel's breakfast special: two eggs any style, griddle-crisped pork, cheese grits and buttermilk biscuits, which went just fine with Ethel's muscadine jelly. Fame for her green fig marmalade (the secret was fresh ginger) and muscadine jelly had led Ethel injudiciously to name their only child and unsteady successor Muscadine, which the wags agreed was truly better than if she had chosen to name her Fig.

In its prime, the Sunnyside Café was ground zero for what passed for the power breakfast in Pincus. The sound of tires crunching across the coquina, salesmen chatting at the counter with their ties undone, local kids lingering over pancakes and milk, vacationing families fresh with energy for the new day's adventure – all these things made the center of town seem alive. Ethel made a point of hiring boys out of jail to wash dishes and bus tables, so they would stay out of trouble and have some pocket money, giving them a leg up and creating a reserve of good will in the community. She shrugged off her generous nature with a sweaty grin, saying she just wanted to be a good egg who served good eggs.

Across the street at Turner's, all was dust and remorse. Row by row, the shelves announced *Paint and Brushes, Garden Implements, Automotive, Cleaning Supplies, Household Organizers, Plumbing*. Loose bins of nails, screws, brads, nuts, and washers sat above dirty brown boxes of paper bags, jammed tight against rolls of braided wire and picture hanging pins. Lonely old cylindrical fuses with faded paper labels waited next to light bulbs in crackled cardboard sleeves. LED nightlights stood arrogantly apart on pegboard hooks, sneering at mock-candle incandescents.

The dry goods were hopelessly stuck at least a generation behind. Vintage auto timing lights were useless, pushed aside by cars too smart for homespun mechanics. Under glass cases in the front lay old-time notions, nose pads for reading glasses, bobby pins, cheap Chinese decoupage pill boxes, eyeglass repair kits with their tiny screwdrivers and flimsy plastic tubes, and a medieval-looking nose and ear hair trimmer. Pressed up against the front window was a collapsible cardboard display of scented Christmas candles. The light scum of dissipation made them sticky to the touch.

Faris' father had kept fishing lures and salmon eggs and a live bait box out back for his oldest customers, along with plug tobacco. Now the bait box was empty and stank of years of fish. Men dipped mint-flavored snuff in packets; only the oldsters chewed. No one knew of a distributor who handled plug tobacco at all anymore, and

Georgia didn't allow anyone to buy it through the mail. The place was all so dead.

Old customers were all that remained. Everybody else drove out to Wal-Mart or left Turner's quickly after their fluorescent irritation therapy. Aside from hair curlers and home barber kits, Turner's no longer stocked minor appliances at all, since no small proprietor had a price advantage over Wal-Mart or Amazon. Faris made a note to get rid of the remaining large appliances, among them a chest freezer with no auto-defrost; two professional electric meat smokers – the old timers thought the use of electricity for smoking meat was a sign of the end; a band saw and bench, they eyeballing kind, not the laser-guided kind; and an antiquated dishwasher on casters that connected to the kitchen sink. He might as well have black and white TVs or console hi-fi record players. While Wal-Mart perfected just-in-time inventory management, Turner's had the monopoly on stuck-in-time.

As Faris stood in the middle of the store for the first time as its proprietor, the old floor seemed to groan with new resignation. This is where his father held court, helping illiterate customers read labels, giving advice when asked, asking after the health of everyone who walked through the door. Oscar was a giver, never a taker. His customers, in contrast, never seemed to consider that they needed to buy something from him now and then.

The store was still a beloved gathering place, though suddenly quieted by the death of its owner. Faris remembered through the thick gauze of time how the men of Pincus had filed through Turner's, as he, in childhood, had tucked up against his father's legs. Some spoke to him or tousled his hair, embarrassing him. Others paid him no more attention than a box of tacks. He avoided the few who would smack him at the first opportunity, hard-bitten old farmers and mill workers who beat their own children and still had some left over. He was sure that the town fathers had given all adults plenary rights to smack kids for offenses universal to their station. Plenty of kids ran around with knots on their head as proof. Not in front of his father, they wouldn't; so, Faris hung close. Sneaks like Miss Bauermeister, the penmanship teacher, got him while he was unprotected, hitting him in school for being left-handed, until his parents found out and made her stop.

Faris made coffee on the large Bunn machine ordered by Pup 'n Suds and then never picked up or paid for when times got hard. He laid open the card-table size "party assortment" of donuts, awaiting the inevitable stream of well-wishers paying respects to his father or simply filing through the store from habit. Maybe they had a new story or wanted to retell an old one, or just wanted to escape from some unnamable something that had them worried.

Faris knew he could never assume his father's mantle in any true sense, because he was as closed in on himself as his father was expansive. No one would ever spill their guts to Faris the way they routinely did to his father. He could never lend money, give advice, patronize old ladies, or perform the myriad acts of mercy that made his father succeed in his own non-material way. The undeclared question before the town was whether the son could turn the father's business into a proper enterprise, something that would sustain him in a place without much of a future. It seemed doubtful that the local consumers would help anymore than they had when his father was alive. For Faris, the question was whether he could finally find his special place in life in this old town full of ghosts. It didn't have to be that special to compare favorably to his past.

Faris hadn't come to much. It might as well have been written on the lid of the casket he had watched being committed to the wet earth, nothing left to pretend. Faris' mind churned like this on its own useless, self-referential tracks, his native intelligence and curiosity betrayed by an utter lack of discipline in thought and complete, neurotic anxiety about his fit in the world. If he had had more talent writing verse or music, he could have been a jazz or hip-hop artist, riffing and huffing and alliterating as stuff lighted up like glitter in his head day and night. His mother always told him he thought too much, without helping him know what the right amount of thinking might be, or whether not thinking might have helped his condition at all. Not that it was an option. He didn't think because he wanted to. He just thought. He couldn't help it. Awake, he wondered if Penny were really Sky King's niece and whether Hop Sing objected to his phony accent in Bonanza. In his dreams he fell out of windows, couldn't outrun bears, missed the last exit, got kicked out of class, lost his trousers, almost had sex, ran over the dog, accidentally shot the neighbor's horse, or got stabbed by a stranger. And that was just during the daytime. Louis Agassiz reportedly said with his dying breath, "Nobody can ever know the tortures I endure in trying to stop thinking." He was Faris' kind of guy.

The school psychologist told Faris' parents years ago that Faris had a different "cognitive style." She said it as if the black plague were a different health choice, susceptible to techniques of human betterment or the right placement in school. Oscar discounted her assessment, noting that she was really just a glorified test-giver working a circuit of public schools in eastern Georgia and dispensing half-baked counseling and test scores that would channel children into their educational futures on the basis of invented metrics. That was that. His parents were besotted with Faris, an only child. They told him they'd had a perfect boy the first time and could wish for nothing more. They believed in Faris utterly, without knowing how to make him behave in order to succeed or how to praise him usefully. If they had a fault, it was praising mediocrity. Knowing he was equal parts smart and odd, his parents redoubled their efforts to convince him he was special, even as the bullies at school pasted him around, threw water on the front of his pants before the morning bell, even put garbage on his cafeteria tray. He couldn't defend himself against such great numbers, especially since he would have voted against himself and joined the other boys in the taunting, if only he could have managed an out-of-body experience. He never had any faith in his parents' praise, sadly seeing through the love. Such was his impoverished sense of self, and no amount of love at home could cure it.

He was a drifty, inattentive student, but that didn't matter in the 1980s, because his standardized test scores were perfect, and no one outside the county paid attention to the grades from Pincus High. In the great American tradition of regional prejudice, colleges outside the South assumed that his grades were assigned by substandard teachers, but that test scores made him a good bet for regional balance in their enrollment. He had scholarship offers from a few universities but chose to attend a New England college of modest reputation, because it was small and far away. An involuntary Faulknerian, he denied hating the South but had to separate himself from its suffocating provincialism. In the cloister of upper class New England, he found an equally well-tended, stultifying regionalism and small-mindedness, like the pathetic rocky patches called farms in upstate New York. The other students were white and upper class, second-tier graduates of Andover, Choate, Kent, St. Paul's, Deerfield and endless other schools he'd never heard of. His peers were the ones who couldn't get into Harvard and Yale and Princeton and Williams, despite their many advantages and legacy connections. Smug despite their plain dullness, they disdained the South for its racism without ever having a routine encounter with a person of a different color in their own lives. That is, unless they might count the kitchen help. They assumed that all Georgians were farmers and ate with their hands, he supposed. His professors' contact with him was nil, beyond a snide remark now and then about how wonderful it must be for a Georgia boy to be able to attend college in the North.

The stigma was a blessing. Hiding in the library, he acquired a great passion for literature and poetry, reading everything that crossed his path in his gluttonous, undisciplined way. He became a first-rate intellectual dilettante and academic water bug, flitting from spot to spot. Friendless, he became an idea man, a peddler to no one in particular of wild dreams that had no chance in real life. He dreamt on a grandiose scale, of writing the Great American Novel, of leading a new Southern school of literature, of spending his life as a mildly (so as not to be too gothic) tortured artist. He might have been clinically delusional, were it not for his firm disbelief in his own value. So, instead of acting on the ideas, he just invented reasons not to. He chose, if choice is the word, to put one foot in front of the other, walking the wide lane that lay between his thoughts and opportunity. To make ends meet, he sewed together a patchwork of temporary teaching assignments for courses no ranked faculty member wanted to teach: Introduction to Composition, Short Fiction, and German Literature. On the side, he tutored high school students for standardized tests. He traveled on the cheap and read deep into each night. And he thought without acting, which he supposed was generally better than acting without thinking, or acting at all.

Faris took a certain perverse pride in viewing life in general through the rear-view mirror, substituting invented meaning and purpose in history for his own aimless lack of initiative. It seemed to him that life only took on the patina of coherence when looking to the past. In his intellectual wandering through 20th century cultural history, he had been taken by Walter Benjamin's view of Klee's Angelus Novus – the angel of history facing backward while hurtling uncontrolled into an unknowable future – like Sybil, only looking in the wrong direction. This small painting was interpreted without compunction by ideologues and art critics and prissily declared as an icon of current historiographical cliché. To Faris, it meant that looking back at life in general spared you the particularity of your own unintelligible life.

Now, he found himself stuck in real life with no help. With the same resolve the weak and trembling Nicholas II must have felt as he stared into the barrel of the Russian revolution, Faris' thoughts turned to his final, simple purpose in life: to do something right and good. When the final doors closed on his father's life, the front door of Turner's opened to welcome his son. With the coffee machine steaming and sniffling, sweet donut smell filling the musty, fluorescent-lit whitescape of Turner's Hardware, Faris felt imprisoned by the death of a relative, locked inside someone else's story, for good.

The tinkling bell at the door sounded the arrival of Henry Jeffords and the beginnings of a plan. After Henry settled his mitts on a large glazed cruller, a parade of others coursed through, slowly passing by the donut box as if it were a self-serve casket, then lingering uncomfortably with powdered sugar or chocolate on their fingers and in their stubble, seeming to feel the ghost of their friend Oscar Turner. Small conversations among men with crossed arms, old suits, and lisle socks with no elastic reprised every small town post-funeral gathering. "It just ain't right," someone would observe. "Pincus won't be the same." "He went too soon." "Is that one cream-filled or jelly?" "Why would a good man have to die like that? "God truly does take the good ones, leaving us with the trash." "Where's the coffee creamer?" By mid-day it was clear to Faris and the remaining trash left by Oscar that they all hoped that Turner's would have a continuing role in the life of the town and its citizens. Less apparent at the moment was that the town fathers were coming around to anoint Faris as the best possible stand-in to play the role of his father, counselor to customers who never bought anything, and uneasy company *cum* day care to old-timers who sat toothless, or nearly so, on the Fifties-style chrome and naugahyde couch across from the cash register counter. All that was missing was a cracker barrel.

The inevitable and continuing subject of debate at Turner's was the decline and fall of Pincus. Much like retirees with too much money and too little to do, the senior citizens of Pincus coveyed up with their own and talked with great conviction about high taxes, out-of-control liberalism, the failure of public education, the dangers of Dead Man's Curve just outside town, the regrettable state of today's youth, the moral corruption of video games, and the steeply sloping decline of the West. Regulars in the debate club included Henry, of course; Marlon Hockett, who called himself Sheriff Emeritus, voted out of office after years of election fraud, and now proud proprietor of 301 Spirits, a package store he had helped license in partnership with the county judge and some friends in State Revenue; Brother Alford Parsons, pastor of the Thankful Baptist Church, spouse of LeDonna and retired county councilman, who fashioned himself the legitimate voice of the African-American community (which, in fact, was several communities that hadn't appointed him official voice, a requirement he waived); Emmett Chesney, a no-nonsense businessman proudly able to trace his family back to Oglethorpe in the 18th century, for all the good that did; Carl Plummer, owner and funeral director at Plummer's Funeral Home, and thanks to financial exigency a minority shareholder in the black funeral home Washington & Washington Funeral Directors (whose proprietor Rodney Washington saw himself as the legitimate voice of the African-American community, and not Brother Parsons); and Sister Angeline Bruce, the former nun from Sacred Heart Convent in Savannah, who had abandoned her religious vocation — but not the honorific title — when Henry's father sponsored her at The Bread Basket, lately the scene of Mr. Turner's demise.

The fact that a woman was included in the group was Faris' only obvious show of leadership. No one else would have thought of including a woman because they barely knew how to talk to each other, without throwing in gender identity to complicate matters. Everyone knew Angeline to have been Faris' first girlfriend in high school. Her abrupt disappearance from town was legendary, announced by a Dear John letter to him confessing that she had found the Lord and preferred Him to Faris. He found it on the first day of school in his senior year, when it had appeared on the bulletin board next to the senior class lockers. Everyone in school had read it, in adolescent shock at her cruelty. It was still great sport to ride Faris for being bulldozed in love by Jesus. He weakly responded that at least he lost to a better man.

In addition to this core, the debate was irregularly leavened by other townsfolk. In retrospect, Turner's may have been the unwitting catalyst in the creation of a public agenda, well before it emerged in full form.

"The problem as I see it has three elements, and they're all more difficult than making a living in town," pronounced Henry one spirited morning. Henry did not offer ideas for discussion, only pronouncements. He had the curious habit of promenading as he spoke. Henry thought it made him look like a law professor, chin high, eyes lidded, purposeful strides punctuated by a military about face, and then another little march. In fact, he looked as a school child imitating the guards at Buckingham Palace. "First, it is manifest that the town is dying, not only economically but civically. Second, the people in town have no voice in the public affairs of Pincus, without which no civic revival is possible. And third, the reason for the first two elements is partly the lack of a proper forum for them to voice their opinions in an efficacious manner." Stage direction: about face, look down the nose.

And then began the round robin.

"All that's fine, Henry, but you can't save a town unless the businesses prosper, and they just can't compete. You can't blame people for going to Wal-Mart or even Home Depot down in Statesboro, when downtown prices and inventory aren't as good. Turner's just can't cut it. You could say the same for the drugstore, Van Perkins,' Ritter's and practically every other business except maybe for the Dew Drop and the funeral homes. I even see some of Emmett's old lunch customers sneaking down to the Wal-Mart for the $1.99 hot dog and coke. "

"These are all facets of the same problem," offered dear Angeline, in a voice that made Faris' trousers tingle in homage to times past. "The recipe for saving Turner's is the same as it is for saving Pincus. So, if we manage one, we accomplish the other." Her sisterly optimism made the bodice of her shirtwaist rise and fall seductively with her eager breath. It left Faris wanting to peek behind the cotton again. No one else seemed to notice his discomfort or her bodice. She used to be a nun, after all.

The discussion went on and on, becoming both more exercised and more tiresome with every breath of its predictability. The Sheriff Emeritus — people called him Emeritus and teased that the E stood for "you're out" and the meritus meant "you deserved it" — offered up nutty opinions about turning out the voters for this and that, but to the others it reeked of a bygone era of passing around farm surplus welfare commodity cheese and peanut butter, and driving bribed voters to the polls. The welfare commodities had disappeared in the 1960s, though the same could not be said for the vote buying. Now people were more cash-minded, which was too bad, in a way. In the old days, at least the kids got cheese and peanut butter.

Marlon dressed each morning to look mean, in a sharp khaki uniform without insignia, shined cordovan boots and a chocolate felt Stetson. Turned out with style and authority, he went out looking for offense. He liked being feared and didn't stand for any of what he called gimcrackery, a broad category of misbehavior of which there was always too much. Marlon thought he was still in the driver's seat, convinced that his turn would come again, once the people realized how important he was to public safety and order in the world. It bothered him not at all that no one else in Pincus shared that opinion or paid him more than superficial respect. Possessed of the baleful countenance of a basset hound that had seen into the spirit world, Marlon was, to the white community, a rough, but necessary man of his times, willing to grease the wheels of criminal justice with patronage. To the black community, he remained a blatant racist and provocateur, a cadger of hate, impelled by roughly equal parts malice, corruption and stupidity. And even his erstwhile admirers were now reluctant to confess to any faith in him, since he stole elections, commandeered a liquor license, and consorted with moonshiners and wildlife smugglers when convenient. Any sound of sympathy was drowned out when the door chime to 301 Liquors sounded, and his two pet mynahs, named Rebel and Tarbaby, no less, would give a Pavlovian response. Rebel would shout "Call the Sheriff, Call the Sheriff!" And Tarbaby would respond, "Don't shoot!" Emeritus thought this was all very clever, as did his limited company of fellow racists, mainly superannuated white men and selected young rednecks toting cases of beer. He was as contemporary as a canvas tent, heavy, musty and stiff with overuse.

Brother Alford blamed the problems of downtown commerce on the lack of attention to black people, whose own consumer preferences were ignored or denied by white merchants. Little black children liked to eat smoked mullet in the summer, but Mrs. Dropcic at the gas station quit selling it when the law made her sell to Negroes through the front door. She also put an Out of Order sign on the toilet when black customers came in. When the Parsons girl was little, LeDonna famously threatened to let her pee on the floor unless

Mrs. Dropcic produced the bathroom key. While the Laurel Oak took pride in its genial atmosphere, no black man felt as welcome there as he did at Ed's BBQ. And white people never shopped at black businesses, except for LeDonna's, and then only for nails, not hair. What white man ever got his hair cut at Ebony Barbers? People didn't even stop for gas at InTown Gas because it's in a black section of town. And then there were the Indians – dot, not feather, Brother Alford hastened to clarify – with their payday loans and convenience stores, selling honeybuns and lottery tickets. Ignoring the differences between Indians and the Pakistani-Americans who owned the local convenience store, Brother Alford was just getting started. Referencing the Montgomery bus boycott of the early civil rights movement, he fulminated, "The black man...."

"The trouble with the blacks," Emeritus began....

Rev. Alford was out of his chair like a scalded cat. "The blacks?' You mean niggers, don't you, Sheriff? Or coloreds. Isn't that what you mean when you say 'the blacks? Isn't that what you say when you're with your friends?'" Cabin pressure plummeted in the room. "Marlon, what you know about black people would fit in a thimble with room to spare. You white people only care about black people before they're born and when they're dead, so that don't count. You steal the black man's business but don't ever – and I mean ever – cross into the black community or have a single black friend you can name. You don't live like we do, but you sure feel easy telling us all about it. How about if I come to your house and tell you how to take care of your children and how loud to sing at church and how you should turn your radio down and whether you should sit on the porch after dark and how you wear your clothes and style your hair and behave in front of black people? That'd be fair, wouldn't it? I believe it was the very King of France who said that rich and poor were equally free to live under a bridge." Brother Alford was getting a second wind. "And, about them damn blackbirds of yours...."

"No, Alford, it wasn't the King of France. It was Anatole France, the novelist, and he said that the law forbids the rich and the poor alike to sleep under bridges."

"Well, Henry, that's exactly my point. And thanks for the unnecessary correction, by the way." Undaunted, Brother Alford put his thumbs in his vest as he had seen Al Sharpton do. The old Al Sharpton, the fat one. Not the new, skinny, TV Al Sharpton.

Several participants defended the sheriff as a good man, who did as well as he could in a difficult time. He kept order, caught criminals, let kids off with warnings and a scare, and made donations to the Boys' Club every year. He was not completely bad, and he was a part of the community. Brother Alford steamed, but conceded their arguments. Unspoken was the truth that moments of virtue didn't make Marlon a good man.

Emeritus, partly redeemed, got up to leave. He was drowning in the shallow end of the discussion and offended that he didn't get to offer his theories of society. He thought of ways he could try to screw the preacher, but it would be difficult, given Brother Alford's popularity and the lack of resources now available to the ex-sheriff. Muttering, "Oh, there was a time, Brother Alford, when you wouldn't have dared speak to me like that," he glared at the minister with hate. The old constable stayed, only at Faris' bidding, flattered into believing that his involvement was essential to the venture's success. But after two hours of talk, the moment had fled. The room had become hot and the participants irritated. Butts numbed from too much sitting and too little circulation cried out for closure. The donuts were gone. Marlon's face seemed to be melting with sweat. Brother Alford appeared to be playing Yahtzee or Tetris or something on his cell. He was, in fact, already filling LeDonna in on his performance.

Henry finally put an idea on the table. "I've been thinking. Saving Pincus does, in fact, depend on the people. But the community is all chopped up and isolated. Nobody's in touch with each other, like in that book about bowling alone. All the togetherness and trust are gone, what they call social capital. We don't have enough because we're all stuck in front of the TV or at work, not doing things together. And folks are unused to speaking up. It's a little like Brother Alford says: We've become like any other town in America, where black people and white people and practically any different mix of people don't really get together, except at Wal-Mart or a high school game. And then they're paying attention to something else."

"Who bowls alone? If that isn't the damnedest thing. Nobody bowls alone, Henry. Come on, now." Emeritus had now lost all sense of what this conversation meant.

Henry persevered. "The kids aren't committed to Pincus, and why should they be? They leave us as soon as they can, for Atlanta or Charleston or Charlotte or Savannah. Would they stay if things were different? That's a question we'll never answer, unless things change. Never mind the Mexicans and Asians coming in and changing things, even though that has its good points, like the House of Mao and El Taco Grande and Touch of India restaurants. Who knows what the new people think? Who asks them? Not us. Shouldn't we? People like us can talk about the town's problems but we never hear different points of view or ideas that might work."

"So," he went on, picking up vigor like a dust mop after lint, "I think the first step is to figure out how to bring out the town to express its opinions and go from there. But meanwhile, I know you all want to move some merchandise. So, my idea is to invite people to use their purchase receipts from Turner's or The Dog Ear to write down a topic describing the problems facing Pincus that they would agree to present for public discussion. The receipt is their ante into the game. We could have a meeting to discuss the best topics from the receipts. The owners of the winning ideas get to make a speech about the topic and get a gift from Turner's for their trouble. Faris gets to unload some inventory, I might sell a few more books, and people might actually offer up some ideas. Otherwise, it's just us talking."

"I think I can get the elementary school auditorium to use for the forum if we can make the meetings when school isn't in session, as long as it's not a religious meeting."

"Who said anything about religion?"

"Nobody. It's just a rule."

"Let's not start listing a bunch of stupid rules, especially godless ones. That's part of this country's problem, lack of respect for God. Most Americans think like I do, that religion is necessary for moral development, and government tries to smother it at every turn. And by the way, why does Turner's get to be the hub for this? Why not the Sunnyside?" Emmett was an intuitive thinker, not too strong on logic and mainly unconcerned with evidence. He didn't know about atheists, how they made it through the day. He did know self-interest, though, and was fiercely protective of the café.

"So, I get the idea: instead of moving forward, let's have a fight over who gets credit for an idea that hasn't even been tried. That's why this town is going to hell in the first place." Sister Angeline rarely spoke in such strong terms and never used profanity in public. Everyone fell quiet. Faris' trousers reawakened for just a second, then slept again.

"Nobody is going to show up just like that. Remember when they were going to de-annex half the town and only 25 people showed up to the city council meeting? Or when the judge wanted to site a halfway house next to the Methodist Church, and only the preacher and a half dozen old ladies came to protest? The only way to get people to come to a public meeting is to promise they'll be exempt from jury duty, or raffle a gun."

"What kind of gun?"

"Maybe they don't show up because they don't think anyone cares," mused Sister Angeline charitably, but with a hint of fatigue.

"They don't show up because they count on folks like us to do the public's business. They trust us so they don't have to waste their own time." Marlon had bought back in, feeling clearly that he understood what people wanted.   Endless wrinkles of vice and cigarette smoke swallowed his smug look.

"That's just the point, Sheriff." Henry was now lathering up Marlon by calling him Sheriff, which the old man loved to hear. And Henry was telling everyone that Marlon was right. So there, Emeritus thought. Henry continued. "As you know, the noted German critical theorist Jurgen Habermas has given us the notion of the public sphere and a theory of communicative action, whereby the people – the real people, not the government – come together in public forums to move their political interests."

The Sheriff stepped into another intellectual hole and found himself over his head again, which was usually the case when he listened to Henry; but he could not reject his flatterer, so he just swept at the brim of his Stetson, which lay on his knee. He tried to look like he got it.

"What about the needs of the black man? The black man's been ignored too long."

"Please, Brother Alford. No need for an Al Sharpton speech. How about staying on the subject for a minute?"

"The black community is the subject, if you ask me."

"Well, the trouble with that is that the town isn't all black, and we're trying to talk about the whole town, not just part of it."

"If you raffled a really nice shotgun, maybe a turkey gun, boy, I'll bet you'd get a crowd. I'd like to have a new gun. A camo autoloader. Course, I'd want a turkey choke for it, too."

Henry intervened again, relishing his role as mediator and thought leader. "Let's look at process first. To begin with, let's organize ourselves as the Committee to Save Pincus. We can have officers and take roll and record minutes of our meetings." Henry was a compulsive organizer, someone who had color coded dividers in his ring binder since childhood, who had played school when not in school and finished first in the summer reading competition at the public library. Henry had apprenticed for years to cultivate the ability to kill enthusiasm with a single verbal blow.

A collective groan called the meeting to a close, with the only agreement to survey the donut box one more time for stragglers and meet again the following week to discuss progress. Several weeks went in similar fashion, only bringing prosperity to the donut shop and incremental girth to the committee. A quiet debate began about which donuts had the best shelf life.

Eventually, though, the group agreed to create some kind of Pincus public forum, more or less along the lines of the original model: ideas in twenty-five words or less written on the back of a receipt from any one of the businesses in town, which would be dropped into a fishbowl at Turner's. The Sunnyside Café garnered most of the business, and The Dog Ear's and Turner's proposed roles were diminished, but the idea was intact. No one was going to make money on this anyway.

The resulting entries surprised with promise. Leo Price, the town's senior curmudgeon, came out of seclusion to participate, as he wrote simply "Quality of Life Crimes." Rodney Washington, funeral home proprietor, offered "The Integration of our Economy." Doreen Wagner, the florist, suggested "Animal Cruelty." Ed Prewitt of Ed's BBQ proposed "Food Safety." While many of these seemed unlikely to change the prospects of Pincus, they might be worthy ways of opening a broader public discourse, thought the Committee. And it couldn't hurt to see what evolved. In the meantime, Faris had agreed to offer one of his spare professional meat smokers as a door prize to a lucky attendee of the first public meeting,

CHAPTER V

Every small town demands at least one Chinese restaurant, at which patrons are served food that would not be recognized in China. General Tso's chicken is not Hunanese, but more likely New Yorker. Chop suey houses are one hundred percent American, as is the version of Egg Fou Yong served in the U.S. Before Asian Fusion became the rage in the mass market, ersatz Chinese had long held the banner of invented ethnic food. The House of Mao flew that proud, phony flag in Pincus. Its owner was Vincent Chin, as falsely Chinese as his menu.

Vincent Chin grew up as Minjoon Park, the only child of a Korean-American family in Midwood, Brooklyn. His parents had a tiny rent-stabilized apartment between Ocean Parkway and Coney Island Avenue, near their Korean grocery. It was a hole in the wall among many others, catering to an ethnic trade, caught in the middle of Middle Eastern, South Asian and black American clusters, themselves surrounded by Kosher and Halal vendors and restaurants, attending to everyone from Pakistan to Israel. Brooklyn's proud cultural confusion was a matter of indifference to his family, as the Parks viewed all the various Abrahamic traditions as flip sides of the same coin. Still, they kept their heads down. Things could get frisky in Brooklyn.

As he grew up, Vincent fell in with a rough bunch of minor local players in the massive global trade in animal parts. He and his buddies made periodic road trips for skins and organs – especially black bear gall bladders – delivering from the Southeast US to Brooklyn, where the goods found their way into shipments to China. The same mob transshipped delicacies from Asia to New York through freight services, so that dried fruit bats, shark fin and deer antler velvet could grace the traditional dinner tables of Brooklyn and Queens. In the 1980s, the bear gall trade was fabulously profitable; desiccated bladders were worth more than gold to the traditional medicine trade in China, Vietnam and Korea. Vincent and his friends worked on the cheap, but they could make a hundred dollars each for a two-day trip to North Carolina or Georgia to take delivery. Smoking pot, driving all night in a rental car and stopping off at some no-name hamlet to box and ship other illicit goods was easy and lucrative. Sometimes, they passed through Pincus, where a nearby farm peddled bear parts harvested from the Appalachians, up country, near the Carolina border.

With benefit of their pot-enhanced genius, the boys thought of substituting pig bladders for bear bladders, which in a dried out or powdered state seemed the same. So, they made a deal with a small South Carolina hog operation to sell them the bladders for the price of chitterlings, which was a lot lower than gold. They used their networks in Brooklyn to sell to two different mob outfits and were making great money at the scam. It worked for a while, until the real bile operators found out. They knew more or less where every scarce bladder came from and could not find a source for the abundance produced by Vincent's gang. The boys quickly learned that the illegal trade in animal parts is run by the same sadistic characters who traffic in children, drugs and arms. Vincent discovered one of his friends bound in duct tape and executed on the floor of his high-rise alcove in Rego Park, with what appeared to be black bear fur forming an outline surrounding the tortured body. Vincent interpreted the scene quickly and correctly and used his money to move to Pincus, which he esteemed to be among the most forgettable locations in America. No one could find him there, thought he, especially as a Chinese restaurateur. He knew about the town from an erstwhile connection to a nearby poacher, who had traded with Jesús.

The House of Mao sat across a gravel parking square from Ed's BBQ, back door to back door. Both restaurants were humble, one-story affairs, suitable for a small food service emphasizing take-out, with a few tables to accommodate those who wanted to eat on site. Vincent and Ed both catered to the parking lot crowd comprised of young men drinking out of paper bags, smoking and telling lies until they got hungry. Both restaurateurs depended on the front door and call-in trades, too, as Pincus families had few fine dining opportunities in town. The air surrounding Ed's and Mao's filled with wok grease and smoke six days a week, reminding passersby of down-home BBQ and American Chinese food.

If ever love was shared between Korean-Americans and their African-American brethren, it was lost a long time ago. Vincent, in particular, had been tempered by conflicts in New York between Korean greengrocers and the poor, mainly black, urban neighborhoods they served. He instinctively disliked Ed, a bias reinforced by the zero-sum competition, in which each of Ed's ribs subtracted from Vincent's profit. Vincent also loathed the outdoor lunch wings Ed served, which pushed smoke through House of Mao's kitchen screen door. Vincent could be heard saying indelicately to white customers that Ed's hygiene wasn't what it should be. Periodically, he would pass around foil pans of Chinese sweet and spicy ribs to the alley crowd, taunting Ed, and crowing in his phony accent, "brack man food no good like Chinese. Try to see." Ed, who knew how to bide his time, vowed to get Vincent. He understood competition, too, and his ethical rulebook had a dollar sign on the cover.

The real war between the two began accidentally, after Ed's suffered a break-in overnight early in the summer. Someone pried the cast-iron grid off the kitchen window and squeezed through to pilfer whatever could be found in the register and refrigerator. Beer and brisket were the main casualties, but Ed worried about his insurance, so he reviewed the video from his security camera, which panned the parking square and entryway.

He saw the culprit easily enough: a young, squeeze-through-sized simpleton named Odeon Williams, nicknamed Odd One. Ed was just about to dial the police on his cell phone when he saw something much more intriguing on the video. It was Odd One's good fortune that Ed's camera, recording at high resolution, had captured footage of Vincent Chin, who appeared to be baiting stray cats by the back door of the House of Mao and leaving the screen open for them to enter for more. But why, Ed wondered, would this no-good ghetto Chinaman want cats? Ed would have to review nearly a month's worth of nighttime recordings before coming to his dramatic conclusion, based entirely on the fact that once the cats entered Mao's kitchen, they never re-emerged. Ed knew it was not really evidence of anything, but it might be. Even if not, he thought it could be made to seem otherwise.

Soon thereafter, Ed's fortune dawned when city fathers announced the scheme to gather citizens together to discuss problems Pincus faced and how to resolve them. Ed decided he would participate. Being black, he decided to approach the opportunity with careful observation first. "Food Safety," he wrote on the breakfast receipt from the Sunnyside Café; he folded it twice and slipped it into Faris' fishbowl.

CHAPTER VI

O n the evening appointed for the first meeting, more than 100 people filed into the Pincus Elementary School Auditorium and Cafeteria, chatting and flitting like finches in a punchbowl full of seeds. No one now knows how many came for the door prize and how many were interested in the town's future and how many others were just looking for something to do after dinner until prime time TV. Self-importantly assembled on the small stage in front of rows of folding chairs, The Committee to Save Pincus adjusted their props and huddled with the immediacy of a football squad in the final minute of play. Lack of foresight meant that the Committee had to sit on children's' cafeteria chairs, since the regular size folding chairs were all taken up by the audience. An old wooden easel to the side of the stage held a whiteboard between its wing nuts, announcing "Town Hall Meeting on The Future of Pincus," written in large green block letters with a felt marker. Facing the crowd, Henry's pulse quickened in the familiar exhilaration of a professor on the first day of class.

The heavy crimson velvet theater curtain loomed behind the dais, smelling mildly of gym class, dust, mildew and cafeteria food, exuding a truffly funk. A rustle of anticipation came from the crowd. Maybe it was the occasion itself, or the promise of something for nothing. Maybe it was genuine hope.

Faris stared into the crowd with worried pride. He had helped bring this gathering together, but had no idea what implications his agency might bring. To occupy his nervous mind, he looked for women he knew in the crowd. Faris had read in a magazine that ladies of the evening took street names from the names of their pets and the streets where they lived. He used this as his own private man joke, pairing dogs and cats and street names with women he knew. He saw Ethel Chesney in the front row. Her street name would be Violet Sparkleberry, which sounded sexy and exotic, even though she and her Pomeranian Violet were the opposite. LeDonna Parsons (aka Precious Hemlock), the owner of the nail salon, fit her street name, with a persona at once chastely erotic and vaguely menacing. Others didn't work well at all. Clementine Scroggins, the nutty old minister's wife, had the street name of Buster Sweetgum, conveying an uncomfortable sexual ambiguity. And, with karmic consistency, Muscadine Fuqua bore the sobriquet Pipsy Landing, which sounded like the motion sickness her many paramours might have suffered during the ride.

Hot lights and high hopes made Henry glow with perspiration as he called the throng to order. He was ready with a carefully prepared inaugural speech. "Citizens and friends of Pincus, as well as those who labor here with insufficient documentation," he intoned, inhaling audibly in anticipation of a laugh that never came. "Thank you for coming to this auspicious first town meeting to discuss the future of our fair home Pincus, Georgia. This town can trace its roots back to the great Governor Oglethorpe and his fellow colonist Arthur Pincus, who first set up a trading post on the Savannah River north of here to trade deerskins with the Yamacraw. Those deep roots of our town are the wellspring of our sacred democratic tradition." He paused, with a self-satisfied air. "Now, as everyone understands, democracy traces its roots to the Greek word *demos*, which stands for village and also for the inhabitants of the village. In those classic days of early direct democracy, each man — sorry, ladies, it was only men – each man who wasn't a slave and who could prove citizenship had political rights and obligations. Fast forward to our generation, fired in the kiln of freedom...."

"Christ on the cross, Henry. Kilns? This is supposed to be about the survival of Pincus, not Greece. And shorten up on the lecture, before you chase everyone out of here." This stage whisper from Emmett deflated Henry and provoked a mild titter from the front row. Emmett was a practical man, not given to sitting still for flowery perorations. He had the support of the crowd.

Henry was wounded, but compliant. "All right, then. I know everyone wants to get started. Tonight's first speaker is Leo Price, who would like to offer his thoughts on how Pincus can be made better, by reference to Quality of Life Crimes, upon which he is prepared to expatiate, after which we can engage in a dialogue. Leo, the platform is yours." The bloviator in chief slumped into his tiny chair, knees practically to his chin, which fell with Emmett's admonition and his own flustered run-on sentence at the end. He had not even gotten to the Civil War in his speech or had a chance to bring Habermas back into the discussion. Philistines were all around him. He hoped no one had noticed the run-on sentence. No one had.

Leo rose from the section of chairs reserved for speakers and slowly approached the steps to the red-draped stage. He was a doubtful avatar of hope. A man of seventy-something, Leo sported a tonsure, thick unkempt white hair on the sides of his head and nothing at all on top, a monk of the Order of the Solitary Grouch. His head was a half-inflated ball. Front to back it was perfectly flat, but the side tufts billowed out like a dandelion bloom. His ears were permanently cocked ailerons, his haircut strictly do-it-yourself: no mirror, possibly chopped by one of those replaceable-blade skinning knives. Wearing a checked flannel shirt with suspenders holding up loose-waisted khaki chinos, shuffling soft shoe in what must have been the first fleece-lined lounge slippers ever made, Leo was a singular figure in Pincus. He wasn't Boo Radley, but surely he was a relative.

Leo was mainly unknown to Pincans personally, but he had established an epistolary persona in the morning newspaper with his letters to the editor on matters of public interest. Mainly, these consisted of reflections on the superiority of his own experiences prior to moving to Pincus, the sad incompetence of local civic leaders, and the low state to which the republic had fallen. This latter owed chiefly to disrespectful youth and permissive parents, leavened by unbridled sex on television. Leo's rants invariably included a suggestion of Southern lassitude, which helped his arguments not at all. He may as well have started his essays with "Dear, You Lazy Cracker" and signed them "Superior Yankee."

Leo carried in his gut a sack of jeremiads wrapped in burlap, struggling to get out. Momentarily, on this evening, the gut was quiet as he approached the stage with the righteous stride of a torts lawyer. Inwardly, he thought himself to be a model citizen, eclipsed by an age without decorum and governed by selfishness out of control. He was quiet, well groomed and abstemious in his personal habits. His house on the corner of Hemlock and Landing was a tall two-story Victorian, the kind every little town cherishes as a remnant of imaginary glory days gone by. In a place where nostalgia was mistaken for character, Leo's house was a heritage site. He kept the house immaculate, painted cream yellow with white shutters and trim, crowned by a steep scalloped shingle roof of charcoal grey. The wraparound porch was an elegant but lonely adornment, wasted on a man who rarely came out except for the paper in the morning, eager to see his letters in print. Unused, the porch still was always freshly swept. Dirt on the porch becomes dirt in the entryway, then in the parlor. Nip it in the bud. Clean porch, clear mind, thought Leo Price.

Tall tulip poplars sheltered the thin collar of dwarf azaleas framing the porch. A noble Japanese privet hedge doubled as a privacy fence and sound buffer. Set back ten feet from the sidewalk, the hedge was mature and evergreen. A feathery trim of border grass bordered the curb line, framing the struggling Bermuda patch in between. The doyens of the Pincus Garden Club moaned about his using invasive privet instead of native plants, but Leo ignored them. He hadn't planted them in the first place. They could stuff their pants full of pansies, as far as he cared. They ought to worry more about Muscadine Chesney's dolled-up trailer house next door. That was a real invasive, in a neighborhood of proper houses.

The whole scene would have been near perfect, if it weren't for the hedge's providing an unintended screen for bad-mannered pedestrians with their defecating dogs, and worse. His lawn between privet and curb was generously flecked with dog feces in varying stages of decay. Leo had come to the town hall meeting to seek redress.

Not surprisingly, his main nemesis turned out to be Muscadine Chesney, whom he thought devalued his neighborhood with her low class trailer and aging pet dog Pipsy, which Leo saw as nothing more than a sewer rat. The two chose Leo's yard as Pipsy's favorite place to relieve himself, and other dogs naturally followed suit. Path dependency was like the dirt on the porch. First one dog, then another, then a third that smells the first two; soon enough, everyone thinks your yard is a toilet. He had tried CURB YOUR DOG warnings. They did no good, even the graphic yellow and black silhouettes with a dog hunched over at the ready. Leo had publicly threatened to kill the next dog he caught *in flagrante defaecatus*. His obsessive anti-stool campaign caused parents to warn their kids to cross the street to avoid Leo's, whether it was due to Leo himself or the dog droppings making his yard look like a turd farm. But everyone was in on the joke: on Halloween each year, drunken teenagers joined the dogs in decorating Leo's yard. Everybody shit in Leo's yard. Kids could have written term papers on the subject.

Now came his moment before the public. "In the great city of New York in the 1980s," Leo began, his radio baritone earning quiet gasps from the crowd. With this single clause, the assembled had already heard more out of Leo than in the many years of his hermetic presence in town. "In the great city of New York in the 1980s, where I resided, we were burdened by quality of life crimes beyond measure. Squeegee men assaulted drivers at stoplights to extort money. Panhandlers harassed innocent people everywhere. Street bums urinated and passed out in the corridors of Grand Central Terminal, which, for you tourists, is the proper name, mind you, not Grand Central Station. At that time, for some unknown reason, Grand Central had rows of lockers that ran down the ramps between levels. They were nothing but a bum magnet. Who in his right mind would leave anything in a locker next to a passed-out wino who had soiled himself? But I digress.

"Apartment houses advertised their dangerous disrepair with broken windows and hanging window planters, mocking city safety ordinances. Prostitutes walked the streets with impunity, exposing their wares to man and child alike. Obscene graffiti covered the subways. Fare cheaters defiled public transport. Bootleggers sold single cigarettes on the street. They called them loosies. Bare-breasted stripper bars were all over Times Square. And the police did little to confront what they called minor nuisance lawlessness. That's just New York, people shrugged. It gives the city character."

It was obvious that Leo had written his speech like his letters to the editor. The crowd must have hoped he'd apply the same word limit. They were sorely disappointed.

"Then, Mayor Rudolph Giuliani arrived, and said 'enough.'

Police started to arrest offenders and increase the penalties for these crimes. Squeegees disappeared, hookers took it off the main streets, Times Square cleaned up, slowly restoring civic morale and public order. Thanks to the reduction in quality of life crimes, New York is a different city today, cleaner, safer and less menacing to all who visit or live there. I was there. I know."

"What on God's green Earth does that have to do with us, Leo? Are you writing a book? We don't care about New York or where you lived in the eighties, and since when did you care about quality of life? All you do is sit on your bony butt in that big yellow house, write letters to the editor and harass your neighbors!" It was uncharacteristic of Muscadine to attend a meeting, much less to shout out in public, but her enmity toward Leo ran bone deep.

The burlap sack in Leo's gut stirred at the sound of Muscadine, and he exploded like a homemade bomb. "Because, miss white trash, EVERYBODY SHITS IN MY YARD, and that's affecting my quality of life, which is what I'm here to talk about." He dramatically enunciated each word for effect, pausing as if he were speaking five sentences: "EVERYBODY—SHITS—IN—MY—YARD. What kind of town allows dogs and children to invade a man's property to move their bowels, day and night? Where are you parents when your rotten teenage kids are taking a dump in my yard on Halloween? Where are the cops? Why should I have to pay to clean it up, and why doesn't the law do anything about it? City ordinances require that residents not despoil private property or threaten public health. I'm getting despoiled and threatened, not to mention insulted by a ninny who changes men more often than her underwear. I came here to get answers, and I'm not going home until I do. Stobaugh, what the hell?" He had turned on the chief of police, who was looking as hard as he could at his cuticles, hoping he was invisible. Leo's face was splotched red and white with rage and embarrassment, the corners of his mouth white with tiny marshmallows of spit. He had lost the positive inertia of his speech, as well as his personal composure, and he had blurted out his complaint without building up to it the way he had planned. But he couldn't care less about what people thought of him. He stood firm, both slippers squarely on the stage's scratched floor.

In a voice Henry had practiced for a school shooting that had never come, he quietly approached Leo. With the care of a dogcatcher after a rabid coon, he neared. "Why, Leo, certainly you appear to have some cause for complaint, and I know for sure that Police Chief Stobaugh will be glad to hear from you after the meeting. But this is supposed to be about the future of Pincus, not the alleged vandalization of your property."

Leo whirled in fury to face Henry, rushing to confront him, in the process losing a slipper. "Alleged? Alleged! You think it's alleged? I'll give you alleged. Come over to my place, and I'll shove a pile of alleged dog crap in your face. Then, you'll know whether it's alleged. Because I don't have a dog, and the stuff doesn't grow out of the ground. And if the protection of law-abiding citizens isn't a proper subject for this meeting, Pincus doesn't have a future. Now, whom do I sue? Little Miss Round Heels next door doesn't have a dime to her name or the brain God gave a goose. She even has to export her dog shit. And those punks from Pincus High and Mt. St. Helen's ought to go to jail for what they leave at my house. So, who's going to convince me not to take the law into my own hands? I have a gun, and I'll use it against trespassers, two-legged and four-legged alike." He staggered back from the exertion, regathering his slipper.

Emmett half rose to defend Muscadine's honor, but realizing he was about nine years too late, he shrank back into his cafeteria chair. Muscadine seethed as she thought about feeding Pipsy more fiber to increase the payout for Leo. She vowed on Pipsy's behalf to drop one every day in Leo's yard, rain or shine, even if she had to walk the dog's legs off.

The crowd was clearly engaged, hoping maybe that Muscadine would go after Leo, or that Leo would take a swing at Henry, or that Stobaugh would arrest Muscadine or put her dog on trial, the way they did in the Middle Ages. Teenage boys in the auditorium fixed on Muscadine's fist-shaking, which made her braless blouse dance and her bellybutton ring play peekaboo out of her crop top. But in moments the excitement fizzled, and the audience sloughed back into its normal state of vague disappointment.

Even though blood was not let, Leo had been the perfect speaker to start the evening. An animated discussion of quality of life crimes followed, at the expense of paying any attention whatever to Leo, whose high dudgeon raged on. Townspeople began to echo his complaints with their own, shoving his aside. Skateboarders on the sidewalks and the steps of the public library; smokers leaving their butts outside the hospital emergency room; public spitters and dippers, leaving tracks on the sidewalks or Styrofoam cups of dip at gas stations; car stereo boom boxes, rattling the windows on businesses with hip hop profanity, at volumes well above the sound nuisance limits; teenagers appearing like bats at dusk to hump at Pincus Park; and on and on. Someone accused "gimps" of reckless driving into people's ankles with their grocery store motorized wheelchairs; gimps railed against ableism, to great confusion, since no one knew quite what ableism meant, or who qualified as a gimp. Leo had struck a chord, though he had not garnered any sympathy at all for his personal cause. Police Chief Stobaugh, Leo's late wife's step-nephew, gently escorted him to his seat. Faris handed Leo his speaker's gift, the ear and nose hair trimmer from Turner's. Leo stared at it, confused and overheated, with a side of vertigo. Fortunately, all this gave Faris the beginnings of an idea, whereby he jotted down "Wildlife Habitats" in his note pad. He thanked Leo for his talk and asked to meet with him the following day at Leo's home.

Leo looked at him from deep in a fog. Faris gave him a pat on the chinos.

After a brief interlude, Henry rose to introduce the next speaker. "Ladies and gentlemen, I think you'll all agree we're off to a rip-roaring start. Thank you, Leo, for your passion. I am reminded of Italo Calvino's mention of Cyrano de Bergerac's allegory on the soul of a cabbage. You'll remember that the cabbage's lament was having its head cut off after living in peaceful coexistence with the farmer. And...."

"Mary, Mother of God, Henry, have you lost the few marbles you had? No one's talking about cabbages. Leo's got a yard full of dog poop, not cabbages!"

"Exactly my point, so thanks for underlining it. Now, remember to stay to the end of the meeting, because there's a great door prize behind the curtain, which I know you all hope to win. But, please, people, let's control our anger, shall we? Where did all this negativity come from? Why so mean? And let's think of us all, of Pincus, not just our own petty interests. We are together, not alone, right?"

Neither receiving an answer, nor hearing from cabbages, Henry moved on. Mrs. Giachetti asked her neighbor exactly who Henry thought he was calling Italo.

"At this point, I'd like to hand the meeting over to Mr. Rodney Washington, of Washington & Washington Funeral Directors. Rodney?"

In fact, Rodney Washington was the only Washington of Washington & Washington, but he thought the extra name added a hint of legacy befitting his profession. A large, unsettlingly handsome man of forty or so, Rodney had style. Equal parts snake charmer and family counselor, he moved in a frictionless glide. His shiny black skin was flawless, as were his tightly groomed mustache, metrosexual eyebrows and Hollywood smile. His tall, well-fed frame was always immaculate in a dark tailored suit, usually chalk stripe, made of expensive wool. Bold-striped shirts with white collars and thick-gauge silk foulard ties set him apart; his cap-toed oxfords always shined. He was a style maker. Though his business was central to the black community, he was not of the community. He lived apart, in a compact apartment above the funeral home, joking that he lived above his station. His was hardly a welcoming abode for the living, which protected him from intrusion. Rodney was visibly present in the public spaces of Pincus, greeting future customers with the measuring leer of Mr. Perkins, the inappropriate tailor. In the mortuary business, this was called pre-need planning, which meant reaching out to the pre-dead.

Otherwise, Rodney was a blank page, without personal connection in Pincus. He was universally popular with the ladies, whom he "serviced" professionally so well in their times of grief that many menfolk worried about being killed as an excuse for their wives and girlfriends to get laid by Rodney. Rodney was called "The Suit," but nobody thought it was empty. Youngish married women in particular speculated about how some parts of it might be filled.

In truth, Rodney had come to his manner through earnest education. His father had been a "historically black farmer" in nearby Catholic Hill, South Carolina, forced out of business by redlining USDA agents, who denied crop insurance, loans and other federal supports to all black farmers in the well-placed hope that they would wither and die. The quiet younger cousin of Jim Crow, economic redlining meant that county agents, invariably appointees of the sheriff or county judge, conspired to apply racial guidelines to farmers' bottom lines. For that reason and others, farmers like Rodney's father disappeared from the face of the South. It helped explain the deep but impersonal venom he felt toward the sheriff emeritus and made more remarkable his success in navigating the white society that had undone his family. Whatever his success in the world, Rodney wore the scar of racial prejudice and the badge of righteousness on behalf of all black people in Pincus.

"My friends, I come to you with a grave problem that eats at the social fabric of our community. Those of you who have lived here for many years remember segregation in all its awful, humiliating aspects. But even after formal segregation ended, racism has continued. It has become so tiresome that no one wants to acknowledge it, even when it hits them slap in the face. In Georgia, it has taken us fifty years since the Civil Rights movement and sixty years since the case of Brown v. Board of Education in 1954 to achieve reasonable desegregation in our schools. It has been fought everywhere in the state and still fails to deliver what our students of color need. We are only recently free of federal government intervention in public education, and it feels a whole lot like being rid of the carpetbaggers. Even that long-overdue victory is soured by daily racism."

The crowd became obviously uncomfortable. Flamingo-like, the seated began choreographed glances, synchronously turned heads, cryptic whispers and clucks, and butt shuffling, as the collective mood turned sour. The subject had unfortunately turned to race. Again. Whites didn't want to hear it from the blacks. Why did the blacks always want to talk about race? And, while we're at it, whites thought, if they didn't like to be called colored, why was it okay to say people of color?

"Now, you may be surprised that I'm not going to defend school integration, but I don't claim to know about schools and all that. I do know that when black people got to come in through the front door, the white kids headed on out the back door. One hundred percent of Pincus High is minority. All the white kids go to Mt. St. Helen's or to the Christian Academy. I guess the Pope won a lot of converts with the civil rights movement, since they're aren't hardly any natural Catholics around. I know: I was born in Catholic Hill, and they're ain't even any there."

"But I'm here to tell you that in or out of the schools, integration is killing the black community, just as surely as Jim Crow did. White people do fine with integration. They choose to leave public schools or to stay. In business, as Brother Alford says often and correctly, the white man takes advantage of new markets to undermine the black business. And, sad to say, whereas black people are somewhat inclined to shop white, no white person is inclined to shop black. No white man goes to a black barbershop. No white woman shops at the black butcher shop. And no white family has ever patronized Washington & Washington Funeral Directors. Ever. Period. The only black businesses that draw any whites are Ed's BBQ and LeDonna's. White people can't barbecue right, so they go to Ed; and LeDonna's got that Mexican working for her."

"She's Guatemalan."

"Damn it, who cares if she's Guatemalan, Mexican or Islamic Jihad? She's not black; she's a foreigner, an interloper, so it don't count. I'm saying that integration means that black goes white but white don't go black. End of story. And it's killing my business. I am 15 percent down over last year on burials and 25 percent down on cremations, which is a growing part of my service. It's all going to Plummer. It's going to drive me out of Pincus, if you people can't do something about it. And I'm warning you black people out there; you will regret it if y'all have to count on the white man to take care of your beloved when they pass. I ask you black ladies, do you want Carl's fat little sausage fingers on you after you're gone and not able to defend yourselves? You think Plummer knows how you like your hair? You think he knows black beauty products? You want some old cracker-ass white man mauling you like a dog on a bone?"

Carl Plummer rose from his seat with the look of a man whose dog, with or without its bone, had just been run over. "Rodney, that's insulting. I'm a professional, just like you. I don't go around playing with dead bodies. You know that we're all respectful of your business. I even have an equity stake in Washington and Washington, so what hurts you hurts me. I thought we had put aside all the unpleasantries of the past."

"The hell you say. Unpleasantries? That means you white folks find it unpleasant to talk about segregation and slavery and lynching and redlining poor farmers. You think it's impolite. But my father was run out of his farm by your unpleasantries. Ended up running a sad little roadside store with drunks falling all over the parking lot. My people suffered under the whip of your unpleasantries. Half the black folk in Pincus were born because some unpleasant white cracker unpleasantly raped a black woman. Over 400 black people were lynched in Georgia, thanks to your unpleasantries. And that's just the ones we know about. Was a time not long ago, in your lifetime, when a white man seen shaking a black man's hand would be thought to be out of his mind. No wonder you white people don't want to talk about race. It is your everlasting shame. And as far as your so-called investment in my funeral home, that's just a takeover, like on Wall Street. I should have never allowed you to buy in. Like the Panthers used to say, burn the mother down!"

Ignoring rape, the whip and slavery, Plummer addressed the current business issue. "Well, that was your decision, and you were on hard times. We can talk buyback terms anytime you want. But the real threat to your business isn't Plummer's. The fact is, our margins are disappearing because of the nature of the funeral business these days. (Carl pronounced it bidniss). We little operators are being eaten up by big bidniss. We used to serve our communities ourselves, but thanks to the regulators and big operators, we just can't do it anymore. Folks know we don't have a crematorium in town, so we have to send our bodies to Atlanta or Savannah or Augusta if the bereaved wants that kind of thing. More than a fourth of our clients in Georgia do that now, and it's on the rise. Over half the Hawaiians get cremated, so maybe that's where we're headed. Not to Hawaii, of course, to the crematorium. You know what I mean. But with cremation, the funeral home gets no charge for a casket, no clothes, no vault, no nothing. And many of the other services we provide — which I won't describe here out of delicacy — are now outsourced at a lower price to Georgia Family Anatomical Services, the same company that helps us with cremation. But they take whatever little profit there is. We used to provide comprehensive services to the bereaved, and now all we do is drive a hearse and move flowers around. We even have to publish a price list. That's what killing your business. What you call the man isn't named Plummer."

"That's just white bullshit, Carl. You all complain all the time about getting run out of business by the big operators, but you drive a new car every year. You don't get it. You never hear black people complaining about Wal-Mart like you do. You know why? Go to Wal-Mart and just look around. They hire black people and they welcome their business, and you don't. Cable company, same thing. But every downtown store in Pincus has done all it can to keep blacks out. Wal-Mart stocks clothes for us; Van Perkins don't, because he can't stand the thought of a black man walking in his store. The difference between you and Wal-Mart is that they know the value of a customer is greater than the color of his skin, and you crackers will never get past your bullshit racist attitudes. Ask them damn blackbirds down to the liquor store." Looks of concern spread through the room; Emeritus was still a man of dark influence, and it didn't do to insult Rebel and Tarbaby.

"Now, I'll give you your point on the cremating, Plummer, but I don't hear you saying to me, let's be partners and build a crematorium. Little old Brunswick's got two! And don't you tell me black people aren't going to Plummer's. I remember when you white people wouldn't even send an ambulance to the hospital to pick up a black body. Now, you can't wait. And the hospital calls you first. You probably give them a taste of the ambulance charge. Getting ahead of you people is like trying to be first into the drink line at a wedding. If we weren't integrated, this wouldn't be happening. What's right is right."

Rodney was speaking to a mainly white audience, so the response was minimal. Plummer started to tell him that St. Simon's Island offered a big market for the Brunswick crematoria, but, suddenly, some old black lady nobody recognized stood up and moaned, "but I don't want to be creamed. And I don't want no white man's hands on me. Don't want Plummer on me." She started to wail. Someone mumbled in a stage whisper, "Hell, you ain't never wanted nobody's hands on you." Henry saw that the dialogue was becoming unproductive and more heated. Maybe Pincus wasn't quite ready for Habermas' public sphere. "Rodney, I don't think Pincus is going to make a commitment to reverse the achievements of integration, which has represented such progress for the people of this country and is living testament to the legacy of the Civil Rights Movement. Right, people?" A general murmur of stupefaction was the response. Many were still stuck on the cabbages.

"Oh, shut the hell up with your speeches, Henry. You're not getting ate up like I am. Even Costco sells caskets, and they're being imported from China. Then I got to use them and do whatever the hell with the shipping cases."

"Just remember," Henry continued, unoffended, "You can move the reflection of a star in the water, but you can't move the star."

"What on the other side of the moon are you talking about? Have you lost your mind? Who said anything about stars? Sweet Jesus, protect me! We're talking funeral business here and the white man's conspiracy to take black businesses. I thought we were supposed to be discussing Pincus' future? Am I not part of its future? Are black people supposed to stand by while the white man screws us some more? Don't let me get started on the Geechee and the Creek Indians. When did you last see an Indian? And the Geechee are all up by Hilton Head weaving grass baskets for them pasty-assed Yankee Easter Week tourists. I will not be a part of that. That day is gone, my friend. Gone! The hell with you and your stars and your damn cabbages. Excuse my language, ladies." Rodney being Rodney, the ladies were wiling to forgive a lot.

Rodney stormed out of the cafeteria, slamming into the double doors for emphasis. Carl Plummer sat down with a tight, smug little tilt to his mouth, thinking about demographics and a business plan for a crematorium. Rodney had a point, but there was no sense in sharing profit. White people in town would be angry with Rodney for his references to racial prejudice. Faris, his brow furrowed by worry, wrote "Georgia Family Anatomical Services" in his notebook. He hoped he'd remember to call Rodney.

It was now nearly ten o'clock, and though people were titillated by the fracas, they were reaching the end of their rope. Exhausted, Henry whispered a suggestion to Faris and Angeline that the meeting be adjourned.

"Friends, this has been just great. We need to work on our profanity and control our passions a bit. Nothing is added by dropping F bombs, but otherwise this is great. That's why we came together in the first place, to do battle for Pincus. We've got a lot on our plate, and I know you'll want to join us next week, when we'll enjoy presentations from Ed Prewitt and Doreen Wagner. You all know them from Ed's BBQ and Plummer's Florist, respectively. We're still taking ideas, if you want to shop at the local merchants listed on the flyer and send in your thoughts. Now, I know you've all been waiting for Faris Turner to announce the winner of our door prize."

Faris sweated nervously as he approached the stage. "Folks, let me thank you again for the many kindnesses you showed me after my father's death. I hope to be with you now for the rest of my....well, permanently, so we can make Pincus better together. Your hopes are my hopes, and I promise to do my best to honor my father and mother." His voice caught and surprised him with a sudden swell of emotion. He coughed lightly to cover it. "Tonight, we're offering a great door prize, which stands behind this curtain. But really, the curtain represents hope to Pincus. We all hope to win the door prize, and we all hope to make Pincus better. This is our curtain of hope. We need to have hope, because, as Coleridge said, "work without hope draws nectar in a sieve." Faris had hoped to invoke poetry to lift up the crowd, but only drew another confused sigh from the audience and a pissy look from Henry, whose thunder he was stealing. Someone asked a neighbor who Coleridge might be, and some lady asked why he had nectar on his sleeve, but mostly people listened to the hope part. He was right, they thought. Hope was needed, even in their little town. Nectar in a sieve.

"And now, behind this curtain of hope, the door prize goes to ticket 1134. Who's the lucky winner?" The alluring but cognitively jarring Doreen Wagner stood in surprise, gamely shouting out "I win, I won!" The noisome red velvet curtain of hope opened dramatically to reveal her prize: a home meat smoker. A meat smoker, what every vegan hopes for. The meeting adjourned.

CHAPTER VII

Pearl Charton, innocent object of Reverend Clarence Mays' lascivious intentions, always arrived first. The Dog Ear Poetry Group met the second Tuesday of each month at 7 p.m., one hour after the bookstore closed for the day. Pearl, the municipal volunteer librarian, liked to choose a seat in advance and arrange her mind for the high point of her month.

As owner of The Dog Ear Independent Book Emporium, Henry Jeffords also presided over the Poetry Group. Henry was Pincus' resident pointy-head, a classmate and long-time best friend of Faris and Angeline. A graduate of Vanderbilt and former teacher and headmaster at the Christian Academy for Boys, he now concentrated exclusively on The Dog Ear, a store heavy on books and light on customers, which sustained itself selling newspapers, magazines and coffee. It also peddled gratuitous advice and surplus dust, both free of charge. The Dog Ear was held up on one side by Turner's and on the other side by the long-closed Rialto Theater. Henry regularly devised plans to knock down the wall between the theater and The Dog Ear to expand his enterprise, but he had nothing to grow into, no concept, he would say. A conceptual man, he hated to say it.

While awaiting a concept, Henry remained an obsessive educator, long after he retired from teaching. Henry had never enjoyed the love of his father, who often observed that reading was for sissies, like Henry. He slapped Henry for being effeminate, a torture that ended when the old man left his family. He just left one morning without a word and never returned. Henry and his mother rejoiced, though they lived a threadbare life without much income. The little boy was inspired by his mother's brother, who, despite not having a high school education, had recited poems from children's books of verse to Henry when he was a fatherless boy. Robert Louis Stevenson's poems were still among Henry's favorites, if only because he could hear the barely audible voice of childhood happiness in them.

At The Dog Ear, Henry hosted small public readings and book signing parties for regional authors, and sponsored a poetry group once every month. Local poets had the opportunity to read before an audience, usually amounting to a dozen or so. Henry rightly surmised that university poets would gladly read for a small honorarium and book signing opportunity, so Pincus became a kind of odd little hub for the humanities. It was the one place that joined students of venerable Keats and Shelley and Dickinson, or James Dickey, Robert Penn Warren and James Weldon Johnson, to the young hip-hop generation with their machine gun rhythms and lively body language. They thought of performance, while he thought of literature, but cultural life was like exercise: doing anything was better than doing nothing. Henry rightly thought of himself as the link to literature in Pincus. It was, too, a bit of revenge for the slaps and criticism dished out by his unlamented father.

The Dog Ear Poetry Group was as diverse a group as gathered in Pincus. Farmers and retired servicemen and housewives and workers occasionally came together with regulars like Pearl and a now-and-then contingent of students. A personal injury lawyer attended, even using some of the young rappers in his TV commercials. They strutted and exhorted, "Call Jimmy! Call Jimmy!" backed up by percussion and gold chains.

Henry was the ringmaster, lifted up by the fact that everyone could be interested in poetry. He lectured constantly, invoking Gilgamesh to explain the origins of the separation of man and nature, the animal glyphs of ancient civilizations as symbols of the equivalency of life and its expression as art. His lectures went down hard, but The Dog Ear people genuinely admired his commitment to understanding the human condition, even if it was still pretty unintelligible and far too mild a salve for the hurts of daily life. On the political front, Henry viewed The Dog Ear as the vanguard of downtown revival, which thus far extended no further, unless Ritter's Outfitter could be counted during hunting season. And if you included Ritter's, you couldn't leave out Pincus Meats, which dressed out game animals as well as selling smoked hog knuckles, turkey legs, smoked Joe Lewis pork chunks, and mullet from a refrigerated case. But that slippery slope of seasonality might end up including the Christmas Store, which was only open from Thanksgiving to the end of December. So, Henry concluded, The Dog Ear stood alone and brave in the vanguard.

Henry looked forward to the Poetry Group meeting with great anticipation, more for his role as literary guide than the fellowship of peers. The Group had begun as another of Henry's grand and not altogether honest schemes: he wanted to put together an anthology of poetry that plain people found meaningful. His tentative title was "The Poetics of Ordinary Life." Since he had no intention of making the project open to suggestions from others, he declined to reveal his authorial intention to the participants. Each month, Henry assigned a theme that members should consider in selecting their poems for reading. The themes corresponded to chapters in Henry's future anthology: Love, Nature, Longing, Remorse, The Gods, and so on. This month's theme was "Parting," which offered group members plenty of ambiguity to roam.

Henry greeted Pearl familiarly with an air kiss. She was his most steadfast and interesting participant, always thoughtful, prepared and early. He sometimes thought her to be an irritant, though. With her quiet confidence, she threatened to amend his vision for the group. She was also sexually disturbing to him, exuding a gender-elusive sensuality in dress and scent. She had a proper set of shoulders, which he envied, and thin dancer's arms that made her sway. Her hands somehow faced knuckle forward when relaxed, highlighting the delicate shades of pink in her skin. Her hair was fine and cut tight on the sides, with plumes on top the feathery consistency of dill. She smelled of lotion and library books, which he loved.

Irritated by her diversion, he continued his preparations. Henry always provided crackers and cheese, olives and nuts, and an inexpensive wine: red in winter, white in spring and fall. The wine was controversial, as an underage member was almost always present. Henry insisted on the wine, but provided soft drinks and bottled tea, as well. The group did not meet in the heat of summer, when Henry might have chosen a rosé. He didn't care for rosés, but he knew them to be *au courant*.

Henry carried his Pearl-envying shoulders and ample waist stuck slightly off-center on thick legs and duck feet. The strain of supporting his middle section and broad butt caused his ankles to pronate inward, his shoe soles gradually taking on the appearance of misaligned tires. He had no straight lines: feet pointing northeast and northwest, left hip slightly back of the right, torso a bit forward, belt buckle off to the right, buttons tucked in to the left, bowtie listing to one side or the other, if not tilting up and down like a stalled propeller. Henry's delicate manner and balletic gait contradicted his portly dimensions, general lopsidedness and bad feet. As the sheriff emeritus was fond of saying, he was an awful dainty-acting fella for being such a big boy. Never married, Henry was friend to every woman in Pincus, but never a threat to their husbands.

He relished the role of town savant. He loved knowledge, and loved even more that he knew things others didn't. It made him. If humanism were to acquire a zip code, Henry was fond of saying, he would volunteer to be postmaster. As befitted his intellectual station, he had multiple projects in play, none of which showed any sign of completion. In addition to the poetry anthology, Henry had been working for years on a life-consuming magnum opus, an academic treatise that started out as an ethnography of Melungeon folk medicine, but migrated to the question of whether the Melungeons of Appalachia originated in the low country of the Carolinas and Georgia. To the devoted, Melungeons were a triracial group descending from enslaved Africans, Native Americans and Portuguese settlers, becoming a bit of a cult subject in the Southeast. The reasons were best known to academics, who found fervent Melungeons from the low country to Appalachia. Their critics said they were nothing but Carolina Brass Ankles or creoles, just like any other mixed people. Everyone wants to be special these days, the skeptics laughed. Henry was excited by the new possibility that they might be associated with the Occaneechi-Saponi of North Carolina. Persuaded that he was onto a subject about which only he might have an authoritative opinion in Pincus, Henry continued his Melungeons research, hoping in the future to include other ethnic isolates in Georgia. Just now he was specializing in matriarchy among the Melungeons and the origins of squirrel hunting rules in hill communities of North Georgia, where the Blue Ridge meets Appalachia.

Of course, Henry lectured endlessly on the Melungeons, whenever he found someone he could trap against the bookstore wall. Carmita, the Guatemalan manicurist, who had never had time to read a book in her life, was interested beyond measure in what Henry said about the Melungeons, because he said they had six fingers on each hand. Of course, Carmita was interested in all things pertaining to nails, even the word that the Chinese sold finger nail polish that smelled like fried chicken, which she found nauseating. To her, Melungeons were just life support systems for more fingernails.

Other poetry group members trickled in. Tim Little came when work allowed. Angeline was a regular, as was Brother Parsons. In fact, the group met on Tuesdays in acknowledgment of Brother Parsons' obligations at the church Wednesday evenings. Ethel Chesney liked to come, and it was an easy walk across the street from the Sunnyside. Emmett or Muscadine stood in for her, but they resented the obligation. Each meeting, a senior student from one of the local high schools was invited, based on a teacher's nomination. This month, Pincus High sent Janita Parsons, the accomplished daughter of Brother Alford and LeDonna. Janita was soon to attend the prestigious Spelman College on scholarship.

"Good evening, friends," Henry began. "It's always exciting to have another meeting of our little group. I'm sorry to see that Sheriff Hockett isn't here this month. I hope it's not because we didn't care for his offering last time." The theme had been "Frontiers of Imagination," and the sheriff emeritus had read some kind of weird cowboy poem about longhorn cattle. Apparently, he had taken "frontier" literally. While the group thought that completely appropriate, Henry had lectured the old man on figurative speech.

"Tonight, though, we have a special new member. Faris Turner has come back to town, as you know. Faris has taught English for many years, including classes on poetry and short fiction. He's not going to offer anything tonight, but I know we'll be happy to have him in the group." Everyone consented, because it would be impolite to do otherwise, though most were intimidated by someone with actual critical skills in poetry. They all felt themselves to be just readers. They also felt they should get a vote before adding someone to the group. Occasional visitors were fine, but this was a group, not a cultural window shopping tour. Faris felt the chill.

"The theme tonight is 'Parting.' Who would like to begin?"

"I have a selection, Henry," volunteered Pearl, who loved to arrive first *and* go first. "It's a beautiful short poem from Japan. It's by Shirome, a woman poet from the tenth century."

If I were only sure

I could live as long as I wanted to,

I would not have to weep

at parting from you.

"That's beautiful, Pearl. It's interesting that you chose something from the Orient. Do you have a comment?"

"Not just yet, but they don't call it the Orient anymore, Henry. That's too Eurocentric and imperial. I like the fact that we can hear a woman's voice from that far back in time. It inspired me to write a haiku I'd like to read."

Eyes spill salty tears,

Wasting the water of life

Soon we will be parched.

Faris was bowled over at the sentiment. Pearl's salty waters ran deep. He looked at Angeline as if to say, "Who knew?" Angeline looked back reproachfully, her eyebrows signaling "Why wouldn't a librarian be literary?"

Henry, stung by Pearl's correction of his reference to the Orient, popped the balloon. "Nice effort, Pearl, but we usually don't read our own work. Are you sure you've kept to the haiku format? Was that a 5-7-5 syllable count? It seemed like a lot."

"I've kept to the count, Henry. But, even Basho, the master of haiku, encouraged content over form. Anyway, I'm not pretending to be a haiku expert. I'm just going with the brevity of style. As to my comment, I'd refer our members to another interesting format that has to do with parting: the Zen death poem. Apparently, certain Zen monks took great pride in crafting their final words in the form of a death poem, which would be uttered as they departed life. I guess it was a kind of legacy. We have a book in the library on the subject, so if anyone wants to check it out, please let me know. It doesn't have to be during hours. I'm always happy to have the chance to serve patrons of our library. Anyway, my favorite is

Frost on grass

Fleeting form

that is

and is not.

"Good, good start. But that's two selections, plus your own. Let's give others a chance. And fitting that last one into our theme is a stretch. Does anyone else have a contribution? Anything?" Pearl sat back into her chair, slightly flushed from the emotion of speaking out in public. She loved the rush, but wished someone had said something about her poem. Henry seemed impatient with her, but she could not understand why. He was irked by her fluency, as he always had been with precocious students. He liked submissive better. She shrugged her lovely shoulders, irritating him further.

Angeline offered a poem by Ted Hughes, from a collection about Ovid. It fell flat, because no one had read the first word of Ovid, and only Pearl knew Ted Hughes by association with Sylvia Plath.

"We should probably take on the classics at some point, but that would turn our group into more of a study group than a poetry potluck. We'll have to discuss that at a future meeting, don't you think?" Henry had no intention of opening the format to democratic intervention. "What about something from the South? Did anyone bring a poem from the South? Let's see if we can talk about something closer to home."

Ethel rose to the challenge. "I've got a Southern one. I like it because it speaks to my heart. It's about a good woman gone. The author is Maggie Anderson, and the title is "Sonnet for her Labor."

My Aunt Nita's kitchen was immaculate and dark,

and she was always bending to the sink

below the window where the shadows off the bulk

of Laurel Mountain rose up to the brink

of all the sky she saw from there. She clattered

pots on countertops wiped clean of coal dust,

fixed three meals a day, fried meat, mixed batter

for buckwheat cakes, hauled water, in what seemed lust

for labor. One March evening, after cleaning,

she lay down to rest and died. I can see Uncle Ed,

his fingers twined at his plate for the blessing;

my Uncle Craig leaning back, silent in red

galluses. No one said a word to her. All that food

and cleanliness. No one ever told her it was good.

"I think pretty near every woman can relate to that, if she makes a home." Ethel glanced at Angeline, worried that she might have been rude in excluding her from the category because she'd never been a homemaker. Angeline was not offended. She wore the same detached smile as usual. Once again, Henry intruded.

"So, group, would we say this is a true sonnet? It certainly has the fourteen lines, but what about the rhyme scheme? Would we categorize this as Petrarchan or Shakespearean?"

"Henry, I just liked the poem for what it said. I thought Aunt Nita was real and wished someone had thanked her or offered some kind of compliment. They acted like what she did was nothing. There's a lot of women out there waiting for thanks that never come, if you ask me."

In support, Faris added that modern sonnet forms were pretty relaxed in their rules. He suggested that this one might qualify as a sonnet without any other criterion than having the word sonnet in the title. Henry did not care for Faris' intrusion so soon after joining the group. And it trumped his pedagogic ace again, which was irritating. Henry added Faris to his doghouse, where Pearl and her shoulders had comfortably settled.

Tim Little saved the moment by martyring himself. "I've got one from the South, too, Henry, by Byron Howard Reece. He was a Georgian."

"Fire away, Tim. Reece is an interesting figure, for sure." Henry had never heard of Reece but felt he could not afford to be thought ignorant of a regional poet. He hoped he didn't have to make more room in the doghouse.

Whose Eye is on the Sparrow

I saw a fallen sparrow

Dead upon the grass

And mused to see how narrow

The wing that bore it was.

By what unlucky chance

The bird had come to settle

Lopsided near the fence

In sword grass and nettle

I had no means to know;

But this I minded well:

Whose eye was on the sparrow

Shifted, and it fell.

"Tim, that's really powerful. Do you think this means that God must keep his eye on us all, if we are to live?"

"Shoot, I don't know, Angeline. I guess. I just thought it was important to feel something, even for this little bird. I didn't go much further than that. And I like this poet, because he had a hard life in the country, like me and my family. He was a farmer."

"Very thoughtful, Tim, but it isn't on topic. This poem isn't about parting, which was the theme we all agreed on for today." Henry wanted to control the meeting, even though it was not out of control.

"Well, if dying ain't parting, I don't know what is. I thought it fit ok." Tim had been the kid who came to class prepared but never pleased the teacher. He scratched his sunburned face, making brushing noises with his stubble.

"Let's move on to our special guest, Janita Parsons, who has been working on her senior paper at Pincus High. You all know Janita and her parents, of course." No one really did know the Parsons family all that well, since no one from the white community attended Thankful Baptist Church, and no one patronized LeDonna's, except Ethel when she had her toenails done.

Janita rose and spoke for several minutes about a volume of poetry from the 1920s, which had the purpose of gathering "Negro verse." She read a couple of the poems, remarking on her surprise at the privileged education of most of the poets and their Northeastern connections. They wrote in a kind of scholarly or formal way, not at all what she had expected. The authors published appeared to have escaped the worst of Jim Crow.

After the first few minutes, Henry started giving Janita signals to hurry up: looking at his watch, gesturing with his hands, and finally drawing a finger across his throat. His antics rattled Janita, so she rushed to finish up.

"I think what's missing from black poetry is a middle piece, that fits between this volume of high culture in the 1920s and the urban poetry of today. And in my senior paper, I propose that we reconsider the vernacular voice of the rural black men and women who have passed from the scene. It's a difficult subject, because I don't like to read poems or stories in dialect or slang. It gives me the creeps. It's why I could never get into Zora Neale Hurston. But people talk how they talk, and country people have their own ways of speaking. It's just harder to capture in writing. Sometimes, it even sounds like poetry. My favorite example is Nate Shaw, an Alabama sharecropper who told his story in a book called *All God's Dangers*. He talked about land so poor that it wouldn't sprout unknown peas. He described competition as "every man sellin' all he could, the devil keepin' score." And when he was courting a sickly girl, he was advised that if he married her "he just might be marrying a doctor's bill." He was so popular as a young man, the girls would 'cut buttonholes' over him. All of that sounded so different, so much like poetry to me. He had his own voice, so who are we to say it's not as good as ours?"

Henry was vigorously slashing his throat with his finger, while looking at his watch and rolling his eyes as if in a seizure. The rest of the group was fascinated, both by Janita and by Henry's histrionics. They seemed to be waiting for one of his famous about face moves.

"So, to finish, we ought to recover these ways of talking from the past and do oral histories of our elders, because this is the voice of black people, too, not just educated poets, but poets of everyday life. Thank you." Janita was disappointed not to be able to go into Geraldine Brooks.

Tim Little applauded. He had tears in his eyes. He was a poor man, too, who talked a pure country style. Brother Alford beamed, wishing LeDonna had been permitted to attend. Henry had said no, because it wasn't the PTA.

The evening had been a success. Henry sat with Angeline and Faris after the others left, drinking the wine that had mainly been left untouched by the group members, who worried about losing their focus. It felt natural to be together again, like they were in Miss Whitman's class so many years ago.

"So, what did you think, Faris?"

"You've got a real thing going, Henry. The people who come are thoughtful and seem committed to talking about poetry and exchanging views. The selections were wonderful. I enjoyed it. I can't get over Pearl Charton and her haiku."

"It sounds like there's another clause coming."

"If I could offer a comment, it's that a lighter hand would create more opportunity for discussion, and that would make the group better. I would have liked to hear more about why Tim chose the poem he did, or how Ethel's choice reflected her own feelings. Like I said, I thought Pearl was a revelation. What in the world goes on in her inner life? And I guess I don't think the form of the poems matters all that much, unless you want to be in the role of teacher."

"Thanks, Faris, but it sounds like you want me to run group therapy. If people want to take poetry seriously, they have to respect the forms. And I think it's awfully early for you to make these judgments, after only one session. After all, I am the reason this group exists."

"You sound awfully defensive, Henry. After all, you asked him. Faris is your best friend, and you did ask him." Angeline was forever trying to put things right.

"Fair enough. My mistake. Thanks. Good talk." It wasn't clear whether Henry thought he had made a mistake in his reaction or in asking Faris' opinion in the first place. Either way, he was put out. With that, Henry began to clean the coffee table aggressively, refusing help, signaling that the others were free to leave.

CHAPTER VIII

Framed in ribbed aluminum, the dated yellow metal flake Formica tabletop gave the small kitchen sparkle. Angeline leaned forward on a placemat as if she were holding it down with her elbows. She watched Faris intently, sipping the last of her zinfandel from a bistro glass while he scraped his plate clean of venison hash and eggs. She was a little tipsy. She reminded herself to watch her mouth. Wine had been known to goad her into behaviors she never would tolerate in herself otherwise.

Faris was a competent cook and better hunter, so much of what he ate came from wild harvest. Tonight it was his home-cured venison ham, diced with potato, onions, and garlic, all crisped in a little lard in a cast iron skillet with paprika and cayenne, a toss of oregano added at the end. Eggs sunny side up in butter nestled alongside in the same pan, with the grease spooned over the top until the yolks' bright yellow clouded. Fresh, thick slices of tomato spritzed with lemon garnished the plate with a leaf of sweet basil from the front garden.

The old Turner house came from the American catalog of

modest comfort, a white frame 1920s bungalow sporting a two-seated swing and a single dormer perched over a welcoming front porch. Tapered wood columns sat on stone pedestals to support the generous overhang. Two idle ceiling fans shared the toothpaste white bead board ceiling. The plank decking and latticework around the crawlspace under the porch were matching battleship grey. Hardy rosemary and grape ivy struggled in the clay garden bed. Pine bark mulch strayed across the borders.

The space inside bore the imprint of the ghosts of Faris's parents: permanent indentations in his father's chair, old crocheting magazines in the knitted bag on the window seat, book smell in the small reading alcove near the stairs. Even the dust seemed to be theirs, disallowing the intrusion of any new scent.

They had talked away most of the evening in the parlor, he and Angeline, just as they had as youngsters. This time, the issues were not love and hope and good books and movies, or whether their friends would be at the pool to swim the next day. Now, they worried over Turner's and the fate of the town, and mourned The Bread Basket, ruined by the great fire. She was the more confident of the two, possessed of a broad vision of what her charity could be, far beyond a food distribution center for the needy. What did it mean to be needy, anyway? It meant lack of opportunity, the shame of poverty, the impairment of society's collective imagination. In her mind, individual responsibility weighed little in the balance. Angeline believed in the beneficent redistribution of wealth from those who had to those who had not. She dreamt of farm to table, work for the homeless cultivating truck farm crops to be transformed into healthy, inexpensive meals for anyone who cared to eat. Loaves and fishes, that kind of thing, only Southern: catfish with fresh, pan roasted okra tossed in cornmeal and hot peppers; sweet corn sliced off the cob and sautéed with red bell pepper and butter; beef brisket, dry rubbed and smoked out back in a barrel all day; chicken smothered in mushrooms; collards with fatback, cider vinegar, sugar and crushed chili pepper.

In her dream she would mother them all with her matriarchal industry, food and expansive good nature. It was a nun's motherhood she dreamt of, without the messy, physical birth and mandatory intimacy required of biological mothers. Her surrogacy was also completely imperious, assuming everything in her subjects, from the will to work to the appetite for wholesome food and fellowship. She wanted to be The Little Red Hen, sowing, reaping, thrashing, milling, baking and eating. Unlike The Little Red Hen, though, she would be surrounded by loving and eager confrères with no less desire than she had to live a moral, sunny life. She painted her dream out loud to Faris as he listened patiently, hoping she would never stop talking. He didn't care what she said. He just liked to watch her effervesce. For her part, she acted as if she loved to cook more than to eat and to serve more than to be served. She seemed to believe in the virtue of others, as if the blight of earthly life were some kind of smothering veil that could be lifted with effort and imagination. Bright and undecorated, given to others, she would have been a wonderful wife, had she not been so sorely and permanently disappointed in men; if her motherly ambition were not so sterile and removed; if she were to allow others to join in defining her singular mission; and if her expression were not so chill. Her vision sounded the slightest bit off-key, like a song of love in a musical that turns out to be an anthem of ambition and unacknowledged self-regard, a song of fellowship that ends up in a solo.

Finally, having filled the room to the ceiling with her voluble self, she fell quiet. He offered more zinfandel. She accepted. The wine's danger lay in wait, but she felt more relaxed now and able to handle herself. This was the lie wine told to her, and she believed it every time.

"What now, Faris?"

He diverted his look from her to mask his unconvincing poker face. He didn't immediately answer, and then rose to clean the dishes.

"You've got something on your mind. I've talked non-stop, so now it's your turn. Tell me what it is. I know you, or at least I knew the person you were as a young man. And you don't seem to have changed all that much." Her deeply etched habits of abstinence blinded her to the answer.

"Well, if you know me so well, you'd know that as a younger man I would have wanted to be all over you all night," he confessed with sheepish honesty, avoiding the true subject, which was his obsessive worry. He was irritated with his shyness, didn't know why, in middle age, he had to be embarrassed over his physical urges or to hide his desires from her. Why should he have to constrain his modest and welcome sexual appetite at this late date? Why should interest in his one great love be cause for censure?

Surprised and flattered, but put off by the physicality of his thoughts, Angeline sniffed, "We're not kids, Faris, so don't be silly. That's all just nonsense, and you know it. What business do you have talking like that, a grown man within striking distance of a Medicare card?" She knew she was attractive, with a good figure that still earned second looks from most men and some women. He reddened, regretting that he had stepped over some line grown thick with the decades of their separation. An idiot again, he sighed inside. Some things last forever. Then, her verbal slap made him angry. Guile was never available to him, and he had long since given up dancing around and crafting what little he had to say. And why should he have to defend himself? What did she mean, asking him what business he had thinking or talking or acting on any subject at all?

"Ok, Sister Angeline, I'm not one of your acolytes, so don't think you can just scold me for the honesty of my feelings. What gives you that right? As an old guy, as you would have it, my answer is that I'd still like to make love to you, but it probably wouldn't take all night. Or it might take all night, but not for the right reasons. The point is that you were my first great obsession, the only one, unfortunately. You gave me something that you think was superficial or sinful, but ended up being my greatest pleasure in life, and it was over before I was even conscious enough to enjoy it. I was a fool to give it up. I have never stopped regretting that, though I've tried hard to smother it with piles of other regrets on top. You are still beautiful to see, as you always have been, Angeline. To me, Wordsworth wrote about you, waiting for you to be born. That's what poets do, you know. They speak for all time, but they also speak to individuals and about great passions. Remember?"

And she hath smiles to earth unknown;

Smiles, that with motion of their own

Do spread, and sink, and rise;

That come and go with endless play,

And ever, as they pass away,

Are hidden in her eyes.

"Well, of course that's nonsense, too," she squeezed out through prim lips. "Nice nonsense, I'll give you that. So, thank you. I'm happy to see you, too. But you didn't really give me up, as I remember it. I did the giving up. It seemed wrong at the time, mean and hard, somehow. But it has turned out for the better in the long run. Being away from you so long truly has been a loss to me, too, but I've only really missed the friendship, which has faded with time. The sex you're talking about I haven't missed. It was more heat than love. Honestly, I'm sure you enjoyed it much more than I did. It was just a children's plaything amped up by hormones. We were friends as little kids, and suddenly our intimacy as friends turned into corporeal love. Not real love, just insistent physical attraction. I wonder if the human race would even continue without the tyranny of adolescent loins. It certainly does nothing for monogamy. Anyway, whatever loss I felt has been offset by great satisfaction in service, with or without the vows. And besides, you were never there, not really. You were all about yourself. Even with sex. You still are. Faris Turner, all alone. That's what I meant when I said nothing has changed." Her neck arched in salute to her scripted rectitude. She stared into her glass of wine, newly empty.

"You sure know how to sound like an old nun, but I remember someone else, a lively, beautiful girl who was hot and wonderful. It was more than the chance to touch and feel each other. We were young together, and I, at least, was in love. Losing you was something I couldn't forget. And on top of that, I didn't get why you took off. I remember the sex and the company with great pleasure, and now fondness and nostalgia. And how do you know it turned out for the better? Do you know how it might have turned out if we had been together? No. You don't. You and I only lived one history apart, so we certainly have no insight into what life together might have been like.

"I guess we're both remembering things the way we want to, you with some kind of scolding superiority, and I only with great good feeling. My memory of us is like a photograph, a still life gone cold. I know I'll never lie next to a beautiful girl in her most perfect young form again, and you were that for me. I never found anyone else who was so warm to touch or so dear in the way she treated me.

In my dreams, I remember you as you were, or probably better than you were in real life. I remember no one else I've ever known that way. Maybe I embellished it in my memories, but you ruined me. And I regret that I was so miserably unaware as a young man. It's been hard remembering myself as an insensitive young dope. Thanks to you and Jesus, we lost time together that we can never recapture. At the time I would have fought Jesus to get you back, but I never had the chance to meet him. And I really didn't understand then how much was at risk."

She laughed a perfect Angeline laugh at the thought of his fighting Jesus. It made her whole body brighten and her eyes shine like a holiday sparkler. She realized she was now a bit drunk. But she didn't feel dangerous, and he had refilled her glass, so she sipped a bit more. Drink more slowly, she warned herself. The wine was taking over.

"I think Jacob and the Angel would be a better image, Faris."

He couldn't resist kissing her square on the mouth, venison and butter and garlic and eggs melding with her zinfandel. She relented, and then joined in, surprised to find in the corner of her heart a tiny opening to him, some kind of subversive feeling she had failed to kill. And as her smiles passed away, they remained hidden in her eyes, just as Wordsworth had foretold.

Ruining the moment, Faris wiped his mouth and began a jumbled dissertation. "See? You can't scold the passion out of me or yourself, either. How did you turn yourself into someone so distant, when you used to be so warm? You seem so self-contained and sure of yourself, when the rest of us are just out there flailing around. I don't recognize that in my memories of you."

"Whether or not you had the right idea of me in the first place, you might concede that decades have passed, and experiences have shown me that I need to care for myself and my goals, not to rely on others, especially men. You were the first chapter in that book, and the saddest, I'm afraid. I have, as they say, moved on."

"That's a pretty lousy thing to say. Wow. I'm the saddest chapter in someone's book. Worse, it's your book. Nice thought to lay on my pillow tonight. So, go back to your first question, instead of ruining the evening. You asked what's on my mind. What's really on my mind is my father's death and what is left for me. I'm not talking about his estate. I mean what should I do? I feel much more finality than I can stand. He spent his whole life trying to learn something and act right, and then he died in a kind of ridiculous way. Everything about him is dying with him, even as we sit here, unless someone picks up for him. Nobody picked up for my mother, but her life was a completely private one, imprisoned in the cloister of the household. If we don't stand in for Oscar Turner, he'll be left a defenseless small-town icon. He'll end up kidnapped by others for their own purposes and reduced to a stick figure in someone else's story. They'll just put a plaque up, with an odd picture of him looking more like Harry Truman than Oscar Turner. It's a danger common to us all: perfect strangers can come along and claim we were loving, brave, happy, and prosperous; or evil, mean, stingy, cold-hearted or cowardly. That's if we're remembered at all. And then even the strangers slough aside, and no one is alive who knows you. Can you tell a story about anyone in the cemetery who's been dead for more than fifteen years? Before we buried Oscar, I walked by just about everybody on the main path of the graveyard, and I can't remember more than two or three names.

"Look at old pictures of my dad and mom and you might imagine a life ever richer and more textured than it was, even as their pictures fade with age; and our own pictures and our memories of ourselves — what we've just been talking about and what we lived some long time ago — are nothing but frozen little episodes, teased out for their story value, innocent of the sadness, pleasures and anxieties of life. It's understandable that people want to remember the lives they never lived, and that relatives like their kin better dead than alive. I've never embraced the romantic side of death, but I'm no more immune than the next person to idealizing my parents as completely mine, even in the face of evidence to the contrary; and I cannot stop thinking about what they wanted from me – which, I guess, mainly adds up to what I wanted for myself. Pretty selfish, I guess. I don't know." He sat back, exhausted and a bit dizzy from his own blather.

"You're right about reinventing the lives of the dead. After all, you just judged your mother into a cloister and valued her legacy less than your father's. But, whatever you think and remember or disremember, they are dead and gone. You need to settle down. You're on the verge of thinking you can actually do something about life. I thought you had decided against acting with purpose a long time ago. Sorry, I know that was unfair. But, listen to yourself. You're swimming in grief; you'll get over it. When I asked what was on your mind, I meant what do you want to do? What, at long last, do you want to be? Or are you just going to float like a clump of dead thatch down the river to the sea?"

She took him by his dead thatch hand as if to read it. He left it to rest lightly among her long fingers. She ran her thumbs over his open palm. They felt like butter on bread. He was embarrassed by his openness and morbid reflection. And his incoherence in the face of life. Here she was, caressing his hand, and he was thinking of death. And himself. And now his palm. And taking her to bed.

"I've always found those questions confusing. When I was a boy, every adult wanted to know. It seemed silly to ask me what I wanted to do, when I didn't even know how to write a check or rent an apartment or get a job. What do I want to do? I had no answer whatsoever and didn't know how to find one. In time, I figured all the everyday things out, of course, but they hardly solved anything. Now, I want what my father wanted for me and for himself: to live my life, to be good and to find some peace. When I say that, people look at me like I'm speaking a foreign language. Everyone has always wanted me to have ambition, to be going somewhere, almost without regard to where or how or whether it matters. Ambition? I started out with none and haven't acquired any. None. What do I want to be is a different question. I know the answer to that. I want to be a good person, an honest one, and a friend to someone. I want to be able to put my head down at night and not feel miserable about myself and close my eyes in peace. That's about it."

"I'm talking about your vocation, Faris. That's what people were asking you: what you want to become in the course of your life. It's about time you had an answer to that. Being at peace as an inconsequential person isn't enough. You can be cynical about doing something that matters, but it's not the same as actually trying. You'd exasperate anyone with your dithering nature." She stumbled over the word 'dither,' which reminded her to stop with the wine. She realized it was slightly too late.

"You're really the clinician, aren't you? I admit to the inconsequential part, but it's not necessary for you to say it. And why isn't it enough? Most people who pretend to be consequential aren't at all. They just inflate what they do in order to feel important. I've at least escaped that illusion. As to a vocation, I've had the thought of an answer for a long time, Angeline, but it doesn't solve anything and causes me too much anxiety. I taught, you know, for many years. English Literature, American Literature, Contemporary Fiction, Introduction to Poetry, all the usual gut courses in humanities. Occasionally, I'd be assigned a specialized course, like Postcolonial Fiction or Twentieth Century Poetry. I was the adjunct professor, so I latched onto whatever the department needed. In my spare time, I wrote. Then, I began to think I'd be a writer, maybe a poet. It must sound ridiculous to you, and it does to me, too, mainly. But I feel it. And I like the fact that even if I don't write anything for anyone else, I have crafted those words for myself. The way you talk about vocation, you'd think the world is out there waiting, standing in judgment, and we're all required to pass some test we don't know how to study for. I promise you, the world is not waiting for adjunct faculty trying to be writers.

"I actually feel that inside my soul I have poetic feelings, and that even if Faris Turner turns out not to be a writer or poet, he is made of words, and occasionally those words seem like poetry. I can't do anything about it, because I've never had a writer's identity and don't know how to find one. I can't find my voice, so I don't have any faith that what I write is worthy of being read. The poets I love are not of my time and place, so I can only nestle in among them for comfort, feeling the power of the written word, like I'm a child of theirs. Contemporary stuff leaves me cold. Too topical. I just don't want to read a poem about urban renewal or the war in Iraq. A lot of contemporary verse is stuffed full of mindless Americanism or one-world global culture crap that has no authenticity. And the identity poetry is even worse. And, yet, I can't replicate or build on the traditions I like, either. The Agrarianists or Robert Penn Warren or Dickey, much less Wallace Stevens and T.S. Eliot, all of them are so distant in time and talent. So, I am paralyzed in a kind of exile. How's that for self-mortification? No one else knows this, but I have a duffel bag in the trunk of my car, full of draft manuscripts and fragments of poems, including some about Pincus. They're not good enough. I've ruined whatever it is I might write by spending all these years stumbling around. I had no idea that when I left my home I would disable some of the most powerful feelings of place that might have guided me and any writing I might aspire to. But that's a ball of yarn that can't be rewound. I'm the only one who's ever seen the stuff. Believe me, I've talked to a lot of professionals about that and more, to no effect. So, I'd rather focus on my father and mother and Pincus and what I might do in daily life. That's not what I am, but it's what I can do. I can't do more. Can you understand that?"

"Do you realize that you wiped your mouth after we kissed? Do you think any girl could ever see that as a compliment?"

Ignoring the temptation to smack himself in the forehead over this blunder, he went on. "I guess you've given me my answer. I'm talking to myself. I just told you something I've never shared with anyone who didn't have a couch in his office, and you scold me for wiping my mouth. Message received. So, let's get back to grieving for my parents. You're right: soon, I'll get over it, and I won't do anything for them. I'll probably do nothing at all. I'll end up closing Turner's and going less often to visit their graves, and then not at all. I'll only think of them when I'm reminded by fading memories, not as part of my self. I don't want that to happen, after all they meant to me. But, on the other hand, I don't want to be a backward-facing Sybil, seeing the past instead of the future."

"Ok. Stop with the Sybil. We're not in class. And I think you're the wrong gender for a Sybil. Is there more zinfandel?" He poured another glass for each of them.

"You know, Angeline, after my mother died, my dad told me that he had held her hand for hours at a time while she was sleeping in the hospital, right up until the moment she died, and even afterward. But he wasn't thinking of their love or their life as a couple, or any of that. He didn't call up memories of their happiness together and the accomplishment of a shared life. As her life faded, and even as her body cooled, he sat there stroking her papery skin, repenting their conjoined infirmity, their chemistry, or whatever it was that made their individual weaknesses even worse after they became a couple. He was sitting there, day after day, regretting the irritation, the arguments, the disappointments, countless lost moments that could never be regained, instead of taking comfort from the satisfaction of a long life together. He looked at her ghost and saw his own. He saw his future as a lonely old man. It hit me as the saddest thought in the world. I knew I didn't ever want to be in that position. I don't want any part of sitting by my mate's deathbed, regretting our life instead of being proud of it."

"Jesus, Faris. That's terrible. Not just Oscar's suffering, but your conclusion about it. Don't you think most people have regrets? How could your father not think about the lost opportunities to be better as a couple, when his wife was leaving him forever? Don't you think most people have such remorse?"

"I guess you're right. I'm just not interested in "people." I'm just interested in minimizing my own self-recrimination, if that's ok with you."

After a long minute, she looked at him tenderly. "Wipe your mouth again; you didn't get it all." They both laughed, without joy.

In the late evening, they opened another bottle of wine and moved from the parlor to the porch. A soft rain had fallen, freshening the air, arousing tree frogs and giving street traffic a wet, percussive sound. Some of the tension between them had evaporated with drink and fatigue. Relocating to the fresh air helped their moods, so they talked some more.

They went inside again, as the evening turned cool and the porch moths insisted on their space. He invited her into Oscar's bedroom to show her something. She thought one thing, he another. She felt sexy, he was melancholy. Faris growled in mock poetic melodrama, as he peered down into his father's funny old chiffarobe. Angeline stared at him, mystified, "The old man must have had fifty pair of socks, all the same black cotton ribbed ones that go with sensible shoes. How many socks did he think he'd wear out in his lifetime? He must have thought he'd go on forever and worried about having holes. Or maybe he just forgot he had so many and thought he needed more. And not a single pair of dress socks." He sighed a great weary breath. "I wonder what else I'll find going through his stuff. At least I don't have any children who'll have to wonder the same thing when I'm dead." He picked up an envelope addressed TO MY SON, and signed Oscar Turner. Tired and sad, straining against tears, Faris put it aside for later, when he could read it alone.

She sat on the bed, as he continued. "Henry thinks we need to get stagier with these town meetings, maybe have a permanent name for them or for the town project, whatever that means. He thinks the school is a good forum, but it lacks drama. And he's bent on using this whole thing to drive his ideas of downtown redevelopment. I was thinking along the lines of "Curtain Of Hope," since I made mention of it the other night, but it doesn't quite work unless we use the curtain more. We could continue to put the door prize behind it or invite the speaker to come out from behind it. It's the one distinguishing feature of the cafeteria, if you discount the kiddie-sized chairs."

"I like The Curtain of Hope idea, and I think people responded to it at the meeting. The problem isn't the staging, though. The issues that are coming up just don't have answers. How are we expected to get anywhere with the questions people are asking? Are we supposed to solve racism, neighborhood feuds, small business problems, the disappearance of a sad little town, the diluted character of the South and the general dissipation of a not very spectacular way of life? It's like when you gave Rodney the portable dishwasher after he spoke. He looked at you like you were either nuts or making fun of him. What was a funeral director supposed to do with a dishwasher? It's a perfect symbol: wrong answer for the right question. The curtain is great. The question is whether it makes any difference. Henry thinks we can talk this out, but I'm not so sure."

He admitted the dishwasher was funny. "How about when Doreen won the door prize? What is a vegan going to do with a charcoal meat smoker, make zucchini jerky? That one made me think there really is a God, and he's a complete smart ass. It reminds me of Bouvard and Pecuchet, Flaubert's retired nitwits who decide to take on bourgeois professions in the service of humanity. You know how that turned out." He began to go on.

She rolled her eyes and stopped him mid-thought. "Faris, stop it. You have the most obnoxious habit of putting footnotes and literary references into ordinary conversation. What is that, some kind of intellectual aggression? I never read any Flaubert past *Madame Bovary*, which made me sick of women and love and small towns. And sick of Flaubert." Now, the wine was definitely doing the talking.

"So, your bad attitude is Bovary's fault. I should have known. Do you have a better opinion of Balzac?"

"Since you brought up Doreen, let's talk about her a little more. She could play an important role in helping Pincus. She's young and smart and militant about what she believes in. She could be a bridge to young people. But she thinks we're all talk and no action, and she's got a great case. She's very impatient with our meetings, thinking they'll just generate more meetings without actually sketching out a plan of action for each challenge Pincus faces."

"Maybe that's because she's young and doesn't understand how hard it is to change the way the world works."

"Maybe it's because she's too much like her father. She's yours, you know." This brutally frank slip never would have passed her lips were it not for the wine. Bovary and Zinfandel, Satan's helpers.

"Did you hear me? Faris?"

"Yes, of course I heard you. I heard the words, but they don't make any sense. How could she be mine? And how would you know that?"

"Because she's mine, too. I'm her mother." Angeline rose to look for the wine bottle. It called to her from the other room. She was no longer feeling sexy. Acid sat in her throat.

"I'm waiting for you to say something that makes me think you're still in your right mind. Everybody's talking like a lunatic around here. When's my turn?"

"Oh, believe me, you've had your turn, and then some." Now, they were talking between rooms, in raised voices. "But it's simple. Just listen. She's my daughter, and you're the reason. You took me to the doctor the day I found out I was pregnant, and you were too dense to figure it out. I asked and asked Dr. Miller if there were an alternative to the unthinkable prospect of abortion. Pills, herbal remedies, anything; but he had nothing. So, he recommended to my parents that I be sent to the Florence Crittenton home in Savannah. And so there I was sent. I wasn't in on the decision. I stayed there until I had my little baby. I wanted to keep her for my own, but I barely even saw her before they took her away. I selfishly felt that the baby might add some purpose to my life. Then, my mother thought up the convent idea. My parents were pretty ashamed of me, so I was ashamed of myself. I'm even more ashamed that I went along. It was all such a lie. I never went to a convent. I used the story as part of a fiction to cover up my pregnancy. You remember girls who used to "go to visit relatives" for several months. It was the same thing with me, only a convent instead of relatives. Meanwhile, my parents arranged – I don't quite know how – to have the baby adopted by the Wagners, whom they knew from church. I really have never forgotten that whole sorry time or what a horrible role I played in it. I can't say I've ever had a good opinion of you since then, either.

"I mean, really, Faris. Can you really say with a straight face that you didn't know I was pregnant?" She waved her wine glass like a flyswatter until its dregs came perilously close to sloshing onto the nice old Turner floral print couch. She drank the glass dry preemptively, and congratulated herself on not staining anything. Red wine and blood were impossible to get out.

"You really, actually, in your heart of hearts thought that I entered the convent to become a nun? A nun? Had you ever heard me say a single word about a religious vocation? Did you ever know me to spend much time in church? Did you think I went to the doctor crying just because I was sad? Were you just a self-deceiving jerk, or were you really too dumb to see what was right in front of you?"

Faris stood convicted, either of stupidity or felonious insensitivity or terminal narcissism, or all of the above. He was a second-story man caught red-handed, trying to explain why he was on the second story. And now he had a daughter and a phony ex-nun ex- girlfriend, along with a thousand questions. He came back into the kitchen, joining her in looking for another bottle of wine. He wanted to open some cheaper stuff, since their palates were already dulled from the evening and wouldn't care.

"How did you find out about her, I mean that she was with the Wagners?"

"When she came of age, Doreen petitioned the Crittenton Foundation for information about her birth parents, and they discreetly contacted me. They've got pretty involved protocols to protect parent and child, so I had to consent to release of my information to Doreen, and she had to ask for it first. I was elated to hear that my dear lost baby wanted to know about me. I didn't even stop to think that she might hate me for what I had done. In due course, she contacted me, and we have been working on things since. I'm not sure we've made too much progress. But she's a smart girl, Faris. A little hard, and a bit angry at the state of the world. She's not well disposed toward me, that's for sure, but I can understand why. Oh, here's the wine. It's not gone after all."

"And how do you know she's mine?"

"Jesus, Faris, you are priceless. You're really no different than you were as a teenager. Listen carefully: I know she's yours because you were the only person I'd had sex with. I didn't just sleep around. I was one of those little fertile time bombs and you lit the fuse. Bang, first time. But thanks for thinking I had so many partners I might be confused. You deserve to be alone."

"So, I'm a dad." His tone was one of confusion and mild happiness.

"No, no. No, that's the last thing you are. You're a sperm donor. You haven't done a fatherly thing in your life, so don't kid yourself into thinking you're a father. You're no different than any other jacked up high school boy who knocks up his girlfriend and then moves off to live his life pretending that he didn't know."

"But I didn't know. I should have but I didn't. You could have said something. We could have gotten married or worked on the problem or something. And what about you? What have you done that is motherly?"

"Thanks for that sophomoric reaction, Faris. Big help. You could have figured it out yourself, for that matter. But, I accept my part of the blame. Look at who we were. We were children. I was scared: pregnant before I really knew my own body, taking orders from people at Crittenton who would never be accountable for the results, signing away control over my body, and having a baby that I would never hold. On the other hand, think of all the girls who chose the other path — had babies and kept them, only to find their futures ruined. I wasn't ready to be trapped as a single mother in a small town, scrambling for little jobs and running around looking for day care in between. But I wasn't ready to give my baby away, either. I sure wasn't ready for the fevers of anxiety and shame that invade me whenever they want, day or night. All these years. It's been like having malaria of the soul."

"You don't look like someone with malaria of the soul. You look fine, and you don't seem all that haunted, either."

"Oh, what do you know? Then, after I left Savannah, I decided I could just declare myself to be a nun. Who ever does background checks on virgins wearing habits? I worked in nursing homes and hospitals, and eventually everybody accepted me as Sister Angeline. I tried to forget about my true past, which of course was impossible. Surprising, really, that a person can't escape a past that doesn't even amount to anything. You can escape a lot, but you can't escape yourself. When I moved back here, people thought I had made good. This has been a rich life for me, Faris, a life of atonement, in ways. But it all depends on a lifetime built on deception. I live a life of lies, and I've had to come to terms with it. There's no sense including you.

"But let's get back to the present. It was trouble enough living the past the first time around without having to explain it now to some jackass man. Regarding the curtain, it's still the nicest feature of the school auditorium, and we're holding our meetings in front of it. I like the title, especially evoking hope. Everybody needs hope, especially in this town."

They agreed that the curtain wasn't too much of a stretch. The Queen for A Day model didn't work, since people were not offering stories that were easily remedied by appliances. The idea of hope was good, since it seemed the only possible reason for people's attendance, besides the door prize, or the fun of watching the fireworks. Title and staging were tabled for the moment, in favor of moving on Faris' idea for Leo. In her bibulous state, Angeline thought his plan was first-rate.

After Angeline had gone, Faris sat exhausted in his mother's chair next to the crochet basket with a mug of coffee and a headache. She came to him then in the weakness of his fatigue, in memories of her, sitting in her chair, watching old art house movies late at night with him. She crocheted and smoked, he ate popcorn and drank lime Kool-Aid and quizzed her on obscure actors of the Golden Age. The films were great: *La Strada*, *Nights of Cabiria*, along with the occasional *Postman Rings Twice*, *Lifeboat* or *I Want to Live*. He fell in love with Lana Turner in *Postman* and Rita Hayworth in *Gilda*, and he cried for Susan Hayward being led to the gas chamber. So many images that had informed his life now roiled his mind and heart: Giulietta Massina's vulnerability as a prostitute looking for love; Susan Hayward's shoe left behind; the malefic Basil Rathbone exposing the tender vulnerability of little David Copperfield; Robert Mitchum's predation of Shirley Winters in *The Night of the Hunter*, especially since her little boy was about Faris' age and aspect at the time. Never mind Richard Basehart being murdered by Anthony Quinn in *La Strada*. How could Anthony Quinn murder a clown, even in a movie? Poor Richard Basehart: the apex of his acting career was getting his head cracked like an egg by an Italian strongman.

"So, Faris Turner has a daughter," he whispered. He unconsciously caressed the arm of the chair where his mother's elbow had rubbed the chenille shiny.

Faris missed his mother terribly, twenty years after her death. She had been as dramatic as his father was subdued, possessed of the deep outrage of people who wonder why life couldn't be otherwise. A person of great discipline, she kept her house, raised her children, balanced the household budget, put good, frugal meals on the table, limited herself to a single glass of red wine, washed and ironed her nylon sheer curtains every spring. She was selflessly kind to her baby and loved life in her own way, with the constraints of class and time that conspired against women of her generation. She settled for the limits of her marriage to an ordinary man, but not always with good will, choking down resentment of her modest station and the equally unimpressive achievements of her mate. She regretted that such bile rose in her, so she worked all her life to bury its bitter taste in service to her loved ones. She knew that Oscar was a good husband and father. She just never allowed his goodness to be good enough.

Her one rebellion was melodrama. "O, Death, where is thy sting? O, Grave, where is thy victory?" She would raise her arms high and practically tear her hair if the dog peed on the floor. "God, give me the strength and the grace to survive!" she would exclaim, as if her end were near, when Faris and his friends fought over the many nothings that caused children to fight. In the end, when she fell ill for the final time, she went oddly uncomplaining, only asking from her hospital bed for the grace of a happy death. Maybe she wanted a good night's sleep, or relished never having to mop the floor again or being excused from Oscar's stories about the hardware business. Maybe the sting of death diminished as she became readier. Maybe she knew that her disappointments would soon disappear, and then be forgotten by others. Her gravestone was wonderful in its way, inscribed with her shockingly lovely sentiment: "I was of time and place. In death time has gone; my place is in the dust." This Georgia borderland verse from a modest, fearful housewife made Faris want to revive her just to know more of what had been in her heart, even as it broke his again.

She had overcome so many fears. She had been raised by severe, poor parents to be afraid – afraid of falling from the swing set, of being touched somehow (she didn't know quite how) by strangers, afraid of men's penises when she was old enough to learn about them. She was afraid to be alone and timid to be in public. She was afraid of black people, not because she had ever been menaced or harmed. She was afraid of being a racist and found comfort in thinking that her fear of black people was the same irrationality that caused her to fear birds. But she was afraid, too, because birds didn't recognize her fear, whereas black people did. She was afraid of pretty much everything she didn't understand, like the Nazarenes and evolution. She was afraid of being afraid, so she mustered courage to continue. That was more than Faris could say in his own defense.

Faris had been unaware of her dark thoughts and deep fears until he became a man and looked at her in a fresh light. She had been his world as a little boy, singing nonsense songs to make him giggle, cupping his face in her kitcheny hands, wiping the sleep from his eyes with her thumbs, telling him he was made of peaches and cream and his hair was silk and cotton. She smelled him like a loaf of bread fresh from the oven. She swore that his dimples were left by angels' kisses. She held him constantly, wore him like a favorite hat, refusing to see it grow older and less well suited to her simple devotion. The day he was able to wrestle free of her and play with other children began the long drift away from safety and innocence toward maturity and loss. Her love of his childhood and of him as a child, which were not the same thing, ended in sadness. He really was her world but didn't know it.

Love for the child had not morphed into an adult relationship. They retained only the faint shadow of their memories of those good days. Now, sitting in her chair, he wanted more than life itself to be that pampered little boy, whose mother didn't think he was an asshole and who didn't have an empty store and a newfound daughter. He wanted most of all not to be an orphan, to have his parents back alive, to bury his face in his mother's lap, to go camping with his father, to stand protected again, holding onto the old man's legs. He felt as if he had never been a whole person, just a shell propped up by the prodigious love of his parents, now gone. He had never wanted to grow up, had never loved life as an adult. He had hoped it would be simpler, more positive. It turned out to be just an extension of his bumbling childhood, uncertainty layered with indecision, wrapped with indirection. Perched next to the ghosts of his mother's hands on crochet hooks, he called out loudly in his mind, directing his voice to the past. "How can I behave well after you're gone, when I failed so miserably while you were here?" The answer lay not with his parents, but with Angeline and Doreen. His thoughts of childhood seared into him a feeling of total failure as a father. He had done little for Angeline, nothing for Doreen. He hadn't even known she was alive.

But, being Faris Turner, he could only embrace this truth as anxiety, not as an agenda for action. Arriving too late to the scene, now he had to set his guilt aside. Fat chance. Instead, picking at the edge of the envelope he had found earlier in Oscar's drawer, he opened it and found a new and unforeseen set of puzzles

Steven Sanderson

You said what should we do

I said we could do anything we want to

I said what could we do

You said we could do anything we want to

But love is a dog from hell

    The Limousines, *Love is a Dog from Hell*

.

CHAPTER IX

Pipsy Fuqua was an exuberant little Pomeranian, the object of Muscadine (née Chesney) Fuqua's unbounded love. Her husband Bobby Lee Fuqua was in jail again for his usual drunken misbehavior. This time he had fixed an old tractor he found in a field, driven it to 301 Liquors, and motored away on the shoulder of the road, drinking Sweet Lucy wine from a brown paper bag. Pincus police made a good share of their budget by hanging around waiting for drunk drivers to exit the package store, and Bobby was a steady contributor. He should have had a plaque on the police station wall. The cops grudgingly gave him credit. Even his old man Vernon had not been so creative, though he did once ride a horse bareback in the rain while drinking cheap rum, until he fell off backwards and passed out in his neighbor's yard. He had said at the time that the sugar in the rum didn't agree with him. Bobby Lee was a lot like that.

So, Muscadine was living alone, at least when she could leave her daughter Blueberry with Emmett and Ethel. Pipsy was her boon companion. She had him groomed like a little lion, with a big mane, short torso cut and no hair at all surrounding his impressive little testicles. Pipsy played the role of a little guy with an over-large ego and embarrassingly obvious pride in his gear.

Muscadine was a beautiful, solid girl with remarkably long, well-shaped legs, who, despite her good upbringing, personified the High Striker midway game at the county fair, where boys would try to ring the gong with a huge mallet. You could ring Muscadine's gong on the first swing, as long as you had a big mallet, So, she had a kid by one man before she married a different one, both subjects having in common an aversion to adulthood and a predilection for jail. Her erstwhile lover Timmy Stobaugh was serving a long prison term upstate for drug trafficking, as a junior member of a particularly dull-witted gang from Savannah. He had been easy prey for the federal drug taskforce working the Georgia coast. Emmett wanted to know where to send a check in gratitude.

It was good that new husband Bobby Lee was in jail, too, as he was insanely jealous of Muscadine and would start a fight with anyone who crossed her path or looked at her obvious charms, which she left barely covered. Muscadine's dalliances — former, current and prospective — dreaded the day Bobby Lee emerged from jail, as did her hated neighbor Leo Price. Bobby was due for release at the end of the week.

Muscadine had been like any other child, with a sweet smile that disappeared as she accumulated the inevitable disappointments of worldly experience. Early in adulthood she had hopes of travel and adventure, all dashed by Bobby Lee's drunkenness and her own slatternly misfortune. She once managed to take a trip to New York to meet a cousin who lived there, and Bobby Lee had made her take Pipsy. She agreed happily, since Bobby Lee had previously kicked Pipsy, and the little dog snarled and gave him a wide berth when he was with drink. On the plane to New York, Muscadine had been so excited she called her entire speed dial list and left identical voice mails: "Hi," she crooned. "Me and Pipsy are on a plane, headed for New York....New York," in apparent concern that people might have thought New York was in Illinois. Not a single caller picked up. Pipsy lay content beneath the seat licking his balls, a seasoned canine contortionist.

"Before I strangled my life with asshole men," as she poetically put it, Muscadine had a poorly-focused sense of adventure, a longing for the exotic. Impulsively, and without the slightest religious vocation, she joined a church mission after nursing school and spent a year in Eastern Bolivia, living in a small indigenous community. It was life changing, but not exactly in the way she intended. The natives were missionary favorites, having been "culturally disorganized" for decades. Which meant they were destitute. The cluster of huts they called a village was without a single amenity, with men hunting and farming, and women raising goats, chickens and pigs. They drank masticated corn beer, which had a filthy taste of soot and vomit, and ate goat meat or large rodents roasted over an open fire pit. The little village was squalid. Thanks partly to poor animal husbandry, the villagers were particularly susceptible to Chagas Disease, a parasitic heart disease transmitted by the bite of the "kissing bug." Naturally, an animal called the kissing bug was bound to find Muscadine. She fell ill and was bounced from the church mission. By age 27, she could add a bad heart and a crazy kid to previously revealed weaknesses that were filling out her resumé. She wore a new kind of pacemaker that combined a defibrillation element along with the standard shocker, so she had that going for her. But like many uncounseled heart patients, she had become a paranoid hypochondriac, or what her mother Ethel called a weak sister.

Emmett Chesney, Muscadine's daddy, was more or less permanently disgusted with his daughter. He faulted her for a weak mind, weak will and weak balance, which combined to cause her to tip over on her back every time she met a worthless man. He could not help blaming himself and Ethel for their daughter's awful life course, a preoccupation he shared with the rest of the town. His fellow citizens were sure the Chesneys could have done better as parents, with scant evidence from the critics' own spawn. Emmett and Ethel were just two more devoted and capable parents whose children turned out badly.

The Curtain of Hope

Muscadine lived in a mobile home she and Bobby Lee had bought after their wedding and set up on a lot he had inherited on Landing Street, next to Leo Price. When not stumbling drunk, Bobby Lee was a solid enough worker and competent handyman. He worked on his home with enthusiasm and noise. He put a foundation underneath the trailer and added two rooms and an extra bathroom by knocking out the back wall. Their home was more than comfortable, with a Ben Franklin stove sitting on terra cotta hearth tiles in the built-on room, an oval braided rug atop russet asphalt flooring with an arabesque pattern, and cotton eyelet curtains on the jalousie windows they had rescued from scrap abutting the stove. Outside, they had a picnic table and charcoal grill on a ten-foot square concrete slab. A pretty willow drained the low margin of the yard and offered the gift of shade.

Bobby always had a project going at the house, which meant sawing and banging and irritating their neighbor Leo. Neighborly harassment was a two-way street, though. Every time Muscadine joined Bobby at the patio charcoal grill for a beer, Leo seemed to appear magically with the world's loudest backpack leaf blower, sounding like an old Harley on meth, sending clouds of dust and pollen into the air, into their beer, and onto their grilling meat. No amount of shouting from Bobby could be heard over the two-cycle roar of Leo's blower. The old bastard could stumble around the yard for hours with that thing on his back.

Absent her murderous hatred of Leo, Muscadine had to admit that she loved their little home and only regretted Bobby Lee's drunkenness and the haunted shudder of the house during the violent summer storms. That wasn't counting the heart thing, of course, but everybody had something. God seemed to be reminding her that she might have dressed up the trailer so that it didn't look like a tornado magnet, but he wasn't fooled. After her experiences in Bolivia, Muscadine took God more seriously. Not in the religious sense; none

133

of that dress up on Sunday and trust in Jesus stuff. God was somebody out there you couldn't see but ought to be afraid of.

Against all evidence, Muscadine was also a proud woman, mixing a stylish lack of accomplishment with self-conscious eccentricity. She didn't miss a chance to parade through the neighborhood with Pipsy. The neighbors chided her for leaving dog droppings in the street, on the sidewalk and in their yards, but she was offended by the very idea of picking it up. After all, she worked in a restaurant. She couldn't believe that anyone wanted her to serve food with hands that had just scooped dog shit. She'd like to meet the idiot whose idea was it for people to pick up dog shit, anyway. Still, to be a good neighbor, she tried to make Pipsy do his business in Leo Price's yard. Nobody but Leo seemed to mind that. Let him see if that noisemaker of his could blow a turd out of his yard.

Sundays were Muscadine's hardest day, as she substituted for her mother at the Sunnyside Café. After church, great numbers of Pincans came to the Sunnyside for brunch, which made the 11-2 shift the most profitable lunchtime service of the week. The staples were always on hand: a steam line teeming with scrambled eggs and cheese, pancakes, stone ground grits, link and patty pork sausage, hash browns with caramelized onions, and canned fruit cocktail. At the end of the buffet were collards and Smoked Joe Lewis, a gristly variety meat popular among the oldsters. Muscadine was known for her jalapeño skillet corn bread, served in great slabs with cold butter and cane syrup. The challenge was the short order service, especially the eggs. Thanks to her pacemaker, Muscadine was obsessed with what she called "electronical equipment," fearing that a cell phone or MP3 player would resonate with her heart and strike her stone dead. She wouldn't come near the microwave, which hovered over the flattop griddle like the black cloud of death. So, her style of preparing any fried eggs was to whoosh by the flattop while pouring eggs from a bowl, stand off to the side until she gauged the eggs to be ready, and swoop past like a matador to plate the eggs on the return. Flipping the eggs called for two passes. She figured she spent no more than five seconds each pass underneath the microwave. Still, by her count, that meant eight to ten minutes at maximum risk on a busy Sunday. Might as well stick your tongue on a power line. She ruined three eggs out of a dozen and finished the day exhausted, all the while giving the diners a regular floorshow of young breasts, long legs and stretching Daisy Dukes. It drove Emmett nuts.

Muscadine's short order shift also included irregular but dramatic Spanish language curses shouted out to Rubén and the other occasional Latino waitresses and busboys. Her time in Latin America had won her a great gift of slang, unspecific to a country, harvested from foul mouths everywhere. "Ahí tienes los huevos con hash, cabrón. Llevatelos." She punctuated arguments with the staff with the grossest insults, delivered with great good humor and charisma.

The help was afraid of her pacemaker story, thinking she might spontaneously combust while on the line cooking and take them with her. The black kids Ethel had scooped up off the street provided their own entertainment with wild patter and good humor. Rahim, née Jerome, would enter the kitchen, doffing his crocheted rasta hat with a cheerful "As-salamu alaykum" as he put on his apron. Wilson, the bus boy, sporting a large comb in his hair like a black geisha cross dresser, invariably answered. "Scrambled eggs and bacon." And the fun began.

The only quiet space in the kitchen was filled by silent Rubén, who held Muscadine in awe, loving her body and bilingual trash talk, grateful for her thinking of him as a human being instead of Dizzy Pickles. Had it not been for his obsession with Doreen, he actually might have tried to proposition Muscadine, or more likely to touch her furtively as she manically brushed by. Rubén loved women, especially when they smiled at him and were nice. He failed to realize that they were flirting with him because he was young and good looking and had a personality from way out somewhere by the end of the world. A brush from Muscadine or a session with Doreen did nothing to reduce his confusion and paralysis.

CHAPTER X

Leo drove home from the town assembly, slowly passing through the dark downtown streets in his sensible old sedan. He was in a black mood, having lost his temper in public and missing his chance at redress, an unforgivable sin. He could not understand why Bobby Lee and Muscadine were such a plague to him. They were surely not worthy of his rage, and he didn't really believe they deserved his contempt. But he could not stand the sight of them, much less their too-modest house next door to his. He resented their youth, their passion, and, most of all, their ignorance of the disappointments to come. Their eyes were facing up. They had not tasted, as he had, the bitterness of love gone cold. They could not feel the weight of living with a wife who showed no regard for her husband's presence, someone who would die for spite, just to leave him without anyone to shut his eyes when his own time came. His late wife had long ago lost interest in him, first by pieces, and then entirely. She became indifferent to his moods, unresponsive to his complaints, bored by the daily affairs of a couple with a house, an adult child, a will, and matters of dust-dry importance to decide. She refused to listen to him, pretending not to hear. He was relegated to the role of a cantankerous old butler in his own home, someone whose presence was tolerated for want of a likely alternative at the price. For him, his marriage was barely better than total solitude, an expensive insurance policy against dying alone. But the wife bested him there, too. She died first. He said it was because she wanted to

137

disappoint him one last time. No one else would care for him. Surely, not their daughter, a child who grew up too fast, seemingly willing herself to adulthood, just so she could escape her home and forget her parents. How could Muscadine and Bobby Lee, these two young nitwits filled with the fleeting enthusiasms of inexperience, foresee the sour taste of a job lost or a judgment gone wrong, a future that suddenly was past? Could they imagine being old, awakening in the night to cry alone and then facing the anguish of being weak? Could they withstand an irregular heartbeat, if they had no one to call? And their house, their miserable dressed-up trailer, a dirty little Cinderella in an apron, just its presence was an insult to his.

Leo parked and locked his car in the garage, shuffled through the trellised breezeway to the back door and hung his keys on the peg inside. He stopped in the butler's pantry, with its comforting creaky oak floor, for a small glass of port to quiet his nerves before bed. Tomorrow would come too soon. And when the new day struck, who would be there to help him forward into the future but Old Man Strother.

Strother was surpassingly different in every way, beginning with his very emergence from the womb. Baby James Canfield Strother was blessed with second sight, thanks to having been born behind the caul. Country people around Pincus used to think that babies born within an amniotic mask had special psychic or religious powers, or were just lucky. Strother had embraced the tradition by beginning to see spirits as a child. Throughout his life, he happily commented to people on their departed kin, causing distress or annoyance whenever he did. In fact, his gift cost him his only real decent job in life, as the county gravedigger. Strother would approach funeral parties to warn them of a little spirit girl buried in an unmarked grave, who would grab at their ankles if they stepped on her. If she appeared to people, they should know that it was a sign that their time had not yet come, and they could return home safely.

This, thought Strother, would be welcome news, but it so unnerved the bereaved that they frantically tiptoed around and left the graveyard as soon as possible after the service. Letters to cemetery management followed. The spirits of the cemetery themselves viewed him with mixed feelings, appreciative of the acknowledgment by a living being, but a bit peevish that he interrupted their peaceful silence and alarmed their visitors. They knew his second sight was real.

Strother was heir to a tradition of conjuring. His father had been a Carolina root doctor, unusual but not unheard of among the white population,. The elder Strother had claimed to be tutored by an acolyte of none other than the famous Dr. Buzzard, who practiced on St. Helena Island, in Port Royal Sound, but no one really believed it. It mattered little, as conjuring, hags and hants were serious business when Strother was little, and only the foolish mocked a root doctor. Strother had also studied a rare seventeenth-century book entitled *The Adventuresome Simplicissimus*, the main objective of which was to instruct the reader in the arts of talking to inanimate objects. He had taken to it.

Strother's appearance went with his origins. His forbears must have included a stork, as he was all angles and bones, long neck sporting a big gular sac in place of an Adam's apple, as knobby as if he had just swallowed an overlarge fish. His body bent frontward, with his head facing vaguely to the right, wisps of feathery hair popping out here and there from pecan-colored skin. He was as wall-eyed as a flounder and equally inscrutable. A man of indeterminate age, Mr. Strother bore the Christian name of James, but everyone just called him Old Man Strother, or Strother. He had been forever old, born old, present at the creation of dirt, which he collected and stored in the deep wrinkles on his neck and hands.

It had been years since Strother had strung two normal

sentences together that made any sense to the living. Now and then he spoke to no one in particular, but he had little use for talk. He spoke mainly in verse and sometimes sang instead of speaking. He lived alone outside of town in an abandoned fish camp next to the RV campground. The campground operators complained that he used their shower without permission, but no one could produce recent evidence of his having washed. Strother spent his days walking around town looking for odd jobs, famously asking if he could haul something off "for a twarter." People generally obliged him by putting some old piece of junk in his ever-present child's red wagon, along with some loose change for his trouble. On the second Friday of every month, the county collected large dry trash at the curb, and Strother reliably scavenged houses on the best streets. He knew Leo's place well.

The old man often wore only one shoe and sock, leaving the other foot bare. As far as anyone could understand, this was due to chronic back pain that radiated down his leg. Strother alleged that the pain was shooting down his leg because it wanted to leave his body, and the easiest way to help it along was to leave his shoe off. So, he did. The bare foot assumed the general dimensions of a calloused skateboard, with nails that would have defied even Carmita's talents, if she had been asked to apply them. Which she had not.

When the city fired him as its gravedigger, he assumed the part of the village idiot of poetry, catching the apples thrown at him by children and eating them all for spite. Since his knowledge had gotten him fired, he stopped speaking to anyone, except as absolute necessity. While he was generally cut off from civilized discourse with humans, he did maintain correspondence with inanimate objects and with spirits. He conjured upon request. And he saw things.

Strother held a druidic belief that certain places could sing – the Laurel oak in the motel parking lot, for example – and he took it upon himself to channel that music to those who could not otherwise hear it. Regulars at the inn had long since stopped listening to his ersatz chants in the parking lot, but tourists were nervous around him. Emmett wanted to install sprinklers around the oak tree, with a motion detector to spray Strother if he came near. Ethel wouldn't hear of it, worried more about wet customers than about Strother getting a much-needed bath. She also had an aunt who was hexed for stepping out with a married man and never seemed right afterward. She retained a country girl's respect for the tetched.

That fateful morning after Leo's rueful performance at the assembly, he saw Strother with a wagonload of old magazines, singing in front of an old sinkhole near Muscadine's house. So, with inspired judgment, Leo decided to hire the old man to de-turd his lawn. "Hey, Strother. How'd you like a few days work in my yard?" Strother did not respond, only looked at him with one chameleon eye while the other glared at the traffic light at the corner. Leo couldn't tell if the old man had heard him or whether he was really watching the traffic light and due to the angle of his walleye happened also to be looking at Leo, all the while muttering monk-like hums *sotto voce*. "Whaddya say? I'll give you a dollar an hour to clean the dog turds out of my lawn and any other trash you might find."

"I'll do it for a twarter."

Well, that's great. But I'll give you four twarters for every hour you spend pulling turds. How 'bout that?"

"How 'bout that," Strother mused, as his left eye bore down on the mailbox, sending the right eye up the fig tree across the street. Leo took that to mean he had a deal and handed the old man a large plastic lawn bag. Strother took it without comment or commitment. Mystified, Leo decided to go in the house and wait to see what happened next. Strother walked down the street pulling his wagon, holding the trash bag like a kid trick-or-treating. Leo congratulated himself on not paying in advance.

That same morning, Faris met Leo at Turner's with an idea to solve his complaint. After abortive efforts at small talk, Faris opened a WILDLIFE HABITATS catalog of equipment for menageries and zoo collections. In a section devoted to confinement of large mammals, they found remarkably lifelike tufted grass that was wired with electricity. Installation was a cinch, no more complicated than stringing lights on a tree and then plugging the whole system into a standard electric fence charger connected to a household outlet. Faris got excited as only a hardware store owner can. Leo didn't get it.

"Look, Leo. This is the answer to your lawn problem. You just buy this electrified border grass and plant it on the edge of your property. Anyone who comes in to foul your yard gets 110 – well, not 110, because it's transformed down to lower voltage – but they do get a baby Taser hit. Believe me, even more people will avoid your side of the street after they get a taste of this. If anyone bothers you, just say you've been troubled by armadillos and thought you'd put in the fence to keep them out."

"I've got nothing against armadillos. What do they have to do with it?"

"That's not the point. The shock grass is the point. Keeping dogs from crapping in your yard is the point. Buy the fencing, Leo. Jesus."

"Can a person really buy a baby Taser? I could use one."

Several useless exchanges later, mainly revolving around whether it was legal for Leo to tase anyone, the old man left Turner's with an invoice for 35 units of border grass, a fence charger, and 100 feet of heavy-duty extension cord. Faris threw in a garden trowel and a warning sign for good measure. He called Green's to order several flats of Indian grass for Leo to mix in as inexpensive camouflage for the electrified stuff. Faris made a little money on the fencing, which made him feel downright entrepreneurial. Doing well by doing good. The Curtain of Hope was showing its first glimmer of practical potential. But Leo was a load of bricks.

Strother, meanwhile, had delivered his magazines to LeDonna's. He appeared to know they had magazines in the beauty parlor, and LeDonna was always good for a twarter. She got Carmita to comb through the magazines for current issues and throw the rest in the dumpster after Strother left. The old man ambled down the street in the same direction he had been walking, as if he intended to circle the Earth. But he crossed at the light and turned uptown, whence he had come. At Leo's, he stopped and stared in two directions. He seemed to be trying to remember why he was there. Whether his conversation with Leo had registered or not, he walked up the small slope from the curb and started picking up dog droppings and the occasional beer can or candy wrapper. Leo drove up just as Strother was about to finish.

"Great job, Strother. Here's two quarters for your work." Already it had been a profitable day for Strother, and it wasn't even noon. Not that he showed any sign of such yeoman pride, or any other particular kind of conscious reflection. He began to hum as he approached the privet hedge, which was singing harmony.

"I'll tell you what. If you plant this special border grass for me, I'll pay you two bucks an hour."

"I'll do it for a twarter."

"That's eight twarters an hour, which is more, isn't it? So, let's get it on."

"Let's get it on!" enthused Strother, in a disturbing spasm of wild-eyed gusto.

As the afternoon sun waned, Strother and Leo looked down on a lawn edge transformed. The Indian grass mixed in nicely with the electrified product, which stood out as a slightly more ornamental species. Nice touch, Leo thought. Strother evinced no interest in the wire leading from the border grass to the garage outdoor outlet, but he was clearly in a good mood after lecturing Leo on the little spirit boy, who ran by Leo's house at dusk every day chasing a little cat. It was more of a dissertation than anyone had heard from Strother in years, and far more than Leo cared to hear. Leo dismissed the old man with eight one-dollar bills for his work. They spent an unfortunate amount of time discussing how many twarters that represented. As Strother trundled off with his wagon and wages, Leo called out to him that he'd be welcome the next week if he wanted to work in the yard again cleaning up. "Just don't touch the border grass."

Strother turned to his new patron and said in simple truth, "If it's don't touch the border grass, don't put it in reach. You want to hurt something, plug it in." Then, grasping his dollar bills, he toddled off home.

CHAPTER XI

For an idea man, nothing serves quite like a retreat, and Faris knew more about retreats than the French. Turning inward seemed essential to understanding the world: you couldn't get it if you were in it. It sounded like a commercial for a monastery. He admired the ancient hermits, wandering in the desert and living in caves, knowing that vision required deprivation. Alone, he could pretend that all the vexing matters of real life with other people were some kind of disagreeable dream. He could imagine that being alone, utterly unto himself, was reality. And the best kind of solitude could be found on a deer stand in the warm morning dark of the piney woods.

Still, he lacked the courage required to live in isolation and feared the risk of completely opening his mind, forgoing all protection. Even modest forays into the glades of silence had revealed their dangers, like opening the attic door at home as a child, finding the scary must of dead things and stored away memories. Opening those doors could cause a man's sorrows to well up all at once, as it had after his mother's death, a wave of sadness enveloping him as he sat at sunrise in the lowland forest. Dogs barking, squirrels rustling and chattering, owls ending their nighttime sentry, and Faris weeping like a child. Grief struck him with total surprise, like the time he had kidney stones and the impatient radiologist pushed iodine into his IV too fast. Flushed and faint, he could taste the metal in his mouth. It was just like that, only it wasn't iodine, it was chest-baring solitude.

He fended off such dangerous self-understanding with recitations of poetry, recalled from youth or from his teaching or his endless efforts to discipline his unruly mind with an ordered memory. He loved the prayerful recitation of words that seemed like litanies to beauty or fond remembrance. He always spoke the words in a kind of sing-song chant, without inflection, like a monk at *matins*.

In the dark quiet of the woods this day, with no light to offer distraction, he tried to remember the lines of a poem by Leopardi, which he had loved as a young man.

O fair and gracious moon! Well I remember

A year hath passed, since up this very hill

I came so full of anguish to behold thee:

And o'er yon forest thou didst shed thy beams,

As at this moment, filling it with light.

But veiled in mist, and tremulous with tears

That hung upon my lashes, to mine eyes

Thy radiance did appear, for dark with woe

Was then my life, and is, nor will it change,

O Moon, Thou my adored! And yet I love

The Curtain of Hope

To bear in mind and one by one to count

The slow years of my sorrow. Oh, how sweet

It is to youth, when hope has yet a long,

And memory has but a brief, career,

To dwell in thought on things for ever past,

Though they be sad and though affliction live.

Faris loved the sad sentiment of youthful hope and aged reverie, but he stumbled badly over the lines and forgot several. He had always found it almost impossible to recite any poem without speaking out loud. Talking defeated the very purpose of a deer stand, so he tried it without vocalizing. By the time he had silently failed on several tries, missing lines or scrambling their order, the day had begun.

Earlier, Faris found himself driving too fast in pre-dawn darkness to his favorite tree stand on this, the first day of firearm season for deer. It was already too hot. A dawn in late summer could only bring momentary beauty, a false precursor to suffocating, white heat. The black air steamed with anticipation, fanning his face through the open car windows. The two lane road revealed nothing but a center line and occasional roadside reflectors. I should have waited for cooler weather, he thought, but sometimes fall doesn't come until November in Georgia, and he couldn't wait after so many seasons away. His eyes scratched from fatigue. Driving by the lighted sign of the Thankful Baptist Church, he read: "One Cross, Two Thieves, Three Nails, Four Ever Saved." He smiled at the memory of having told an out-of-towner to turn right off the road where the old smokehouse used to be, forgetting that the directions would be worthless to anyone who hadn't been here before the smokehouse burned.

His heartbeat was happier than his heart today, because to go out on the first day of deer season was to be a little boy again, too exuberant for one's own good, pushing aside worry, standing at the school door a half hour early in new jeans with new crayons and a sack lunch. He didn't suppose that either crayons or sack lunches figured in today's world, but little boys and their man-child morphs still arrived too early for things to begin, imbued with the irresistible electricity of renewal. Ever the boy, Faris continued to suffer excessive hope, the kind that routinely spawned crippling headaches before big occasions, as if his excitement had to burst from his skull. Age had not diminished his willingness to greet the day, only his expectations. Today, his excitement told him he had already failed at being without the world. His remaining hope was to be a hunter. He did not expect to succeed at that, either. But he could hope.

His mind would not leave him alone. His dead father sat beside him in the truck, a pleasant ghost of past camping trips, but a ghost all the same. Never an outdoorsman, Oscar had nevertheless been a great Boy Scout parent. He and Faris cooked in foil, kept a clean campsite, fished with dough balls, and hiked at the front of the troop. They trenched around their tent against rainwater and vermin. They were first to identify poison ivy, or Broadhead skinks in the leaf litter. Oscar told the best ghost stories at the nightly campfire, turning his son's nighttime fears into pride and love. Faris held onto his father's sleeping bag as protection against the dark. He found in his feelings for the woods a pale reflection of happy times with Oscar, wondering only now what his father thought about his boy's mainly empty merit badge sash and his weakening grip on the unimpressive middle of the troop. He turned to ask the ghost riding beside him, but Oscar had fled. Faris' father had hidden all disappointment in his son with a magical veil of love and devotion.

Faris felt cold without its protection, and irritated by the intrusion of memory into his aloneness. He glanced to his side once more to make sure Oscar was gone.

Parking the truck and walking through the dark, Faris traced the rutted path to the deer stand and climbed the metal ladder. Absurdly perched twenty feet up a fat loblolly pine, sitting on a thin, camouflaged cushion, trying to remember poems, Faris cradled his deer rifle across his legs. A strong, compact man, he didn't suffer on the small camp seat, but sitting still in a pine tree trying not to move took commitment. He thought of it as a kind of country mindfulness, cracker meditation. He had chosen the tree as a younger man. Now, it was too thin for his weight and waved in the afternoon breeze. But it had always yielded game, so he forgave the tree its instability. His vertigo disappeared with the fine first light. After giving up on old poems, he listened to the forest awaken, Barred owls who asked in the night "Who cooks for you? Who cooks for you all?" handed the day to mockingbirds and warblers. He listened for screech owls, but heard none. Maybe they avoided this part of the woods because of the big owls. Pileated woodpeckers hammered messages across the canopy with admirable industry, as an incorrigibly happy cardinal whistled its tune. Brown thrashers in the understory and pine warblers dashing from tree to tree kept him alert. The variegations of color in the woods revealed themselves, as first light turned to dawn and dawn to day. The crepuscular morning light was divine revelation. Trees appeared from pure darkness, then myrtle bushes followed by grasses and ground cover – partridge pea, beggar's lice, ragweed, switchgrasses and greenbrier. Gray half tones gave way to dappled green and tan, black sky turning to daytime blue. The light betrayed motion, too; leaves and stems shuddering with tiny puffs of air, random dancers of the wild. In Faris' childlike spirit of romantic reverie, he unclosed his trembling eyelids to the kiss of day. At least he remembered that line from Shelley. The poem worked. Promise hung in the air.

Faris' thoughts jumped again to past memory, from years ago, when walking along a trail as dusk became night, he heard and barely saw a Great horned owl soaring low between the rows of pine trees in the single patch of open sky over his head. Recalling the beauty, with his grieving sensibilities and wounded heart, he recognized the Owl of Minerva, spreading its wings at dusk. It was his memory, his alone, unshareable.

That was dusk and this was dawn. He returned to himself on the stand. A pair of red foxes listening for field mice inspired Faris to be still. A faint reminder of a skunk hung in the damp. The occasional silver and black fox squirrel hurried in the forest openings. Killdeer called from the cornfield, mixed with snipes searching for bugs. What looked like a Cooper's hawk sat as his partner, silhouetted far away in a spindly gum tree. He really couldn't identify the bird from such a distance, but it satisfied him to think otherwise.

Daylight tricked the eyes, turning dark forms that might be deer into simple bushes. As early light surrendered to the full bloom of morning, the sky was painted beautifully false in bluebird blues and fairy pinks, as in the dome of a Venetian chapel. The full brightness of August in the morning baked away the subtle beauties of the morning in favor of sun and flies. The convection of morning heat boiled up quickly, and soon he was soaked in sweat. Mosquitoes found him and drank his blood.

Faris worried again over Turner's and the future of Pincus, which were nothing more than projected worries about himself. Had he, at age 50, found his mission in life? Was he to represent the people of Pincus in their effort to halt the decline of their town and its community? More modestly, could he keep the doors of Turner's open, and if so, for what? Am I again foolishly thinking I could mean something in a meaningless world, he mused, setting myself up as an ever-repeating joke, a clown on the dunking stool? Now, on the deer stand, such unanswerable questions were bringing forth the idealistic silliness of his younger years, when he discovered socialism, thought he understood the way the world went round, read Trotsky late into the night, opposed world capitalism, argued the merits of Maoism, all the while ignorant of the slaughter that traveled under that flag. How had he thought a man in his twenties could have it all solved? And what had it come to? Had he just now, in his middle age, discovered another world that had been hidden from him in plain sight, only to fail to move it? How could he reconcile what he represented to others and how he viewed himself? His mother was right. He thought too much. It was barely dawn, and he was already mentally exhausted.

Ah, and then Oscar reappeared, this time not as a camper but a latter-day Abraham, torn between duty and family. The tree stand was too small for a grown man and a ghost, too. Faris asked his father if his humility had falsely hidden the sin of pride. Didn't Faris' father step out of his modesty through service to others? Giving was its own form of taking, after all. Oscar smiled, unoffended, but left the deer stand without answering. Thoughts of Angeline took his place, in love with her own vision. But it was a vision of good, of making a better world, so what was wrong with claiming it as her own? How could he chase his father off the stand with accusations? How could he doubt Angeline, his one romantic love in life? Better to return to doubting himself, with which he was more familiar. His mind buzzed louder than the flies. The mosquitoes called in their friends.

His hyperkinetic mind games were interrupted when the light showed him a target. A bit more than 100 yards away, in the gently sloped boundary among field, forest and swamp, a White-tailed buck appeared magically — one moment nothing, the next a young male.

This must be how the ancient forest myths began, of shadows becoming life. Though he had hunted all his life, the sight of prey quickened his blood every time as if it were the first. After all, to kill an animal is no small thing. This time, it was a young four-point, barely through his second summer, possessed of antlers hardly worth the name and not appropriate to shoot, a handsome boy who would grow to size and stature in a couple of years. None of the marks of maturity were evident: the thick, one-piece neck and breast; the tarsal stain from past ruts; the softening of his belly with weight and age; and a real rack of breadth and beam. Faris relaxed, and wondered at the clarity of life embodied in the buck. He had no doubts, no ambiguity of purpose. He was to sustain his genetic information by impregnating does. Then, he was destined to die as a prey animal. Simple. Faris cleared his throat loudly to startle the buck back into the forest bottom. He thought for a moment about the necessary connection between predator and prey, how the deer would not be so sharp-sensed and fleet of foot if it did not fear for its life. Faris might not be so attuned to his own weaknesses if he had not been given the luxury of self-absorption. As a predator, he would not have been so picky if his family had needed food. His own well being and the buck's were connected. And, of course, he had no family, just himself.

The little buck was the last animal he saw that morning. At nine thirty, he climbed down from his stand into the rising heat and the smell of toasted dust in the road. Leaving the quiet of the woods behind on the tree stand, but still dragging around his neuroses, he re-entered the world and headed for a plate of eggs at the Sunnyside. His head throbbed.

Steven Sanderson

I know a lady with a terrible tongue,

Blear eyes fallen from blue,

All her perfections tarnished – yet it is not long

Since she was lovelier than any of you.

John Crowe Ransom, *The Vanity of the Blue Girls*

CHAPTER XII

E thel Chesney luxuriated in her Jacuzzi tub on the one day she could call her own. It wasn't a true Jacuzzi, just a big tub with a few submerged jets that spewed bubbles. It was relaxing enough to an overworked fry cook, wife and grandmother, who had once been a girl. The only reminders of that tender youth were little adornments in dress and home, and the prodigious energy that had always possessed her spirit. When dressed in her pink and white seersucker candy striper's dress and butcher's apron, Ethel was a tornado as a line cook. Many of the old farmers called her "Twister," because of the speed with which she moved her round little body. She served up short orders from a vintage diner menu on melamine platters, the plastic clatter combining with the shouted orders to create a warm white noise for hungry customers. She sported several tattoos, most prominently a small script "sassybaby" in lower case cursive on the left side of her neck. Body art notwithstanding, her pot roast, three-meat meatloaf, homemade sausage and greens soup, and chicken a la king would have received raves anywhere in the diner world. Twenty-something chefs in Charleston made their reputations on less.

Sunday line cooking at the Sunnyside Café belonged to her daughter Muscadine, starting with a late brunch service instead of the six-day breakfast menu Ethel slaved over. Muscadine, too, was quickly moving from innocence to age. She made Sundays at the café a mess, because she was a total nut case at work, as she was at home. Still, Ethel felt utterly committed to her day off, hiding up to her neck in scalding water topped with a meringue of suds, humming noise and forced water laving her whole body, basting her mashed potato arms floating about the surface with their bottom flab submerged. She held her biceps up, her forearms angled, manicured hands dry. She was a lolling pink manatee, with the back of her head lightly tethered by a mat of red-grey hair and a folded wet hand towel. Only her feet and forearms rose above the water, her hands extended upward as if in praise of God. Her painted toes, each one bearing a portrait of a favorite cartoon character – Mickey and Minnie on the big toes, Snow White and the Seven Dwarves on the rest – were a triumph of Carmita's art and testament to Ethel's childlike persona. She could not normally decorate her fingernails because of her job, but on Sundays she painted them herself, always glossy baby pink to go with her cartoon toes. She loved her painted toes almost as much as the new tattoo of The Little Mermaid on her ankle, an idea borrowed from a lady she saw one time in a Charleston dollar store. How she loved Disney. And little Ariel made her feel so young.

On that one day, Sunday, in the tub alone, Ethel could think of herself as a little girl again. She had been a beautiful child, and imagined herself that way: no daughter, no husband, and no granddaughter; just hot water, plenty of suds, and fresh-painted nails.

She was in a fine mood, looking forward to the Paul Harvey radio replay on WPNC at noon, after the morning commodities report and before the mid-day news. She was also eager for the announcement of her forthcoming 40th wedding anniversary on Afternoon Town Talk at one.

Many a listener lingered over a second cup of coffee with

Paul, though they certainly would have called him Mr. Harvey to his face and become nervous if he had knocked at the door. Housewives who still ironed the family's clothes found rhythm in his Voice of God timbre and his rock-ribbed views. Long after he ceased to broadcast in this world, his mellifluous, honeyed tongue would reach back across the river with cornball epistles tailor-made for AM radio broadcasts in the heartland. He had been a fixture in rural and small town America since the 1960s, when his discourse on what Satan would have to do to bring the world to final perdition struck a deep chord among those who believed that post-WWII the world was going to hell in a hand basket. Along with his homily "So God Created a Farmer," and testimonials of golden wedding anniversary celebrants, Paul Harvey was oil on troubled waters to a world in need of mythical happy yeoman farmers, steadfast spouses, Christian virtue and good neighbors in small towns. Towns like Pincus imagined itself to be.

To Ethel, Paul Harvey and Lawrence Welk were at the center of the media pantheon, legends who didn't have to be alive to be popular. Every Sunday, her old-fashioned gold and cream plastic analog clock radio sat on the stamped vinyl vanity stool by the tub. She wanted to hear every word.

The fly in the buttermilk this peaceful day was Ethel's granddaughter, Amy, whom the family called Blueberry, because she was a fruit like her mother Muscadine. Blueberry was a sweet child of six, but she was in the advanced placement group for ADHD. She had the subtlety of a cheap blender: one switch, off or on. If her eyes were open, she was on. Ethel recognized herself in her granddaughter, but didn't care for as she thought she should, and so felt guilty. Her torment was further deepened by Ethel's collateral resentment of her daughter, who had been a difficult child and then had run off with Timmy Stobaugh, who promptly knocked her up before going to prison for manufacturing and distributing methamphetamine. If Ethel thought that ace could not be trumped, Muscadine then married Bobby Lee Fuqua, a congenital drunk. Emmett called him shit heel so often that one day, with Blueberry in the car, Emmett cursed another driver who had cut Emmett off, calling the driver a shit heel. Blueberry sat up in her car seat, looked around anxiously, and said, "Daddy?"

Loved though she was by her parents, Muscadine now lived with Shit Heel in exuberant chaos in their trailer and left Blueberry too often with Emmett and Ethel. Blueberry had embraced her lead role as the grand torturer of her grandmother in the recurring nightmare of Muscadine's youth, which the senior Chesneys did not deserve in their advancing years. Plus, Blueberry wasn't right in the head. She had the maturity of an Easter peep and no more sense of direction. She stuck raisins and cheese in the electrical outlets, put Vienna sausages down her panties, and still peed the bed at night every time she ate watermelon. Ethel, now obliged to raise yet another hellion, wondered what sins she must have committed to deserve such penance. She wondered why God did not use the merit system in handing out his punishments.

Still, all it took to make her happy was a hot bubble bath, as she was by nature cheery and easy to please. This morning she had left Blueberry finger painting in the kitchen, which seemed to be the one thing the little girl would stay at for more than ten minutes. Ethel hoped for a few moments of peace before hearing the call of "Mamaw" from little Blueberry. It was Paul Harvey time.

Paul Harvey's replay was edited to skip the news, which was twenty years old, and to focus on the eternal values so comforting to his listeners. Paul had just begun the feature portion of his program.

"Page Two," he intoned, with a hint of a question mark.

"Let us remind ourselves of the virtues of a long marriage,

being lived by a couple who has just celebrated 65 years of wedded bliss.   Arthur and Mary May Wallace, of Lookout Mountain, Tennessee. He went off to war; she wrote him every day. In 1945, together again, they started their little family, raising three children in a Sears house. All the youngsters graduated college and showed their parents the love they deserved. Now in their ninth decade, Arthur and Mary May still hold hands at church and still read from the family bible inscribed with their children's names. How timeless is the institution of marriage, how outrageous to think of any version but the true one," Paul declared, in his best baritone. Ethel imagined the happy couple still holding hands, long after Paul had anointed them.

God, how right you are, Paul, thought Ethel. You were a prophet for our age. How could the gays ever understand? Not that she was intolerant. Sometimes she wished Muscadine had gone the other way and run away with a girl, rather than rolling over for those trashy men. At least she'd have one nice girlfriend.

What good words would Paul have on Page Three? She flipped on a little more hot water with her toes, careful not to chip a Disney. Emotion came with the water, and she pushed back a tear, thankful for her blessings. She had a good marriage, too, just like Mary May of Lookout Mountain, Tennessee. The offspring part of her story still needed work, though, before it became Paul Harvey quality.

But today she was as lucky as the commander of the Lost Patrol. While Ethel held her water-pruned, pink-nailed hands up in a papal wave, into the bathroom marched Blueberry, wearing Ethel's terrycloth Goofy bedroom slippers and carrying a finger painting of herself and her Mamaw's dog Violet. "Look, Mamaw," was all she managed to say, before the too-big slippers caught the edge of the shag bathmat, sending her hard little forehead into the vanity stool, which, in turn, slid Paul Harvey, still plugged in, into the tub with Ethel. Ethel bolted upright to attention. All the circuit breakers in the house tripped. The lights went out. Paul Harvey fell silent. Blueberry's little nose bled. Through her snot and tears, she cried out for Mamaw, as an eponymous knot rose between her eyes. Except for Mamaw's hands and feet, she had slid beneath the water. Mamaw, Violet Sparkleberry, Ethel Chesney and the girl she had once been, were no more. Murdered by Paul Harvey, with an assist from Blueberry.

"Page Three." Paul Harvey went on, oblivious to the passing of a most loyal fan.□

Lorne Stobaugh sat in the Chesney house waiting for the ambulance and coroner, his patrol car idling and flashing its lights lazily. He had rushed over from his usual Sunday post, directing traffic as it exited the late service at the Methodist church. The faithful on Sunday mornings tended to overflow with Christian zeal as they left the parking lot, competing to get the best tables at the Sunnyside brunch. The late service crowd was especially difficult. They knew the brunch was soon to end, and they wanted to get fresh food and not the stuff that had been sitting on the steam line. The end of services posed a high traffic risk, considering it was a Sunday morning in Pincus. Lorne viewed the Sunday church shift as part obligation and part community outreach. He managed to glad-hand as much as the old preacher and fancied himself more popular.

When Lorne arrived at the Chesney place, he found Lew Givens, his only other officer on duty, sitting with little Blueberry, a hanky to her bloody nose. He had restored the electricity and drained the tub. Ethel lay under a bedsheet. "Chief, Blueberry keeps crying that Paul Harvey hurt her Mamaw, which don't make no sense at all.

Ain't he dead?"

"Shuddup, Lew. She's a little bitty girl who just saw her granny poached like an egg, and she's took a pretty good shot to that nose, to boot. I don't think you need to be taking a statement from her. But maybe she knows somebody named Paul Harvey. How do I know?"

"Paul Harvey is dead, I'm telling you. Has been for years. Somebody re-runs his radio show on Sundays, that's all. I was just listening to it in the ambulance. Now, will that make you guys shut up?" One of the EMTs, on call for the weekend, was already aggravated about having to come out on Sunday, when nothing happened most of the time. He had enough age on him to remember Paul Harvey.

Lorne had been police chief in Pincus since failing to gain promotion in Statesboro, due to his brother Timmy's criminal record. In his opinion the city fathers were unduly sensitive to his family history, but unfairness at work wasn't any different than the rest of his life. His parents had liked television better than their kids, with good reason. Timmy had been named for the kid in the Lassie TV show, and Lorne had gotten his name from the star of Bonanza. They were fed, clothed and dropped off at school. At night, they ate frozen dinners from the toaster oven, then sat in front of the television. Otherwise, they were pretty much on their own. Lorne had followed Timmy through life, stepping in his messes and trying to distance himself from his entire clan. He had become a policeman partly to escape his family's reputation and partly to escape his own fear of cowardice. As a child he had been small and afraid, and it worried him terribly as a teen. He went out of his way to get into fights, play violent sports, drink until drunk, and whatever else affirmed his adolescent sense of courage. A fantasy of becoming tough explained his initial choice of law enforcement as a career. In the course of time he had mostly outgrown it. None too smart, he was the perfect authoritarian personality, rough on subordinates and submissive to superiors. Prisoners hated him. Still, he was a good, honest cop.

"Just in case, put out an APB on anyone in the county answering to the name of Paul Harvey. This thing stinks. And get Ethel off to Plummer's. Belay that last part; here comes Plummer's ambulance up the drive."

CHAPTER XIII

The school auditorium filled early for the second Curtain of Hope assembly. The ladies' police auxiliary set up a folding table with lemon bars the color of tennis balls, tweedy zucchini bread and iced tea (sweet and unsweet), hoping for donations. A pleasant frisson animated the room, since Pincans who had missed the inaugural session had heard about the fracas between Washington and Plummer and the rant by Leo. Excitement was rare in a small town. No one wanted to miss the next installment. Everyone was ready to see more of Muscadine in motion, especially the high school boys.

The otherwise effervescent mood was soured by the tragic death of Ethel Chesney and the mindless but predictable speculation about its implications for the Sunnyside Café. Ethel was known by everyone and pretty well liked. Even those who for one reason or another didn't care for her, and there are always some, acknowledged that she deserved a better death than electrocution by a radio in the bathtub. Some twerp on Channel 7 News said that only about 60 people die each year from home electrocution nationwide, and now Ethel was one of them. As if she would have wanted the distinction. Snarky gossips muttered that if Muscadine had taken better care of Blueberry, none of this would have happened. Too many grandmothers are raising their children's children, while the younger set runs around like whores. That's what's wrong with America. Whores or not, Ethel was poached like an egg, Lorne said to anyone who would listen and some who would not. He seemed to like the imagery. No one else did.

Muscadine stood front and center in the auditorium decked out in a gingham halter top and Daisy Duke cutoffs, one hip jutting out in welcome. She chewed gum and licked her lips with intention, self-consciously staring at her nails. She could even manage to look slutty while accepting condolences for her recent loss. She missed her mama, but the tragedy was the greatest thing to happen in this town in years, and Muscadine's own second-best personal highlight, right after Chagas disease. "My mama," Muscadine would begin, teary-eyed, before launching into a completely irrelevant and selfish long story about her own heartbreak and bad luck. "I wish my mama was here to see this," she often said, in circumstances she knew would mortify poor Ethel's ghost. Muscadine, good at heart, was still all about Muscadine.

Emmett, the new widower, was not in evidence. He was truly brokenhearted. He loved Ethel to his core, had known her all of his adult life, loved to pat her hair at night as she slept and even liked to hear her snore. Dear Abby or somebody in the newspaper once said that a person ought to be grateful that someone chose to snore next to them in bed, and he guessed that was true, at least for him. Although it had not been true when he went to deer hunting camp with his friends, and they snored. Without Ethel, he thought his breastbone would split. He could not bear to think of her lying cold at Plummer's, much less to consider cremating her, as she wished. Plummer said cremation was definitely the deal, partly to cut costs, but also because he couldn't get her in a box anyway, with her arms raised in the air that way. Emmett saw no reason to tell a man something like that about his dead wife. Plummer was an asshole, but that was hardly a news flash. Poached like an egg, Lorne said. No cremation, Emmett said. No way. She's been burnt up enough. How could he live his life alone, after all this time with her? Before she died, he wasn't even a "he" any more. He had become a "they." They went to sleep together, woke together, worried together, worked together, ate together. They were a single entity made up of two young kids who had never been adults without the other. Now half of his self was gone. If God baked all the Ethel out of Emmett, only a flavorless rusk would remain.

"Folks," Henry began with a handclap, "please sit down so we can get started." Slowly, the crowd found seats, scraping chairs and scuffing the buffed gloss on the hardwood floor before settling in for the show. "I want us all to take a minute to remember our dear friend Ethel Chesney, who left this world so suddenly. I know I speak for us all when I say we're shocked." Some teenage jackass in the audience snickered at the reference to being shocked. Before continuing to speak, Henry deployed his most fearsome teacher's stink eye, pinning the kid to his seat. "Ethel was the soul behind the Sunnyside Café, and no one can ever take her place. She was beloved of Emmett and a matriarch in our community. I have it on good authority that the first roasted squirrel heads from a fall season were delivered to Appalachian matriarchs as a kind of homage, and Ethel would have liked that." The crowd rolled their eyes at Henry and his squirrel heads and wondered where in the world this came from and where it would lead. But people managed to focus on Ethel, filling the empty spaces with sniffles and clearing throats. Henry went on. "We are all grateful to have known her and to have broken bread at her table. She was a person of honest devotion, a wife of great virtue and a mother burdened by personal struggle."

Muscadine glowered, knowing that Henry spoke of her.

"How like Marsyas of ancient myth our flesh is flayed in life before eternal release."

The assembled stared at Henry like picnickers on a nuthouse lawn, marveling at people who had lost their minds. He saw that they had parted company with him. He tried to re-gather them.

"Not because we challenge Apollo to a flute contest, of course, which is what got Marsyas in trouble in the first place. I know that. But, you get the point. Ethel had too much trouble and not enough joy, and then she was called away too early. Anyway, I'm sure there will be many remembrances to come, but let's all pause to observe a moment of silence."

The crowd was certainly thankful for the silence, bringing as it did the end of another one of Henry's pompous, weird dissertations. A suffocating quiet followed, lasting just a bit too long, the distance between too brief and too protracted being very delicate. Henry never opted for brief. Finally, he cleared his throat and rapped the lectern with his knuckles twice. He had seen that once at a Rotary meeting after someone had died and was pleased to be so authoritative.

Pirouetting slightly toward the speakers, Henry shifted his voice from emcee of grief to host of The Curtain of Hope, introducing the evening. "Tonight we have two more citizens desirous of making a contribution to our great civic discourse. First, we'll listen to Ed Prewitt of Ed's BBQ, one of our most venerable dining establishments. He'll address the question of food safety, which is certainly on our minds as we learn more about listeria, salmonella and other frightening bugs." He extended the pronunciation of bugs so that it seemed to have two syllables and sounded particularly ugly. "Following Ed will be one of our youngest presenters and the winner of the inaugural Curtain of Hope door prize, Doreen Wagner, who wishes to address us regarding the matter of animal cruelty. These are portentous subjects, as we all recognize. Let's give a hearty Pincus welcome to both. Ed, you have the stage."

At 63, Ed had seen it all, or at least pretty much all he wanted to see. Raised on a little farmstead between Pincus and the Savannah River, he had spent his young years harvesting pecans, growing okra and other row crops, and working timber crews off the farm. His father had a family deed that went back to Reconstruction, but the farm was doomed by prejudice, Jim Crow banking practices, diseconomies of scale and the general desuetude of abandoned properties around him.

Ed had stayed home to help his father until the old man's death. Once Ed came of age, helping his father meant going to Pincus at dusk after work every day but Sunday to climb on a Jensen Farms truck with a handful of other young black men schooled in the bitter enterprise of chicken catching. He would spend almost all night in a hen house grabbing five or six chickens at a time by their feet and hustling them into crates for transport and slaughter. Bent over, sweating, lungs full of powdered sawdust and chicken shit, he represented low labor costs to the feed mill that owned the hens and contracted them out to poor farmers like Ed's dad. Only white. Ed was paid by the chicken, with the tally often shorted by the job boss. Nowadays, long years later, undocumented workers from Central America did such work, but the black man was not complaining about the loss of opportunity. Ed always said that when someone says poor people don't want to work, you can bet he never stooped for onions or caught chickens.

After many years of hashing along on his little farm, Ed's father died. Ed happily sold the place for more than it was worth to a car dealer from Beaufort, who thought he could turn the old place into a gentleman's hunting property. The proceeds allowed Ed to start his BBQ place, where the work was hard but the aromas were smoked meat instead of chicken dust. He never did serve chicken, except fried gizzards and hot sauce, which were a great moneymaker. Otherwise he wouldn't touch them. Goat, pulled pork, and brisket were his specialties. Fried catfish appeared from time to time, depending on the price of farmed fish, or the current in the river and the placement of his set lines. He always staged a weekend oyster roast in the summer, between July 4 and the beginning of school, when things were otherwise lazy and dead. Smoky heat, grease on the walls, classic R & B playing on the old boom box. Everyone in the county knew Ed's, and even TV network people had visited for a segment on Georgia Today, but it never aired. At least, it hadn't yet.

Ed stood up to the podium all cleaned up in a white short sleeve uniform shirt and forest green gabardine trousers, supported just below his belly by a pair of black braces with leather eye straps. His powerful arms, burn-blistered red hands and gently drooping beltline were all of a piece. Carefully unfolding a handwritten speech, looking around the room intently, and squinting through reading glasses, he read with obvious reluctance but in strong voice. "I have been here all my life, and I'm pretty near certain that everybody in this room has eaten Ed's BBQ. You know me, and you know I stand for good food and responsible business. I charge a fair price and pay my people as well as I can. And I try to bring along young people with their first paying jobs. You all can probably name a lot of young men who found their way forward working at Ed's through the years."

"I ain't asking for nothing and never have. I got nothing against an honest man, woman or child, black, white or anything else. But I have got to stand up tonight and tell you about some bad trouble in our town. I'm not one for a lot of talk or extra words, so, as I see it, here's the deal: Somebody appears to be paying somebody else, so that the House of Mao can get by with selling cat for chicken. That's right. You heard me: cat for chicken. Maybe in China they do that. I once heard they even milk dogs for wine there. I don't rightly know about that, either. But cat for chicken don't go in Georgia. If y'all knew the whole story behind the House of Mao, I'm telling you that you would start gagging up rice, washing your mouth out, and spitting on the floor. I can't tell you what and where to eat, but in this town, you can't serve cat and call it chicken. Period. It's not legal and it's not right. Somebody needs to look into it. This town needs to uphold its laws on this kinda thing. And y'all need to come to Ed's, where a goat's a goat, the pork doesn't meow and the brisket came from an actual cow. That's all I got to say. Thank you for the opportunity."

Vincent Chin stood enraged. "What you say? House of Mao good restaurant. People like. White people like, black people like, too. Not right you talk like that." Chin, owner-operator of House of Mao, spoke in a cartoon pidgin that sounded more or less like what he thought folks expected from Chinese English. He wasn't even Chinese, of course, and really didn't know how he should sound. He had taken the name Vincent Chin from a story about Vincent "the chin" Gigante, the New York mobster. Along the way he had learned to cook just about the entire menu of every hole in the wall Chinese joint in the country, and morphed into a Chinese-acting Korean as part of his business plan. Pincans thought he was Chinese and the House of Mao was great. His bowing and scraping and funny talk made him a colorful character, even though no one knew where he had come from, what was in the food, or who General Tso was, for that matter. Ed had uncovered a few choice things about Vincent Chin, though, which he would be glad to reveal in due course, if necessary. But even at this late date in the South, it was not wise for a black man to be too closely identified with a direct attack on anyone else. Ed thought this was a good enough start, unless white people were dumber than he thought. Which would be hard.

"Hope is the midwife of ambition, Ed, as you well know." Henry wheezed out, to general bewilderment. "So, let's not prejudge what's going on in the business matters of another upstanding proprietor in Pincus." Henry was a particular fan of House of Mao shrimp puffs, Styrofoam-like fried crackers that he dipped in little packets of duck sauce. He could, and did, eat them by the basket. "We have a public health inspector who regularly reviews food safety in our dining establishments. I'm sure we can call on Agnes McGriff to advise us on the findings of her latest inspection." Agnes, who in an earlier time could have played a prison matron in drive-in movies, stood up and treated the assembly to the tortured standards of the public health authorities – no meat stored above vegetables, proper refrigeration, no fly paper over the grill, hair nets for food handlers, that sort of thing. She punctuated her conclusions by declaring that House of Mao had received a Grade A just weeks ago.

Ed was ready. "Agnes, the only restaurant in Pincus that didn't get an A in your last evaluations was The Pancake Joint, and that was because the crapper was backed up and you caught someone standing on top of one of the booths washing windows, while you were eating your waffles at the next station. Fifty dollars in a coffee mug by the steam table has been known to work wonders with your grading. Or do you just like to eat cat at Chin's?"

Ed had overstepped, but on the right toes. Agnes was a lazy time server, who did little besides depositing her paycheck. She ate free everywhere in town and was not above taking a gratuity from a restaurant now and then, when she bothered to inspect at all. She called it professional consideration. Agnes had earned public contempt for always inspecting the Sunnyside Café during Sunday brunch, helping herself to the buffet and a corner booth. A chorus of murmurs rippled through the auditorium, each person with a private story of hair in food somewhere or a waitress with dirty nails. Some even repeated the urban legend of a severed thumb found in a vending machine honey bun, which, in view of the bountiful waistlines in the room, hadn't deterred honey bun eaters. The fact that Agnes' remit did not include vending machine foods made no difference.

Henry struggled to restore order, happily pounding the gavel for effect.

"Ed, we're going to get to the bottom of this, but nothing is served (pardon the pun) by ad hominem attacks on our neighbors, Ed. I'm sure Agnes will review the findings of her last inspection, and then we'll know if Vincent deserves an apology. Now, I'd like to segue to Doreen Wagner, who has expressed concern about animal cruelty. Doreen, the floor is yours." Henry loved that he had made one of puns, which were priceless to him, and him alone.

Ed sat down disappointed that he'd been cut off in peak form, half his cards still in his hand. Still exercised, he popped back up and shouted, "I won't apologize for telling the truth. And ad hominem my neck! I'm telling you I got video of Vincent Chin snatching stray cats and taking them into his kitchen by the back door. You think he's starting a shelter? Them damn things is ending up in the wok!"

In hushed shock, the room watched as Vincent Chin ran from his seat, fists raised, to attack Ed, bleating "Rya! Rya!" Remarkably, he stayed in faux dialect through his fury. He did not appear to have a plan to execute when he actually got to Ed, though. A big man, Ed slammed the palms of both hands into Vincent's chest, effortlessly knocking him back into the first row of folding chairs. "Back off, Chopsticks. Channel 7 is showing my security video on the news tomorrow night. Then we'll see who's a rya." Chin gave Ed a cat murderer's glare as he got up and left the room; Ed took note.

Henry leapt to the stage, showing agility that defied his size. "Wow, neighbors, talk about excitement! I know we'll all be watching the six o'clock news tomorrow night, but in the meantime, hold back on the stir fry, girlfriend." No one laughed.

"But seriously, let's settle down. This is good, very good, very exciting. But we have another topic to take up, and our speaker is our own Doreen Wagner, so let's give her our full attention. Doreen?" Henry, titillated by the reality show air of the assembly, inhaled audibly through his nostrils, filling his lungs with the self-generated aroma of leadership, and minced to his tiny chair. He stared with mock interest at Doreen as she began.

Every little town and village in the world somehow manages to produce youthful beauty. Lovely flowers bloom in the desert, delicate vetch springs from sidewalk cracks, and beautiful children seem to be sprinkled uniformly throughout the Earth. Doreen Wagner was living witness. She was stunning, the only young woman in town more desirable than Muscadine Chesney and infinitely more intriguing. Muscadine had chosen the traditional route of mistaking handsome for responsible and ended up with criminals and drunks as her consorts. In her father's pensive moments, Emmett admitted that she was "a bit too nightly." Doreen, in contrast, had no known history with the local boys, and in fact exuded an alluring gender-free beauty, as exotic in Pincus as Mata Hari might have been. She was the anti-Muscadine.

Tall and willowy with inky cropped hair, Doreen ignored the anarchy of her thick eyebrows, never dirtied her alabaster skin with makeup, and rarely wore anything but an untucked black oxford cloth shirt, open over a snug, ribbed black cotton shell and faded black work jeans. Her slender frame was perfect: wasp-waisted and low-hipped, with small well-proportioned breasts. A forward cant to her hips and a slightly tired pose of the shoulders announced a gamine of rare and unaffected beauty. Her languid motions suggested a cat after dinner. She wore a sated smile, defined by a diamond-shaped tip to her nose and the faintest lines above the cupid's bow of her lip. Her teeth were bright, wet and clean, with sharply turned canines hinting at menace. Oversized eyes of faintly pink cream and black rested on puffs of under eye, adding to her aura of passion mixed with melancholy. A silk of gray shadow dusted her upper lip and outlined

171

the turn of her jaw, as if she had been born in cottonwood fluff. Below her long neck a bony sternum drew attention to the top of her cleavage and the delicate skeleton beneath the shell. A latter day Audrey Hepburn or Leslie Caron, painted in careful shades of ash and peach. She gave the appearance of a tough puppy, showing teeth but also a bit too much youth to inspire fear. Doreen herself was superficially sweet, smart and cryptic, whatever her appearance. Boys and girls alike felt dizzy, and more than a little aroused.

As her nail-head clogs clumped up the aisle to the stage, Doreen's shy smile seemed to turn from housecat to panther, parting gill-red lips to show her canines, a warning that delicate beauty belied her conviction. She was prepared and passionate about her subject, reading from a prepared text she seemed not to need.

"Mr. Jeffords, Mr. Turner, thank you for allowing me to speak on behalf of those who do not have the power of the spoken word: our brother animals. They, like we, are God's creatures, and we too willingly ignore their plight in favor of our own vanity." Doreen in no way believed in God, but she knew her audience. "They cannot speak, so we must. I remember when I was a student in your English class, Mr. Jeffords, and we read ANIMAL FARM. It seemed so wrong to me that Orwell made the animals ugly by assigning them human qualities; I've never forgotten it. Animals and nature are not cruel; humans are. Around the world, people misuse animals every day. We own them, eat them, experiment on them and use them for cruel purpose. This very day, the gall bladders of Asian bears are being "milked" in bile farms in Korea, Vietnam and China, just so people can have traditional medicines without violating laws against trade in endangered animals and their parts. In the mountains of Peru every year, panicked wild condors are strapped to bulls' backs, just to celebrate some primitive festival. In the US, poultry beaks are clipped, pigs forced into breeding cages, surplus baby lambs left out in the cold to die, and bulls electro-ejaculated for breeding." Doreen's disquisition went on for some time, veering from canned hunts of exotic animals in Texas to rare parrots being stuffed into packing tubes smuggled into the US. When she started on mad cow disease and chronic wasting among White-tailed deer, a few of the old timers catnapped. An ancient farmer in the back row gave out an apnea-induced snort. Teenage boys were stuck on electro-ejaculation, not knowing quite what it was, but eager to find out. She went on, undaunted.

"Here in Pincus, we are hardly innocent of such cruel practices, one of which Mr. Prewitt just talked about. We shouldn't be eating animals at all; surely not little cats that want to come in for a saucer of milk. But the House of Mao isn't even the worst. It's WILD ANIMAL KINGDOM and its owner Jesús Santamaria. He makes his living off the exploitation of poor animals, and he's doing it in violation of federal law. An investigation would show that he's got animals he acquired illegally, and I'm sure he doesn't follow government regulations for their care. If Pincus is to be the progressive community we all want, we've got to close that terrible menagerie on the edge of town, which is such a total hick eyesore as it is. I think it ought to be turned into an animal sanctuary, where God's wild beasts can live their lives in happiness without having to perform like – well, like performing animals. Thank you." Ignoring references to unpopular themes such as the federal government, progressive values, hick eyesores and regulation of industry, the crowd had actually listened to her. Her skin glistened with perspiration. On Doreen, the shine looked like victory.

Vincent Chin, who had reentered the room for the sole purpose of ogling Doreen, stiffened and looked around him at the mention of bear gall. He was happy to hear Doreen move on to Jesús and made a mental note to ensure that her crosshairs didn't accidentally turn back to him. Jesús, in turn, was not present to defend himself, as he never took part in community affairs. He was at his juke joint taking the measure of a bottle of gin while working with a new White Bearded Silkie chicken he had bought from a hatchery, trying to teach it to walk backward, with little progress. He had killed the last one because it was too stupid to learn. He wondered if he could just buy some Easter-colored chicks to sell and make a profit that way. The only representative of WILD ANIMAL KINGDOM present at the meeting was Rubén, who stood transfixed at the rear of the auditorium, deathly in love with Doreen.

"Doreen Wagner, everybody," enthused Henry, as if she had just finished singing the national anthem. The assembly applauded, more or less, still wondering what she wanted. As an adopted child, Doreen was a rare curiosity in Pincus. Before the Southern Christian Home closed, there were more orphans around town, blending in eventually, as they grew and went to high school and took jobs in the community. Now, it seemed most people kept their love accidents. No one knew what happened to the rest.

Doreen had been the pride of Mt. St. Helen's Catholic School, so much so, that the old nuns there hoped she would assume a religious vocation. She decidedly did not, matriculating to NYU on scholarship for one year before realizing that no matter the financial aid, she could not afford her living costs. She unhappily left college and roamed a bit in the Northeast, to do whatever she did that did not require further discussion by her and was no one's business but her own, especially not the nuns. She had been unhappy to return to Pincus' familiarity. She rationalized that it was only for the time being. Mr. Plummer, possessed of an unhealthy passion for young girls, had asked her to take over the funeral flower duties at the flower shop where she had worked as a teenager and offered her the apartment above the store. Now, a few years later, she ran the flower shop itself. She was involved all over the community, quietly playing organ for Plummer's funeral home, arranging flowers for the dead, and drawing attention each year for her great Mt. St. Helen's homecoming parade float. Her appearance at the Curtain of Hope assembly marked her as a public intellectual, in defense of animals. No one quite understood why. Probably some kind of hippie thing.

As she left the auditorium, Mr. Green asked if she would be interested in selling him the meat smoker she had won the previous week. She named an absurdly high price, underlined with her troubling smile. Disappointed that she was not inclined to mark it down, he demurred. That was Doreen: willing to keep something she didn't want, just to deny someone the pleasure of a bargain.

Walking out of the hall, she touched Vincent Chin on the shoulder. She knew who he was. She had been in New York when his buddy was killed, and a photo ran of Vincent and his two friends in the newspapers. She would use this. "Mr. Chin," she blinked. "Two guys who said they were from New York were at the shop today asking for you. They said they were hunting black bear and heard you knew all about it. That didn't sound right to me. Does that even sound right? Do you know about black bears?" Vincent blanched and ran from the scene. Doreen's canines glinted. Her lie about the visitors had worked.

CHAPTER XIV.

My Dearest Boy,

I hope that you and I will have a chance to meet again before you read this letter, as it is intended only as a substitute for a fond embrace and a more personal declaration of my intentions after death. If you are reading this, it is because I'm gone, and with me the last person who with complete devotion has loved you all of your life, your mother having preceded me on that path.

First, you surely must know that your mother and I loved you beyond measure. You were a gift to us of a kind that every person should receive but I imagine few do. You made our modest lives rich. We were addicted to you in a way that made later years, when you were gone, poor by comparison to the happy days when you were little and entirely ours. I know that seems selfish.

The one GREAT TRUTH is that we are born to die. Everything about that mournful subject has been said, but we all march differently toward the grave. The final act of life is equally singular, but almost imperceptibly so, like one person's gait or complexion differs from another's. I shall not fail at dying, if only because death is not graded on technical and artistic merit, and you who survive have no direct experience of death yourselves, so you're not in a position to judge. Everyone dies, and no one fails at it, though some do get better style points than others.

My life has been a modest one, which was a source of some disappointment to your mother. She wanted more. I was happy, though, in my way. I loved Pincus and the store and my friends, and I particularly loved the idea that people would come in to ask for help. It meant that I was the kind of person they thought might be generous, and generous is mostly what I wanted to be. Ambition is a fool's drug.

But we all have egos, and I want to leave a mark, not just some meaningless hole in the ground. That's what motivated me to write my will the way I did and to accompany it with this letter. Two messages are important to me. The first I have already delivered, that I love you in ways I could never say. I hope you will hold that fact dear. My love is undiminished by the second part of the message, which is that I'm leaving everything except the house to Angeline. I love you as my son, but she loves Pincus, which is my place. I'm bequeathing her the store and a fund to go with it, as long as she uses it for the benefit of Pincus. Of course, I'm thinking of The Bread Basket, which is a wonderful cause. But, beyond that, it's up to her.

If I had a magic wand, I would use it to bring you back to Pincus and see you in our family home, rich in the bosom of your friends as your mother and I were. But that may not be for you, and certainly it's not for me to say.

Your father

PS – make them play some spirituals at the funeral if you read this in time. Maybe I'll be listening.

Enclosed with the letter was a copy of Oscar's Last Will and Testament, reflecting his wishes for his real property, such as it was.

So, the Great Ruth was really the Great Truth. The note in his father's fire-damaged journal was a scrap that he incorporated into this letter. You had to give the old man credit for doing the right thing with his life, and then topping it off by doing the right thing with his estate. And he could always write a good letter. Faris remained in his chair, utterly still, ruminating over the letter and the loss of his inheritance. He didn't care about the store, but he knew his father had, so it took on the significance of an heirloom – something precious to his father that he, too, might have cherished. Oscar had urged Faris to love something deeply, but it had been beyond him. And now, this derivative love, Oscar's love of the store, was passed along to someone more worthy. The pain of failing to be someone more estimable to one's parents settled in Faris' spine, to ache every time he moved. Still, forced by life itself to move and shuffle and try, Faris got up from his chair, washed his face and headed for Turner's.

The regulars filed into Turner's for the weekly Save Pincus meeting and donut festival. Everyone was in attendance, and the mood was perceptibly lighter, now that the Curtain had gotten underway. Ken Carstarter, the dean of local estates and trusts law and chair of the city council, was also present. He was well known to all, so it hardly seemed cause for concern. Faris' mood was pensive, but that wasn't unusual.

"I want to begin today's meeting by sharing some information that changes things a bit. Let me ask Ken to explain." Faris nodded to Carstarter. "Ken, let's just hit the highlights."

Carstarter enjoyed everyone's respect as a decent guy and good enough attorney for the town's needs. He had been elected repeatedly to the town council, which was an honor few seemed to crave. He had written everyone's will and many people's divorces. He closed real estate deals, created trusts, and represented children in the state Guardian ad Litem program. With that exception, he steered clear of criminal law. He was a man of courtly manners and deep central Georgia accent.

"Gentlemen. Miss Angeline. Faris has asked me here to explain his late father's wishes, which took shape in the form of a letter to Faris and a formal Last Will and Testament, both of which I have had on file in my office. Without going into details, the upshot is that Miss Angeline here is to become sole heir to Turner's and to have sole access to a bank account with Oscar Turner's savings, which he would like to be used for the benefit of Pincus. In point of fact, he explicitly said that he'd like Turner's to become more useful to Pincus and its citizens, and he acted on that wish by giving over all his worldly goods to that purpose, save his family home, which goes to Faris." These few sentences took twice as long as a New Yorker would need and fairly dripped with honey and incantatory rhythm.

Before Carstarter could warm up to part two of his presentation, Angeline interrupted. "Ken, Oscar wrote me a letter, too, and asked me to open it only after he was gone. I think you should have a look."

Carstarter glanced at the letter, which precisely confirmed what he had said, embedded in a statement of deep affection for

179

Angeline and belief in her mission at The Bread Basket. A little bruised by the surprise, with its possible implication that Oscar had not trusted him with absolutely everything, Carstarter asked to make a copy of the letter for his records. He drew a breath in preparation to read the letter aloud, only to be blocked by Angeline for a second time, this time with a muscular announcement.

"Ken, the key is that Oscar wanted me to turn Turner's into an expanded version of The Breadbasket. He recognized long ago that the location we had on the edge of town was too far from the clientele we try to serve. There's no point to our business model if we can't reach the needy, and they don't have transportation to the old site. Needless to say, Oscar didn't foresee his death and the imminent availability of Turner's as a site for the Breadbasket, but there we are."

Deflated by the interruption of his oratorical moment, the lawyer turned to Faris and asked if he had something to contribute. Oscar Turner's son had apparently found something of great interest in the remains of a small bug he had crushed on the windowsill, which he now was rolling around between his thumb and forefinger. Down the thumb he dragged the bugs remains, then across his forefinger, then up above the first knuckle, circling to the top of the thumb for another lap. He took a minute to respond, then spoke without looking up. He seemed to be talking to the dead bug. "Everybody knows that Turner's is dead as a hardware store, and, no offense to the elders here, it hardly makes sense as an old man's club in the absence of the old-man-in-chief. You all can imagine how hard this is for me, but Ken has summed up Dad's wishes, and I certainly don't think we have any business questioning his wisdom. I haven't been around enough to stake an honest claim to this place, and I can't think of a better use than to leave it in Angeline's hands. It's not mine to say otherwise, or yours." He punctuated his feeling with a small, smiling sigh. He was reminded of his newfound status as an orphan, deprived of father and mother, standing alone before the ditch. He and the bug.

Henry sat paralyzed, his face the color of putty, his hands mottled purple. His mentor and friend Oscar, a father-like figure who had claimed to be committed to Henry's vision of downtown revival, had betrayed him in death. Not only had Oscar crushed his hope of realizing that vision, but Henry's best friends and only son had endorsed its demise. "And the night falls, without the hope of dawn," he whispered.

"What did you just say, Henry? What's the matter?"

Henry ignored them.

"Are you ok? Say something. What were you saying about the dawn?"

Henry had the aspect of a stroke victim, and the elders of Turner's worried about him like hens. They all secretly loved an acute health event among friends, which had become the main source of their conversations. Perhaps this was another. Henry was no help to them, babbling and blinking back tears.

"And the night falls, without the hope of dawn. That's what I said."

"It's Akhmatova," Faris offered unhelpfully. "Anna Akhmatova. It's a verse from a poem she wrote as a confession of despair. Henry loved her poetry because he was a hopeless romantic, and she was a hopeless Russian. He's been that way since we were kids. You all know that."

"Henry, snap out of it. We don't know what you're saying. What's the matter? Say something we can understand."

"If he said something we could understand, it'd be the first time." Everyone glared at sheriff emeritus, whose bottomless supply of bile had a puffy layer of sarcasm on top.

Suddenly, with pepper spray red eyes, Henry slapped his thighs and rose to respond. "What's the matter? I don't know how you can't see what's the matter. I'll explain, but only once, so try to listen, for a change. The matter is that I've spent years committed to this block and to the revival of cultural life in Pincus. The Dog Ear has been my wife and my child and my community. I've never made a dime, never gone away to see the things I'd like to see, never saw the museums in New York or Washington or Boston, never loved anyone or anything better than Pincus. At least Oscar had his wife and son, and he had Angeline, of course. Everybody has Angeline, the patron saint of Pincus. Oscar had all of us, his friends. Now, Oscar takes what little I have and gives it to Angeline, so she can give it to the bums and the takers and welfare deadbeats and anyone who doesn't want to fend for themselves. It's not right. What about me? Faris may not care about the store or about us, but I do. That's what's the matter. I've been passed over like I was never here."

Angeline rose from her chair and went to him, in the posture of a nurse in a Milledgeville mental ward, standing to his left and slightly behind, hands on his inadequate shoulders, her face and tender parts out of range in case he lashed out. "Henry, collect yourself. Nobody's passing over you. You'll be okay. We'll be downtown partners."

Again, Henry stared past them all in silence.

"Would you like me to call a doctor?"

"Yes, please," he rasped. "Call the doctor who specializes in fixing people whose hearts have been broken by their friends. Call the guy who removes knives from people's backs. Call someone who makes malignant people disappear. Call the doctor who cares for normal people more than for saints and their bums. But before you make your calls, get your hands off me and leave them off."

"Henry, please calm down. I'm your friend. We're all your friends. We don't understand why you're so upset."

"No, of course you don't, even though I just told you why. That's because you only think of yourself. You waltz around town spouting the beatitudes and looking at the sky, never thinking about anyone else, except as stage props for you. St. Angeline of the Poor Pincans, an order of one. The rest of us grind along in the dirt while you glide by on your way to Lourdes, or some damn place. No wonder you don't understand. You're not real. But maybe you can understand this. You'll need a zoning change to allow you to bring The Bread Basket to Main Street and make Turner's into a do-gooder magnet for your trash. I'll oppose it. The town won't stand for it. Imagine people having to step over bums and drunks and food stamp hustlers to get into The Dog Ear. Talk about quality of life! You'll ruin me and Pincus together. I won't have it. I'll fight you with the city and in court. And I promise you no one will be on your side, Angeline. Everybody may love you in principle, but nobody loves your clients or any of the other transients, drunks and dope heads you're likely to attract in town."

With that finale to his transmogrification of people in need to dope fiends and criminals, Henry gave a repulsed shudder, loosening Angeline's embrace from his inadequate shoulders as he gained his balance, scanning the room as if to record the face of every accomplice to this offense against him and the future of life in Pincus. He began to mince out the door with a flourish. The bell on the opening door tinkled his departure as a boatswain piping the captain ashore.

183

"Wait just a minute, Henry." Carstarter spoiled Henry's Gloria Swanson moment. "I chair the zoning committee, and Angeline doesn't need a variance." His pronunciation of variance sounded like the tailpipe rumble at Daytona. "Look at the building code. Any building in central Pincus is entitled to pursue nonresidential commercial use, without restriction. No additional permits are required, because The Bread Basket is not a food establishment per se or a liquor store. As long as Angeline isn't turning Turner's into a rooming house, she's ok within the current town plan. And I'm not sure you'd have standing in the eyes of the court, since you just lease your store from its owner, the late Oscar Turner."

"We'll see about that, you officious old bastard." Henry was a man possessed by rage and disappointment, barely able to contain himself as he left. He slammed the door so hard, the bell rang like a telephone.

The group dispersed, leaving Angeline alone with Faris. Her mind was in disarray. At the beginning of the year, she found herself renting an old shotgun house near the now-gutted Bread Basket: two rooms, front to back, each served by a door and simple casement windows. For transportation, she rode a little Italian scooter that was old enough to have been in a Rossellini film. She had little income and no savings. Now, she was heir to Oscar's wealth. She could afford her own home. She had taken to driving Oscar's truck, on Faris's invitation. It wasn't much, but it was better. For over forty years, Oscar drove a now-vintage coral-colored 1970 Ford pickup with a manual transmission on the column, an inoperative five-button AM radio, and a minimal blue strip of tinting at the top of the windshield. The windows rolled down manually, but only if pushed against from the side. The single bench seat was woven plastic with beaded trim. A heater blew dust from the dash. He loved it dearly for its spare steadiness. Angeline had come to know it well and to love it in his memory. It had been put into service for The Bread Basket, hauling food and people. Now, it was hers. The truck, which breathed Oscar in every aspect, was now hers. It was perfect for her. Truck and driver alike comprised an unadorned portrait of abstemious virtue, faded but reliable icons, venerable because they had endured. Georgia gothic.

However enriched by Oscar's bequest, Angeline had suffered another deep loss with Henry's enmity. She felt superficially that she was to blame. Whatever was in her that caused her to repel or lose those she cared most about? Oscar was dead, her last comfort gone. She refused to back down to Henry, who was clearly wrong in his feelings toward her work. Even if he were right, what would be left of her if she admitted it? And Faris: he had expressed residual love for her, and she had frozen him like late summer corn. Why? What was wrong with a good man who cared for her? How could she find him lacking, when the bill of particulars against him described her own weaknesses, too? What was she waiting for? Was she to remain tangential to others' personal lives, without one of her own? Could she serve her clients without finding her own self and making peace with it? She felt like she was turning into a type – a sere, aging frontierswoman whose mate somehow had disappeared; a fresh young maid once encountered by Ulysses or Jason, and then left to disappear as an incidental character of myth, mentioned no more; Eurydice, sinking for the final time into the underworld, seeing her life finally slip away. Given Angeline's aloof, icy nature, she would have no grounds for complaint as she turned toward the lonely dark.

She shook herself visibly with a kind of mental shrug and tightened the elastic forbidding her hair from flowing loose. Enough self-punishment. She Was Angeline Bruce and had a job to do.

"I thought that went well," she laughed, trying to make the least of Henry's bitter departure. Tears welled up in her eyes.

"Henry's not going to settle down for quite a while, Angeline. I think we should give him a lot of room and wait for him to get back together with us."

"Is there an 'us?' Who's included in the 'us'? What exactly would 'us' be like?" This was asked as a tired dare, which no mature man would have the nerve to answer. Faris, more tone deaf than mature, asked to take the subject up later. He gave her a chaste kiss. The taste of lost opportunity faded slowly from her lips. They left for their separate homes.

CHAPTER XV

The night after the second Curtain of Hope Assembly, Ed Prewitt's security video of The House of Mao appeared on the local Channel 7 News, at 5, 6 and 11. The lead on the screen shouted "House of Mao or House of Meow?" The story included a background of an old novelty tune someone in research had dug up. The production crew used it as the lead-in. They were having fun with the story.

There is something, honey baby, that grieves my mind.

I'm thinking about your future, when I leave you behind.

It's got me up a tree – here's the thing that worries me:

Who'll chop your suey, when I'm gone?

Who'll corn your fritters Sunday morn?

Despite competition from a tornado in neighboring Colleton County and an Amber Alert for six children from Florida, Ed's video led the news. The footage itself could not have been better if Vincent Chin had been wearing a body camera. In slightly overexposed grey half tones, the back door of the House of Mao was clearly outlined, showing Vincent grabbing a smoke before returning to work.

Minutes later – edited for the news, but bearing the fateful time stamp on the video – Vincent Chin opened the door again bearing two saucers of milk. The feral cats in the lot responded instantly, with the unique sounds of ownerless cats, meowing with menace and complaint. As they lapped the milk, Vincent picked them up one by one and took them into the restaurant. For each disappeared cat, a replacement appeared from the darkened alley, and in the space of a few minutes nine desperate pussies went from being outside cats to inside cats. The House of Mao's rear porch light turned off, leaving only the tall alley light to guard the scene.

No one saw the cats killed, skinned, wokked and served. Vincent may have been the felinophile he claimed to be. The cats appearing on the scene might have been the same cats entering with Vincent earlier. He might have fed them and let them out the front door, only to have them return to the alley and get in again. There was no evidence of a crime, only the inevitable idle speculation. But no matter. The eternally vigilant cultural police of social media pounced. Channel 7 had orders of magnitude more Facebook likes and Twitter retweets than any local station in Georgia history, though where that record book is kept remains unclear. Avenging denizens of the internet tore into Vincent Chin, recommending that he be killed and cooked in a stir-fry; thrown to Chinese tigers; and subjected to various unseemly tortures involving cat genitalia. Another video surfaced with a figure looking a lot like Vincent picking up stray cats at the public boat ramp, where they subsisted on charity and leftover baitfish. The erstwhile restaurateur was tried and convicted in the digital courtroom, where due process was an inconvenience. Vincent became a national figure, sure to draw the attention of those still looking for him. Late night TV hosts made hay with jokes about cat litter in the PuPu Platter and references to Hello Kitty Bars. The popularity of Vincent as a criminal far outweighed whatever crime he may or may not have committed.

Bright and early the next morning, Ed arrived at his place, only to find the back lot filled with protestors, with another cohort at the street entrance to the House of Mao. They found a sign from the Georgia Department of Public Health, closing the restaurant pending investigation of charges that House of Mao illegally harbored more than the ordinance limit of eight cats. Alongside the notice was another, postponing Save Your Groundwater Day due to staff deployment to the House of Mao investigation. The second notice was unnecessary, as no one was aware of Save Your Groundwater Day in the first place.

By this time, Vincent was miles away. For some long time, he had kept as much cash as he could in his apartment, a caution left over from his quick exit from Brooklyn. Except for the money, he left everything in Pincus, including his fake name. He hit the road for someplace anonymous in the West, Montana or North Dakota, maybe. He could open a new restaurant, he thought, maybe Korean this time, with a judicious name change. He would travel under his own name of Minjoon Park, until he could think of a replacement.

Doreen and Rubén sat transfixed in her apartment's tiny living room during the House of Mao news story. His hand was on hers, fingers interlaced, his thumb stroking the thumb side of her forefinger. He had loved her all of his adult life, which was now over six months. Before that, they had been together for three years, but secretly, since she was twenty-one when they fell for each other and he only fifteen. No one, but no one, knew about them, which made his love for her more tantalizing and edgy. He followed her lead in every way. She gave him voice, and, Svengali-like, reduced his anxieties by exempting him from bearing his own burden of talk and decisions. Before Doreen, he had been painfully alone, though not lonely, as he knew society only in his role as a victim of cruelty. He wanted no part of it. He still could not talk normally. The only subject he was even able to bring up with Doreen was his worry about the lack of rainfall. She had no response. He marveled at her fluency in society. With her and his mother as guardians, Rubén needed no one else. Doreen also had introduced him to the world of physical love, the only person in his world ever to reach inside his belt and down his trousers. Comfortable only with her, sometimes he would silently ask for sex, especially after he had done what she asked. Beautiful and remotely pleasant, she was Rubén's dream of heaven, a reward for suffering on Earth.

For Doreen, the attraction to Rubén was only partly physical. She kept him around because he was useful, and she was a woman concerned mainly with instrumental purpose. She had a healthy appetite for sex, but no desire to court it from the bumpkins she knew, so he served a purpose. He was remarkably good looking, distinctive enough to have been a model in the Renaissance, where he would have been all the more sought after for his docile nature. He demanded almost nothing, which matched her capacity for giving. Rubén was a sleepy dog of a boy, the kind that followed you like he was tied to your leg with a short tether until you hated him. He was a needy puppy in a chiseled body, waiting for his next instructions. For now, Rubén fit her needs perfectly, with a psychic sensibility that was either a millimeter deep or buried in the Earth's core, the difference to Doreen being an academic one. Doreen and Rubén declined to explore deep questions with each other, he because he couldn't, she because she wouldn't. Along with many in their cohort, they preferred to be alone together, in naked embrace or in front of the TV or their cell phones. The appliances carried the conversation. She loved the quiet.

Unlike Rubén, though, Doreen suffered the twin burdens of impatience and ambition, kept warm by anger as deep as a peat fire. She had been handed around. Passed from one to another caretaker, she depended on well-meaning child managers who cared for her material needs, but did not include in their work plan her development as a person. First, she was adopted by a young couple that inconveniently died in an auto accident. Absent willing relatives who would raise her, she became a ward of the state. A series of foster homes followed, teaching her the wisdom of keeping her mouth shut and her head down. Finally, because she was a healthy, compliant child, she was adopted by the Wagner family of Pincus, becoming that rare foundling who landed with a family at the advanced age of eight, no longer a fresh baby, long after the blush of innocence and malleability of infancy had faded. The Wagners themselves were an older farm couple, who took care of her in their way, sadly not extending to material indulgence or abundant good cheer. Her last foster home promised that the Wagners were impossibly wonderful people – Mrs. Wagner a great cook and homemaker and Mr. Wagner a devoted breadwinner. In the event, they just needed someone to help with chores and couldn't afford to hire an adult. Mr. Wagner molested her, and Mrs. Wagner ignored it. Still, she knew enough to be thankful. Her value to others had always been ornamental or simply functional. No one, including the Wagners, ever seemed concerned with her soul. They only wanted her to behave in school and do her work at home. She left home as soon as she turned eighteen.

After her return to Pincus from New York, she was known to frequent 301 Liquors, where she flirted with the old sheriff and fed treats of banana or grapes to Rebel and Tarbaby. From time to time, she bought a bottle of Campari to sip at home with soda and a twist of lime. Hardly anyone else in Pincus bought Campari, so everyone at the store knew her. And, of course, she was the dramatically alluring Doreen. She befriended Amy Richard, the girl at the liquor store whose nails Carmita painted with her telephone number. Amy thought they were soul mates; Doreen thought Amy could come in handy.

While she understood that co-vegetating with Rubén was the

price of sex and control, she had bigger things in mind. She, too, wanted to make a mark. She hated the cloister of Pincus, saw how the town ladies looked at her with mixed appreciation for her beauty and disdain for her style. She was neither big city anonymous nor small town acceptable. And she certainly was not willing to paddle in the pond in which she found herself, or to live out life with a simple fraction of a man whose best features would disappear with age. She had lived in New York. She wanted more of that, less of this.

As Rubén petted her hand, Doreen found herself thinking of her quandary. She had put herself forward as Pincus' leading animal rights activist with her speech at the assembly. Now, she would have to take some kind of position on the stray cat issue, which was a surprise and completely uninteresting to her. The Curtain of Hope speech was only intended as a setup for her next project, taking Rubén's father down, destroying him for his mean and bitter self. She reached for the bowl of popcorn that nested in Ruben's lap. After Jesús would come Angeline. Rubén pushed his popcorn crotch toward her and smiled.

CHAPTER XVI

Henry sat down in a corner booth at the Sunnyside Café, facing Ken Carstarter and Emmett Chesney. He had asked to meet them as old friends and as pillars of the business community in Pincus. Together, Henry thought, they made up the core of Pincus' burghers, civic leaders and bourgeois professionals in the best sense.

"Ken, first let me apologize for my outburst at the reading of Oscar's will. You are a good friend, and I had no business lashing out at you for something you didn't do. I don't consider you to be an officious old bastard, really. I have been feeling out of sorts because of Oscar's death and all."

"Don't worry about it, Henry. You're certainly not the first to want to kill the bearer of bad news, and you lash out with a good vocabulary, so you've got that going for you. But that doesn't make the facts different." Ken wore a worried look, but it was no different than the look he wore when he ate ice cream or opened his tax refund. He just looked worried by nature, as if it were his vocation. Pincans expected their lawyer to look that way, and he knew it.

"I wanted to talk with you both because of my enormous

respect for you and the roles you play in the community. I am desperate to block Angeline from relocating The Bread Basket next door to The Dog Ear, which will ruin me for sure. I need your help."

"What is it that you would want us to do?" Emmett was drumming his fingers and glancing nervously at Muscadine in the background, as she flew around the flattop griddle, serving up today's lunch special of pulled pork barbecue, crisped up and piled on a bun, with fries and slaw on the side. No substitutions. At $3.49 plus free unsweetened iced tea, it was popular to a fault. Emmet made extra on the drink substitutions, because no one in Pincus liked unsweet tea, but they couldn't complain when it was offered free. The only people who drank unsweet were either too cheap to drink what they wanted or came from somewhere else, like the North, or Atlanta. Muscadine glistened with sweat, tongue tipped out of her mouth, eyes slightly crazed. The microwave was just dying to zap her pacemaker, she was sure. From the looks of the bus boys, they had bets on it. "Dizzy," Emmett yelled out, "get those guys working. We've got tables to clear and people waiting in line. And go get another butt out of the smoker. Come on."

"Yes sir, Mr. Emmitt," answered Rubén, sighing at the sound of his nickname.

"I want you to join me in a delegation of town leaders. I propose to call on Angeline formally with you and others to protest Oscar's bequest and to ask her to locate The Bread Basket elsewhere, maybe down by LeDonna's or near the Boy's Club. Anywhere but the heart of town. She'll listen to us if we are all together on this."

"You mean over by the black businesses. That's what you're saying."

"Well, it's not what I'm saying, but it's a fair point. After all, Angeline's clientele is mainly black. They'll probably feel more comfortable in a neighborhood they recognize."

"Well, Henry, there you are. You may not be a complete racist, but you could play one on TV. The fact is that more than half the poor people in our county are white, not black. You're just making a whole lot of nasty assumptions and trying to put poor people on the other side of the tracks. You'd be right to think that black people recognize that sort of thing. I'll give you that. They ought to, by this time.

"But none of that matters, as far as supporting your plan goes. I believe we've got to honor Oscar's wishes and to support Angeline, who is as good a person as you or I know. I can't be part of turning on her, after all she's gone through. And I advised Oscar on his estate planning, as you know. So, I guess you could say I'm in on it already, but on the wrong side, as far as you're concerned. And, frankly, that's fine with me. What you're proposing stinks."

Emmett fidgeted as he took a rough survey of the café and estimated the gross. He was trying to figure how many people were ordering a soft drink instead of the complimentary tea. The margins on fountain drinks were great, a dollar for a drink that took a few pennies to produce.

"How many signatures you got on that petition you been passing around, Henry?"

"That's part of the reason I wanted to meet with you. I only have two, Mrs. Dropcic and Marlon. I need a lot more."

"Henry, for Christ's sake, Mrs. Dropcic is the one who stood in front of the public high school opening day and called the black children 'gobbich.' And Marlon has two blackbirds named Rebel and Tarbaby. Is this your coalition to save Pincus? Or are you starting a new Klan chapter?" Carstarter shook his head and gave Henry a jaundiced smirk. Henry reddened.

"And why do you suppose it's so hard to get people to sign?" Emmett looked at Henry with a pitying eye.

"Why don't you tell me? You seem to think you know."

Ken intervened. "Henry, you don't want to have this conversation, especially now, when Emmett is all worked up about the lunch crowd. Right, Emmett?"

"It's up to him whether he wants to have it. It don't make no difference to me. I always have plenty to do."

"Well, sure, I want to hear it. I feel like someone's not telling me something. I'm left in the dark. Tell me what you think, Emmett." Henry had the look of a veal calf taken from his mother.

"Awright, Henry," sighed Emmett, "you asked for it, so here it is. I'm meaning this to be friendly, but it's not going to sound like it. The simple truth is you've lived here all your life and you're still not one of us. You spend all your time insisting on not being one of us, because you don't want to be. You're too busy making sure everybody knows you're unique. You don't go to church, which is fine, I guess, but you make all kinds of loud comments about how stupid it is for a person to go to church. A lot of us do go, and your unwanted opinion is hurtful to people that get comfort and friendship and counseling from belonging to a church. What do you belong to? Who helps you make good decisions or behave right? Where do you go when someone you love dies? Why do you think you get to pronounce on all that for everybody else?

"And then, there's The Dog Ear. People like the bookstore and your programs, but they don't want either one of them shoved down their throats. And they don't want you looking down your nose at what they buy or read. These days, you ought to be happy that anybody reads. Your customers get enough crap from you without having to pass some kind of a smell test. You don't want them to bring their kids in, except for Tuesday morning kiddie corner. They have to drink your coffee, instead of what they'd bring in from the car. You don't want them loitering while they page through magazines. You don't want the teens in there after school. And you still want them to care whether The Dog Ear makes it or not."

"But...."

"Just sit there and let me finish. I won't take long. You've always wanted to be the smartest kid in the room, and mainly you've succeeded. But at your age, you ought to stop raising your hand before everybody else and spend more time trying to be part of the rest of the class, instead. Not everybody likes it that you know more than they do. You may know all the poets — or more of them than any of us — and who married Frank Sinatra and who started World War I, but that doesn't mean that no one else knows anything worthwhile. People you probably don't even care about can deliver a calf or plant a field or fix a tractor or start an IV or run a little business. People might want to read all the things you do, but they can't because they're too busy feeding a family, or they didn't have the privilege of going to college. They work hard all their lives at stuff you don't know anything about. The people you don't pay attention to are changing the oil in your car or serving you lunch, partly because you don't know how. Don't you see? People admire that you know things, but you don't ever return the favor. How do you think you'd do taking over for Muscadine during the lunch service, for example?"

"She likes boys more than I do," Henry mewled inappropriately, thinking he was being funny.

Emmett flared. "That's not what I hear, but I don't think you'll want to make another smartass crack to me about my daughter just now, so then I won't have to slap that grin off your face. We were talking about you, not her, and this is exactly the kind of crap that makes people hate you."

"Hate me? Me? Why would anyone hate me? I can't believe it." Henry had the aspect of someone looking at the corpse of his pet cat. "Who, specifically, hates me?"

"Henry, look out the window. Anyone you see hates you. Not hate hate, but casual hate. They don't like you, think you're an asshole, and you hardly ever present a reason not to think so. And now you want to wreck the dream of the best person in town, just because you think people down on their luck are not as good as you are."

Henry looked to Carstarter for help, but found none. Lip quivering, a latter day St. Sebastian, heart shot through with arrows, he rose to leave. "Thank you, Emmett, for your candor, if not your friendship." He exited the Sunnyside like a cartoon Simon Legree, head down, hat covering his teary eyes.

Emmett called after him. "And Ethel's family is full of Melungeons, and they sure don't appreciate all that stuff you're saying about them, neither!"

CHAPTER XVII

Henry stood at the front of the auditorium, waiting for the final stragglers to finish their butterscotch brownies and carrot cupcakes and settle into the rows of folding chairs for the third Curtain of Hope assembly. The room was loud with chatter about the House of Mao, with some blaming Ed for chasing a good Chinese restaurant out of town. Others wondered about the future of Turner's. A third group criticized the quality of food at The Sunnyside, now that Ethel was gone, lamenting Emmett's mental state since her death and Muscadine's unlikely prospects as Ethel's successor. Henry scanned the room in agitation, searching the familiar faces of the crowd, finding only blandness and petty nattering about the day's trivia. Henry despaired that his efforts to sway this sea of mediocrities would give the same limited satisfaction as singing to a hog. Personal pride drove him forward, fueled by a child's faith in reason and lubricated by his sense of superiority.

His reverie came to a halt at the shock of seeing Strother standing in the back of the hall, holding himself vertical by grasping a PVC stanchion set into a tractor tire, which usually served the more useful purpose of supporting the girls' volleyball net. Strother had his gaze fixed on Henry, except for his wandering eye, which was still looking at the exit. The old man appeared to smile through his grizzle. You could never tell. Not really.

Henry called the crowd to order with a walnut palm gavel he had been given for a talk on Melungeons at the Rotary Club. The brass plate on its side had been inscribed "BLOVIATOR IN CHIEF" in good-natured friendship, but the humor wounded Henry's delicate feelings. Still, he thought using a palm gavel made him distinctive. He rapped it thrice.

"My fellow Pincans, please settle in so we can proceed with the evening's agenda." He paused authoritatively. "Let me begin by thanking the ladies again for the refreshments they've provided. And thanks, too, to all of you for coming to our assemblies. *Homo civitatis* is still alive in Pincus.

"The topics chosen for tonight's assembly are deeply interesting. A shopper at Dropcic's wants to discuss traffic congestion in and around the Mt. St. Helen's Homecoming Parade; another how to pay for roof repairs on City Hall; and a third wonders whether a special assessment might be required to repair the downed fence at the back of the cemetery, which has allowed feral pigs to enter and wallow. The concern is that the hogs are disquieting the dearly departed." Henry alone enjoyed his alliteration.

"These matters, however, are for the ordained councils of town government and far from the admirable purpose to which the Save Pincus committee has aspired. I suggest that the agenda I've just listed is a not-so-gentle hint to our elected officials to stop hashing around and start addressing public complaints. We, the people, cannot do their jobs, to which they were willingly elected and for which they are happily compensated. For us Pincans, the challenge is to make good on our use of the public sphere, to devise a course of action for our own betterment and to take action as democratic citizens.

"So," Henry continued with his cheeks pinked up and the arch of his neck professorial, "I propose to discuss a matter of equally great importance – nay, greater importance, even – which can reclaim that high ground toward which our previous assemblies were marching, by appealing to the masses for your support." He loved "nay." It sounded parliamentary.

"And off we go," muttered one of the masses from the audience. Henry ignored him, as did the rest of the audience, which was still stuck on who was a *homo civitatis*.

"As I was saying, many topics have been suggested for tonight, but I want to bring to the fore the greatest and most immediate challenge facing our town's future: the disposition of Turner's Hardware, in light of Oscar Turner's bequest. You all know by now that Oscar, in his characteristic combination of humble generosity and sweet surprise, has declared that Turner's should become the property of our dear Sister Angeline Bruce, along with a sum of money intended for the betterment of Pincus. Oscar declared in a side letter that he would like Turner's to be used for the benefit of The Bread Basket, which we know became the instrument of his tragic death when it burned to the ground. Oscar did not require that The Bread Basket be relocated to Turner's, but that is Angeline's express intention." Angeline closed her eyes and dropped her head, Mary Queen of Scots awaiting the blow.

"My dear friends," Henry continued, speaking to an audience that was comprised of anything but, "I confess to being worried about the future of Pincus, now more than ever. The House of Mao is closed and no tenant is in sight. Wild Animal Kingdom is imperiled by accusations of cruelty. The Laurel Oak Inn has suffered a terrible blow with Ethel's death. Against our hopes, these assemblies have revealed great division in the community. And now, Oscar has bequeathed Turner's to Angeline. I regard Oscar's bequest with love and admiration for him, but also with trepidation because of what it inevitably means for our town. If we surrender Turner's to The Bread Basket, it means nothing less than the end of downtown, to which I am committed to the death. Let me repeat: to the death. In that spirit, I have argued to the town council leadership that a zoning variance would be required for The Bread Basket to operate on the site of Turner's, in light of its clearly inappropriate purpose; but the authorities have refused my disambiguation.

"Now, my ministrations to the poor are well-recorded, as I have served for many years on the United Way board in our county. But, I believe that the entire master plan for the revival of our fair town is at risk if we allow a public food distribution center to be located right in the heart of our metropolis. Tonight, I'd like to offer my thoughts to you on that subject. I will be frank at the outset in saying that I seek your support for my opposition to the relocation of The Bread Basket downtown."

"You mean next door to the Dog Ear, don't you, Henry?" Henry couldn't tell who had spoken in the glare of the dais light. He chose to ignore it.

"Friends," he continued, reading from a prepared speech, "we are Southerners, uniquely devoted to place. Pincus is our place, as Oscar so clearly understood. Carl Degler, in his classic book *Place Over Time*, which is available in paperback in the history section at The Dog Ear, made a most sophisticated argument connecting our deep rural traditions to specific places and to the great traditions of the South. He pointed out that we are not just Americans, but Southerners. He suggested that our distinctiveness was Faulknerian, not geographic; that we are sons and daughters of a great tradition, not just a physical region. I say more: we are not just Southerners, but Georgians; not just Georgians, but Pincans; not just Pincans but revivalist Pincans; visionaries of our own future. And now is the time to advance that future, which is the very womb of our own individual destinies."

Reluctant to emerge from the civic womb, many trapped listeners began to fiddle with their smart phones or pick at their cuticles. A few escaped from the sinners' seats in the back and exited through the equipment room, rightly thinking this could take a while.

"The reason I cannot support the relocation of The Bread Basket to Turner's Hardware has nothing to do with my own self-interest. The intellectual heart of The Dog Ear will continue beating by force of its own importance. I simply know that visitors to Pincus will not want to see our needier brethren going into what amounts to a trashy food bank to pick up supplies. The curs of misery cannot be allowed to wild through the streets of Pincus, each one devoted to picking on a weaker dog."

"Oh trifle not with wants you cannot feel, Nor mock the misery of a stinted meal."

This outburst came again from the darkest part of the hall. This time it definitely sounded like Strother's voice.

"Did you say something Strother?" Henry was incredulous.

"It don't matter. You heard it." This was a different voice from somewhere else in the room. It sounded familiar, maybe someone from his poetry group. Sheriff Hockett? Impossible.

"Yeah, Henry, it don't look like you been missing too many meals. Why you so hard on those that don't have nothing? How is it trashy to feed the hungry?" This, again, from the darkened crowd, which was now becoming an uncontrolled chorus.

"Now, hold on, folks. Let Henry talk. He's got a point of view we ought to hear." Ken Carstarter gained no redemption from Henry for the support.

"And what's your deal with The Bread Basket? When my sister Janie's husband got laid off, they were able to get groceries there when they needed them. Everybody here knows my family and knows they work hard. You calling them trash? They ain't trash. I don't believe they embarrassed anybody by walking into The Bread Basket, and they were bashful enough already because they had to go. You act like they parade around. Worse, you're telling us that they're chasing away tourists. Where does that come from?" This from a big man Henry didn't recognize, who jabbed his work-thick fingers in Henry's direction as he spoke.

"What visitors are you talking about, Henry, the ones in your head? Who in God's creation do you think comes to Pincus, and so what if they don't like it here? They can keep on moving down the road, as far as I care. Which they do, anyway, unless they stop at the Sunnyside. You're not crazy enough to think they're coming here to visit your sorry ass bookstore, are you?"

"Dey Gobbich," let out Mrs. Dropcic. She sat in front, lower lip drooping, arms crossed beneath her ample bosom, emphasizing the lace trim on her matronly bodice.

"And what about our memories, Henry? Don't they count? Moving into town and losing your neighbors and what held you together, that's no good. A place isn't a place without something to hold it together. And it sure don't seem to me that anybody's putting together memories at a bookstore. That probably don't mean much to you, since you don't count on anybody. But you're not everybody." Henry didn't recognize this woman and couldn't gauge how to respond. Was she a customer?

Angeline stood up and raised her hands as if in benediction. "Please, everybody, Henry's our friend. Let him finish. It's only fair."

Henry returned to the dais, flushed, searching his note cards for where he left off. He was too angry with Angeline to acknowledge the life ring she had just thrown. He looked hard again at the back of the room but didn't see Strother.

"Where was I?" He looked back into the audience, seeking eye contact with a friendly face, anyone. He saw nothing hopeful, just lights and shadows. "So. Here we are." Henry took a deep breath and wiped the beads of sweat from his upper lip. He could feel the heat from his face. His eyes were watering, who knows why. He began to read from his speech, which he suddenly hated, because it sounded so scripted. "My proposal is in your best interests as citizens of Pincus, as well as my own. Let's see here. Ah, yes. You people have your roots in the countryside, but you freely chose to come to the city to live." He began to race through his notes. "No one forced you. You recognized that your prospects were better in town rather than in the country. The romantic agrarians notwithstanding, it is the age-old story of civilization to leave the *vita rustica* for the cosmopolis. I'm just standing up for your own good." He regained himself and offered a modest smile to the lights. They burned so bright and hot. Mrs. Dropcic scowled in support of his disdain.

"Now, wait just a minute here, Henry." Tim Little, the cotton farmer and day worker who had spoken at Oscar's funeral, stood to speak. It must have been his voice earlier. Bit by bit he was revealing himself to be a populist of modest and thoughtful rebuke. "I don't know all of what you know, Henry, and that's fine. Good for you that you're educated. But you don't know up from down when it comes to country people and what we care about. We didn't move into town because we wanted to. We had to. You're the big historian, so how about remembering how things really were? My daddy lost his farm after World War I. You probably don't know, or maybe you just don't care, that the Depression started in farm country a long time before Hoover and FDR. So, my people got tossed off their property and then hired back as farm hands for the man who bought up our old homestead. Except it wasn't really a man, it was a bank. Just like Reconstruction. Then, in the thirties FDR said to plow it under. The government made us. They said prices would go up again. Course, they didn't go up, at least not until the war started. But who cared if prices went up for crops you had just ruined, on property you had just lost to the bank? Same thing after the War. Daddy come home from the war and found no work, because there wasn't no army to buy up the cotton and meat and hides and sugar. We all had to come to town to work. You only knew my daddy as a farm worker, but that's because you only knew a piece of him. That's not all he was in the beginning. Ask Ed Prewitt or Rodney if it wasn't even worse for colored people. Ask them how they grew up. Then, the money boys from what I guess you'd call the cosmopolis, or whatever, started buying up land again, so they'd have something to do on weekends besides count their money. We got hired part time as dog handlers or cooks or handymen for people who didn't even care who we were or where we came from. The same people made subdivisions out of little farmsteads and taxed or priced us out. How many people saw their taxes raised until they couldn't pay them, then some rich guy buys it up and resells it or develops it. Or, either, the timber companies vacuumed up our small farms to plant pine and had us planting or thinning or burning or mending fence. Or the feed mills contracted out to folks like us to grow chickens and turkeys on their feed and take all the risk. Any way you went, we ended up working for nothing again, owning nothing, getting nothing, and then being told what's what by folks like you. Henry, look at your hands and see if you can find a trace of honest work. I mean a callous. Just one. Bet you can't. So, don't tell me why I live in town instead of on my farm. If that ain't the damnedest. Ain't it the damnedest, folks?" Loud murmurs of assent rose from the assembly, with a few "amens" sprinkled in. It was the damnedest.

"And now you just want to make Pincus pretty and fill it with new people. We don't know the new ones. They're not our neighbors, like the ones we used to be able to turn to, the ones that went to our same little church. I can't ask a stranger for help, especially when he can't speak English." Amen.

"Dey gobbich!" said, Mrs. Dropcic again, forgetting that she was one of the new people. She brushed at imaginary lint on her lap. Amen.

Henry reflexively looked at his hands. They didn't show a life of hard work. They showed the truth of what Emmett had said days ago. These people really did hate him. They had just been too polite to say so, until he made them mad.

Then, Muscadine stood. She couldn't stand Henry ever since he gave her a "C" in English for liking e.e. cummings. She didn't want to pile on, though, only to explain. "Henry, when I was in Bolivia, all we talked about was *necesidades sentidas*, felt needs. It was our job to figure out what the local folks wanted, what their felt needs were. Sometimes it didn't make any sense to us, just like now, when people want to worry about the fence around the graveyard. The dead don't care. But that wasn't the point. We couldn't just tell them what they were supposed to feel, which is what you're doing now." One of the young boys in the row in front of her said he'd like to tell Muscadine what his felt need was. For that, he got a sharp punch in the back from her. She had a bad heart, but she wasn't deaf. And she could punch.

The rest of the assembly was for Henry a sweaty blur of

criticism and complaint, which found him defenseless. A member of the poetry group, his own poetry group, accused Henry of elitism, saying he didn't approve when someone read Ogden Nash or Robert Service, but heaped praise on fans of Wallace Stevens. Not many actually got that one. Someone else attacked him again for his scholarly work on the Melungeons, alleging that Henry's work had undermined the one thing somebody's aunt felt special about, or something like that. Henry felt like a Chinese mayor in the Cultural Revolution, surrounded by Red Guards. This wasn't China, though, and nobody beat him up or made him wear a dunce hat or sign a phony confession. Gradually, people tired of the one-sided shouting and left.

At the end, only the Save Pincus stalwarts remained in the hall, halfheartedly consoling Henry. He walked home by himself, to his suffocating loneliness. He sat through the night in a club chair next to his little dropfront secretary, practically without moving, eyes closed but not sleeping, mind unquiet with starbursts of thought, every one blinking out in the dark of his despair. He was truly alone, as he always had been. He thought he had created a family in Pincus, but it was a poor substitute. The people he imagined to be his closest intimates had their own families, real ones, for better or worse. At the end of the day, they had someone to love or disagree with or criticize for their deficiencies. At the end of life, they had someone beside them while they whispered their last. He had nothing, not even Faris and Angeline, who themselves were no better than he. It was like the Cultural Revolution, after all. Everything was backward. He was the student. The people were the teachers. And he had misunderstood the assignment.

A little before first light, his path became clear to him.

CHAPTER XVIII

As was her custom each day, Muscadine dressed to take her precious dog Pipsy for his constitutional. Pipsy, despite advancing age, was ever eager, standing on his hind legs at the front door, ready to pee on the first deserving bush or clump of Spanish moss blown down from the oaks. He wore a bright red harness for his public outings, fixed to a metal link leash with a leather strap. Muscadine dressed in what her father once quipped was the style of a vagrant: she had no visible means of support. This particular morning, she wore one of her endless crop tops, made of a cut-off t-shirt, paired with Pincus High cotton gym shorts rolled down at the waist to show her navel ring at the top and a hint of butt cheek at the bottom.

Pipsy's grand promenade began with a slow stroll down the alleyway behind Muscadine's house. The vigilant little dog was a canine *boulevardier*, all nose, constantly sniffing out the trail of raccoons, possums or other interlopers. They headed in the direction of Hemlock Street and then turned south to Landing. On the northeast corner stood Leo's house, now guarded by his ridiculous border grass hedge. Muscadine thought it was funny that he had chosen two kinds of grass instead of one. Leo was a weird one, all right. Fortified by his morning kibble, Pipsy had a plan for Leo's yard. It went this way every morning; only the dress and timing differed according to the seasons. The result was the same: Muscadine was showing her stuff, and Pipsy was going to the Pincus Bank of Leo to make a deposit.

This sunny morning, the dew was still on the grass, which was greener than usual for this time of year. The fall rains had been soft and regular, almost spring like. Approaching Leo's, Pipsy stepped lightly over the border grass, but dragged his arthritic left rear leg. Sparks flew as he brushed the electrified grass product Leo and Strother had installed for just this purpose. Pipsy yelped and flew into the air like a bottle rocket, coming straight down onto another electrified clump. Over and over, he howled and jumped, unable to get past the continuous border and not understanding what was inflicting such pain. Pipsy's age was a disadvantage, as he jumped neither as high nor as fast as in his salad days. After several big shocks, he lay on his side exhausted in the yard, tongue lolling, eyes rolled back in his head.

Meanwhile, Muscadine played crack the whip with Pipsy, being jerked around on his leash in all directions. Frantic at the snarling and yelps of her beleaguered pet, she stepped onto the border grass herself and was promptly popped. Her heart jumped. Ever anxious about having her pacemaker interrupted, she swooned at the sharp jolt, whereupon she collected more shocks, chirping "Ow! Ow! Ow!" at each spark. Finally, she fell unconscious. There they lay, dog and maid, two carp on a dock. The widow across the street peered from her window. She watched Muscadine and Pipsy every morning, convinced that they were making a drug drop. This was no drug drop. She dialed 911.

Emmett felt doubly sad as he looked down at his daughter in

the emergency room: sad for her slutty ways and for her diminished mental state in the wake of her heart ailment. She was modestly dressed now in a hospital gown, sedated, but able to mumble frothily to him about "going to see Mama." She asked about little Pipsy before slipping into light sleep. It made her look angelic. The doctor said she would be fine, but recommended that she see a counselor about her morbid cardiac fears. These fears were normal, he pointed out, but should be treated. But as Emmett stood by Muscadine, and she purred with soft snores, he wondered if anything about Muscadine could be labeled normal. He feared that his dear daughter, never a bad person, had disappeared for good. What would return in her place he did not know. Without further consultation, he decided to have Pipsy put down. He could blame it on Leo.

Muscadine recovered, after a fashion, but, as Emmett feared, was never was quite the same. The effervescence had been shocked out of her. She became an old woman in a young woman's body, as her come hither became where am I. When people asked after her health, she just whispered, "I ain't quite hunnert percent." She still smiled, but without regard to what went on around her. Her ears rang constantly, so she only heard part of what was said to her. And she spontaneously burst into tears or giggles. She refused to work the line at the Sunnyside, even after Emmett had the microwave pulled off the wall. She said she'd wait tables, which she did.

Unfortunately, everyone who came into the restaurant had to hear the latest about her heart condition and the many risks that came with her kind of pacemaker. She delivered the wrong orders to customers. She was inclined to bare part of her chest to show where the implant had been made, which caused great flutter among the regulars. Muscadine told them about the kissing bug and her long-lost doggie and her no-good shit heel of a husband. In this alone, she pleased her father.

Emotionally, she had been dealt an ungodly series of blows, even discounting the pacemaker. Her mother was dead, the father of her child in prison, and her dog euthanized, thanks to her next door neighbor Leo Price. She wept and moped and complained all the waking hours of her day, taking Bobby Lee to task for not having defended her in the first place and not seeing to redress after the fact. What kind of man was he, she asked? She asked several times a day, which took a toll on Bobby Lee's liquor-weakened psyche. After all, he wasn't even thirty yet and sure hadn't signed on to take care of a shocked out ninny. It wouldn't take a clairvoyant to see that Pipsy wasn't the only thing that was going to pop. Bobby Lee wasn't quite hunnert percent, either.

The calm,

Cool face of the river

Asked me for a kiss.

Langston Hughes, *Suicide's Note*

CHAPTER XIX

Romantic suicide attempts that begin with high drama sometimes become low farce. Extended emotional adolescence, combined with visions of Cleopatra or Madame Bovary, or even the real-life melodrama of a rock star who shoots himself, can cause otherwise ordinary people to imagine the world grinding to a halt at their deaths. At least this was the case with Henry Jeffords. After the debacle of his speech at the Curtain of Hope meeting and a night of solemn self-pity, Henry had decided that his life in Pincus was over, and that he could no longer face his fellow citizens. But he had nowhere else to turn but south. Armed with desperate conviction and a bottle of bourbon, he headed out in the cold pre-dawn darkness to the cemetery, which bordered on a bitterly damp and forbidding cypress swamp fed by the remains of Pincus creek. There he disrobed, joining the other organic litter, intending to die a quiet death of exposure. He imagined being found by surprised duck hunters or kayakers, or maybe a fisherman. The town would mourn its loss in shock and wear its guilt like sackcloth, or so Henry thought in comforting fantasy.

After slipping down the wet slope from the graveyard fence, Henry trudged through thick muck until he could stand it no more. The swamp sucked at his feet, impatient to eat him up. Tired in every way, he sat foolishly in the shallow water with his back against a cypress. He had chosen his spot poorly. The cypress pressed unrelenting against his tailbone. Shallow water barely lapped over his heels. He drank with serious purpose, thinking it weakened the body's response to cold temperature. But the hours passed without death, bringing only drunkenness and soggy cold. He felt like he was freezing to death without actually managing to die in the process. His underpants took on the tannin of the water. The curd-white skin of his belly trembled in the dark. His nose ran from crying and, oh god, the cold. His back ached and his frozen feet burned with pain. Wet muck painted his bare legs. He drank some more. He began to doubt that anyone would find him and instead imagined that raccoons and coyotes and crows would pick at his dead flesh, violating his fantasy of being found as fresh and frozen as the character in Silas Marner. Eppie's mother, the dope fiend. He must be really drunk; he couldn't remember her name. And it was one of his favorite literary death scenes. Or, he might be found as Shelley supposedly was, artistically washed ashore in baptismal drowning. But what matter if he was found at all? He would be too dead to enjoy it. He cried some more and coughed.

How long could this suicide take? He regretted not having done more research. Molly, that was her name, Eppie's mother. She died in the snow. In the novel it didn't take all that long, as he remembered. But that was literature, and this was life.

Then, Henry was redeemed by the bare first light of a magical cypress swamp. The delicate thermal alchemy of the morning birthed a sudden tuft of mist, a little swirl of moisture that joined the water's surface with the fluid envelope of air. In his extreme emotional state, Henry was little different than a hermit in antiquity, fresh from rolling in thistles, being visited by God. A delicate sylph had appeared, all beauty and innocence, barely there, almost expressionless. It was the specter of Strother's little spirit girl, the one

215

who warned the living away from the graveyard, coming benignly to him to say it wasn't yet his time to die. She neared and seemed to wave to him, as to a friend in a passing life. Then, hanging in the ether, her insubstantial little body evanesced into the vapors of the swamp. Her touch lingered on his cheek. Henry had felt her kiss him back to life, had felt her caress. He bawled like a baby and threw up. Then, he arose, stiff-legged, sore and drunk. The erstwhile champion of Pincus' revival tugged on his sagging, mud-smeared pants and like an overgrown little boy who had messed his britches, staggered spraddle-legged back to his car to drive home.

The first white person to receive the benefit of Rodney Washington's embalming services was this same Henry Jeffords, who in the wake of his redemption had drunkenly left the narrow shoulder of the road on his return to town. From the tire marks it appeared that he had briefly recovered control of his car, only to careen into a culvert that catapulted him into a tree. His unmarked chest was crushed. The spirit girl had been wrong. It was his time.

Henry's pasty, cold body, covered inexplicably in swamp litter, did not diminish the importance of this milestone for Rodney, who had to suppress a feeling of pride at crossing over to service the white dead. As he looked down at Henry, Rodney reflected, as he often did, about what exactly was the difference in the restful face of the dead, what separated its flaccid peace from the tight-muscled tension of a living person. In this case, Henry had a slightly beatific look, the visage of a middle-aged, portly corpse, formerly inhabited but now empty and slack. In death, he was no longer a pompous ass.

Rodney prepared Henry's body with care, inflected by professional sympathy and genuine affection for a man he had known. Even the loss of an acquaintance creates an empty spot in the lives of the survivors. For hours, he personally groomed the body, dressing it and applying the makeup himself, to present the late Henry Jeffords in the best light. He could not have said why.

Henry's closest friends, Angeline and Faris, were left to manage his last affairs. Their alienation from him in the last days of his life had disappeared with his death. Because Henry had been such an ardent critic of organized religion, it seemed inappropriate to them both to impose a church funeral. But they had to have a service. Rodney offered the use of his small funeral chapel, which Angeline and Faris gratefully accepted. It would be another first: Washington and Washington's Funeral Parlor, full of white people grieving.

The chapel was a smallish interior room at the funeral home, with artificial stained window alcoves back lit by fluorescent bulbs and dusty silk flowers in planters softening the room's corners. Rodney hated the silk flowers because they were always hungry for dust and were impossible to clean. They were marketed to him as affordable color, but they everybody knew they weren't real flowers. The pews were simple painted wood, trimmed in blond oak, with hymnals backpacked above the kneelers. The nondenominational blandness of a dark wooden cross framed the center of the space where services were conducted. The cross could be slid from sight on wires rigged like a tenement clothesline. For Henry's service, a grey portable lectern stood in front of the altar niche, and the cross had been removed to stage left.

The funeral itself was as quaint as Henry Jeffords, though not as long-winded. The small room created the illusion that the whole town had come. Those who couldn't find a seat either stood against the rear wall or simply signed the guest book and left. They would come to regret missing a singular occasion. The front row filled last, since no one wanted to be trapped in case the service ran long. They had learned that much from Henry's events. Faris, Angeline, and notables from the Save Pincus committee sat on either side of the lectern, facing the attendees. A metal casket, "Going Home Model 1095," stood athwart the room, painted in a color called by its vendor Silver Dusty Rose. Rodney had bought it on closeout some months before, but the color was tricky, and when it had not found a buyer, he donated it for Henry's service. He could claim the retail price on his taxes. Doreen had outdone herself with a floral tribute of white carnations in the shape of an open book. It hung affixed to the open casket, covering the manufacturer's garish stenciled silhouette of prayerful hands. Henry lay beneath the open pages, eyes closed, dreaming of reading, his skin a mortician's blush. Members of The Dog Ear poetry group flecked the crowd.

Faris stood pale and forlorn, head down as it had been at his father's funeral. He paused to gather himself, then began by clearing his throat.

"On Henry's behalf, thank you for coming to remember him today. He would be pleased, I'm sure, since he cared so completely about this town and worried about your good opinion of him. I am especially grateful to see members of The Dog Ear poetry group, which was Henry's pride." Faris briefly mentioned Henry's family, about which little was known, focusing instead on his teaching, pointing out several people in attendance who were erstwhile students and mostly appreciative veterans of Henry's pedagogical tyranny.

"I want to say something by way of explanation. I want to explain Henry a little, if I can, because I'm not sure how well we really knew him in life. He was not the easiest person to figure out, but understanding him was always worth a try.

"For one thing, Henry truly loved us. I mean as a concept. Henry was very conceptual. He used to say that he loved us all in general, but sometimes didn't love us at all as individuals. And leave it to Henry to tell us all that he stole that sentiment from Dostoevsky, not a cartoon strip. But the point is that he did love us, and he loved Pincus more than anyone I ever knew, except for my father.

"Who's to say why a person is so moved? I think with Henry it was the absence of a family of his own after his parents passed, which led him to think of us all as some kind of relatives that he had to scold and put up with and tell stories about and roll his eyes over when we disappointed him. And he wasn't very good at loving himself. He felt he had to be smarter and more driven and better prepared for people to care about him, and in that he was wrong.

"Henry had hopes for us and for himself. He was a hopeful man. He hoped to amount to something, to leave a record. The Curtain of Hope was really his idea, too. Like most of us, he didn't want to think his life was just a moment in time that wouldn't amount to more than a memory lasting a little while after death.

"I know this to have been a deep and true feeling of his, because in his desk at The Dog Ear I found a fragment of a poem by Laura Riding. You poetry folks may recognize it. I did not. It's from the 1920s.

Measure me by myself

And not by time or love or space

Or beauty. Give me this last grace:

That I may be on my low stone

A gage unto myself alone.

I would not have these old faiths fall

To prove that I was nothing at all.

"Henry wasn't nothing at all. He was a dear friend and an intellectual and a force for good. Above all, as I said, he was a man with hopes for Pincus, Georgia. He recognized it as a place in time. A Faulknerian place, he said, not geographic. I don't imagine most of us understand exactly what he had in mind. Whatever it was, he surrendered to it, and Pincus consumed his life and his energy and now is awaiting his earthly remains.

"It would surprise him to hear me speak for him with another poem I know he loved, by Stanley Johnson. It calls for us to pay attention to this man's passing, and it says something of how I will miss him. I don't have a lot of friends and only had one friend like Henry. His death has left me poorer, and I'll hold his memory dear for the rest of my life. The poems called 'An Intellectual's Funeral.' We all know that Henry would be proud to be thought of that way, even though it made him a pain in the neck."

On such a day we put him in a box

And carried him to that last house, the grave;

All round the people walked upon the streets

Without once thinking that he had gone.

Their hard heels clacked upon the pavement stones.

A voiceless change had muted all his thoughts

To a deep significance we could not know;

And yet we knew that he knew all at last.

We heard with grave wonder the falling clods,

And with grave wonder met the loud day.

The night would come and day, but we had died.

With new green sod the melancholy gate

Was closed and locked, and we went pitiful.

Our clacking heels upon the pavement stones

Did knock and knock for Death to let us in.

Faris sat, fighting a great urge to vomit or cry, or both. An awkward silence followed, as no one had thought to choreograph the service overall. Henry would not have forgotten a single detail about the staging or the speakers' list, but his voice was present only in the shadow of the box in which he lay. Rodney, standing in the most visible corner of the room, stood stone still, with his eyes on the furthest wall and his hands folded. It wasn't up to him, he was thinking. He was counting white people. Angeline was sniffling into an old-fashioned embroidered hanky, apparently oblivious.

Then, hesitantly, a member of the poetry group who was a staunch ally of Henry's in the zoning dispute, stood and read, choosing Thomas Wyatt's bitter Elizabethan poem "They Flee from Me." The self-serving tone and angry pout of the poem did not sit well, even though it fit perfectly. Later, a townswoman would say it was "arch." Another from the poetry group offered his own original poem about Pincus, which was dreadful, but genuine. Henry might have said genuinely dreadful, and he would have been right, but wrong to say so. The offerings continued for a while, and people gradually seemed to get comfort from the verse and pleasure from speaking out. The poetry offered a way to speak that didn't confront the complexity of their feelings about Henry, which was just as well.

In death, through poetry, Henry was still teaching.

Toward the end, a handsomely dressed young black man who practiced law in Savannah and who had been a student of Henry's, stood up to speak.

"When I was in school, Mr. Jeffords insisted that we black kids think about and learn of the contributions of our own race to Southern culture, which we all refused. We told him he was racist. And we told him poetry was gay. We stupidly thought we were real men and didn't need culture. Even more stupidly, we thought we didn't need to know about our own. He gave us readings and memorizations and tried, in his old white guy kind of way, to speak to our hearts. And I guess it worked. As I got older, I realized how singular his kindness toward us kids was. I repent the fact that I can't thank him to his face. I came today to remember him in a way I should have during his life, but didn't. I imagine that's partly why people cry at funerals. They're sorry for not being better to the one who's lying there." He paused to take a breath, obviously moved by his own thoughts.

"I didn't know people would be reading poems today, and I really didn't come prepared to say anything at all. I don't go to many white funerals, so I don't know exactly how they go. But I still remember one that he made me memorize when I was in his English class. It was right after my granddaddy passed. He had lived such a hard life and had such little chance to succeed. I have never forgotten that poem, and I will never forget Mr. Jeffords or my granddaddy and how they both believed in me, in their separate ways. The poem is by Angelina Weld Grimké, who was one of the first African-American poets I ever knew of. If Mr. Jeffords had not made me read the poem, I probably wouldn't know her even today. It's called 'Surrender,' and it still reminds me of my granddaddy. Now it will remind me of Mr. Jeffords, too."

We ask for peace. We, at the bound

O life, are weary of the round

In search of Truth. We know the quest

Is not for us, the vision blest

Is meant for other eyes. Uncrowned,

We go, with heads bowed to the ground,

And old hands, gnarled and hard and browned.

Let us forget the past unrest, --

We ask for peace.

Our strainéd ears are deaf, -- no sound

May reach them more; no sight may wound

Our worn-out eyes. We gave our best,

And, while we totter down the West,

Unto that last, that open mound, --

We ask for peace.

Many were weeping openly by now, sharing in the guilt and beauty of grief, and the community of loss among those who have one less companion between them and their own end.

Interrupting their sad self-indulgence came Strother, who had been standing outside the funeral parlor for some time. He left his little red wagon parked in the porte cochère and made his stork like entrance with a flourish of wall-eyed looks. One foot was shoeless, as it often was, but this time it wore a bright green sock, apparently in celebration of the occasion. He stood in the center of the aisle for a long moment, suddenly giving forth in song:

Little Sallie Saucer,

Sitting in the water,

Crying and a-weeping

For what she has done.

Oh, rise, Sallie, rise

And wipe your weeping eyes,

Turn to the east

And turn to the west

And turn to the one you love best.

Strother closed his wandering eyes. The room fell still. Admonished by Strother's verse, and more than a little fearful of what he might do next, Angeline stepped into the breach. Pretending to wipe away tears that had not come, and blowing her nose loudly, she gathered herself.

"Thank you, Mr. Strother, for bringing us back to the living. And thank you all for your offerings today. Henry's spirit is surely full of joy. Who would have thought that a life ending in tragedy would bring our little town together, black and white and rich and poor, to remember what is good and memorable in all of us? Who could have imagined that Mr. Strother would sing the coda to Henry's life? Please, let's all leave this wonderful service remembering to be more like little Sallie Saucer, turning to our loved ones who are still alive and can still hear us. And let's be grateful for our dear Henry, who is lost to our lives but not to our hearts." Her voice tailed off.

People began to file out quickly, signaling that things had gone on long enough. Or, perhaps they were just eager to get to the bathroom or the buffet line at The Dog Ear, which was set up in Henry's honor. Some old lady said, "Who was that young black fella? He seemed nice." Emeritus responded that the young man would have been better off altogether if he had chosen not to talk at a white funeral. Angeline told him to keep his racism to himself. The Sheriff took offense. Faris, Angeline and Ken Carstarter walked out together.

"Faris, I don't mean to be inappropriate, but Henry's affairs are a bit of a mess. He had no heirs and died intestate. The only record I'm aware of was a letter he wrote to me after you came back to town, designating you to be his executor and giving you full power of attorney. I'd like you to come by the office as soon as you can to talk this through. Henry didn't have much, but it was a bit greater than nothing and needs to be dealt with."

Faris mumbled something about coming by Ken's office the following week. Then, they all went to the reception.

CHAPTER XX

O n a sunlit Sunday morning in a corner booth of the Sunnyside Café, Angeline Bruce and Doreen Wagner sat over tea. Tea service was not the strong suit of the Sunnyside, but a person could find a little Earl Grey and hot water with lemon. Doreen's cool gaze focused on Angeline, while her left forefinger caressed the rim of the cup. Angeline returned her stare, two fish in the same bowl, each one trying to find elements of herself in the water-refracted mirror of the other.

Rubén stood vigil at the kitchen door. Angeline had requested the meeting, which caused him vague worry. But he always suffered vague worry. This seemed different, but as usual he was unable to articulate how, exactly. It might be different, it might not. Unable, also, to restrain his love for Doreen, he momentarily forgot his anxiety about Angeline to focus on how Doreen's beautiful shadow bathed the floor. He was a panting dog on a leash. At the other end was an unpredictable owner, with a firm grip on the tether and a pocket full of treats.

"Well, Miss Angeline, what is it that caused you to spend time with me this fine morning?" The question had an unmistakable edge.

"Doreen, I'm glad to spend time with you, pretty much anytime you want. You've made it clear that you don't want my company, though, and I've respected the distance you've expected from me."

"Well, how convenient for you. But let's not worry about it. I'm in pretty bad shape by now, if I can't get along without the parents I never had. So, again: What's the subject of our little tea party?"

"Since you want to get straight to it, I'm wondering if you've looked into finding your biological father's identity, dear, as you did mine. You know that I'm bound to respect your wishes in these matters, but I'd like to know where you stand."

"If you mean do I know that Faris is my biological father, the answer is yes. What else?" She treated Angeline as an interviewer, exuding a catlike indifference to her affectionate tone. Doreen was not overtly unkind, just yet, only indifferent. Angeline might have been asking what books Doreen had on her nightstand, for all the emotional affect in her answer.

"Don't you think it'd be nice...."?

"Look, Angeline, forgive me for saying that this is a funny time for you to be wondering what might be nice or what I think or what I might do or what I know about my origins. I might have asked you twenty-four years ago whether you might have thought of alternatives to giving me up. I might have said, 'Mother, don't you think it'd be nice to keep me?' But I couldn't ask. I was a baby, and, oh, yeah, you weren't there after the first day. I might have asked, 'Mother, don't you think it'd be nice if Mr. Wagner decided not to fondle me?' Or, I might have asked what your thoughts have been all these years, as you've lived your life and forgotten mine. But I haven't asked, because I don't care, and, oh, yeah, you haven't been there. The same is true for Faris Turner. I'll bet he doesn't even know who I am. But, if he does, who cares? He left Pincus a long time ago, kind of made a big nothing of his life and now he parachutes back in and starts telling people what they need to do to fix the old hometown. Why would anyone care about his opinion, when he's not even part of this community? Because of his father? And why would I care about him now? With your experience, you may concede that giving birth isn't the same as being a mother. How much less involvement is there for a fugitive man? Am I supposed to call him daddy?"

"I can't say you're wrong, Doreen, but you're being pretty harsh."

"No, Angeline, you're confused. Harsh is being put into a baby lottery and forgotten. That's harsh. Harsh is hearing you tell some made-up story about how your parents arranged for me to live with the Wagners, when, in truth, I was passed around like an old sweater and played with by an old man like a sex toy. And harsh is ending up in a shit town with no future and no chances for anyone under the age of dead. Sorry. That's harsh. And while we're being harsh, when was the last time you asked me how you could help me, now that we know who's who, and you're so concerned? And how about your fake nun thing? How's that working out? If you'd asked me, which you didn't, I would have said you could have managed to stay a virgin without the charade. Why, you're even cold to the touch. But maybe you turn down the temperature just for me. Maybe you're hotter for Faris Turner. God knows why."

Rubén saw the tension in the conversation and started to come over. She gave him a single look that tugged his leash, stopping him in his tracks.

"I'm worried about you, Doreen. That's all."

"Too little, too late, Angeline. Or should I call you Sister." She hissed the word. "But you should be worried. You old farts on the Save Pincus committee, or whatever you call yourselves, are just a bunch of coffee shop militants. You think that talking is the same as doing something. It isn't. By now, you can see that all sorts of terrible stuff goes on in this town, and all you can worry about is whether main street looks like a postcard. Well, news flash: I don't intend to allow the town to turn a blind eye to racism, animal abuse, corruption and the rest. I'm doing something, just so you know what action looks like. Not because I care about Pincus, because I don't. This dump is dead and doesn't know it. I just can't stand the hypocrisy and whining. All of you people sitting in a mud puddle crying that your pants are wet. One thing you don't have to worry about is me, your daughter for ten minutes. Not that it's kept you awake before. I plan to be gone."

"I'm so sorry you've become so angry. It doesn't suit you. You're so beautiful, and smart. You have your whole life ahead of you." She reached out to touch Doreen's hair in a motherly way. Doreen flinched and showed her teeth, as a beaten dog that sees a broom.

Angeline shifted. "Doreen, I need to ask you: did you set the fire that burned The Bread Basket down and killed Oscar Turner?"

"Angeline, you've got a lot of nerve asking me that. I'm not going to honor your insult with an answer. Jesus."

"I saw you that night, didn't I? Standing in the shadows, in a black slicker. What were you doing?"

"I don't have to answer to you, Angeline. You're disgusting. First, I'm your beautiful daughter, now I'm an arsonist. You need to find some help. And, what do you care about what suits me? Just so you know, I'm not angry, Mommy, I'm impatient. And it does suit me, at least better than being a fake saint." She spat the word Mommy as bitter weed caught in her throat. "While you're making up things to worry about, look at Emmett Chesney over there. He's lost his wife, and he's still better off than you are. You never lost anything. You just gave it away. So, worry about that while you're growing old. Alone. You lied to the one man who loved you, just to get rid of him. And you gave your baby away." The heat from her anger made her voice hellish. *"You gave your baby away, Angeline.* Live with that. Sister."

With that, Doreen rose and walked toward the door, causing every man in the Sunnyside to gaze as if the president were passing in review. It wasn't the president, though. It was Pincus' own avenging angel.

Angeline sat in the stocks, condemned for her sins. She had, as Doreen said, given her baby away. She had spurned her mate and declined to be a mother. Worse, she had forgotten the baby and lived her life as if the child were dead, just a memory growing fainter by the year. Worst of all, she had forgotten who she was herself and what emotions she must have felt when she made those fateful decisions. She had only the dimmest sense of who Angeline Bruce was when she lay with Faris Turner to conceive the child who became Doreen. She remembered it as summer, but not much else. The sex had been liberating, only because she had never been naked with a man before, had never felt a man, had never yielded to another person. The actual intercourse had been fumbly and fast, and now poorly recalled. But the act of surrender and appropriation of another was indelible. Her thoughts of pregnancy and birth at the Crittenton Center had become more and more stylized through the years – all waiting and sitting and worrying, a certain sadness, but nothing about the baby, really. With childbirth, she knew, memories of pain and labor fade, so that considering a second birth is possible. Though Angeline's memories did not uniformly favor her, on balance they

230

offered a reprieve from pain. But not forever. Her guilt and shame surprised her like a recurrence of cancer in a weakened patient. During her remission, she had neglected to use the respite for something. Now, corralled by her past, she had only her nunnish ways, which themselves were false in origin, a patina burnishing an empty shell. And she suspected her daughter of arson and murder.

CHAPTER XXI

D oreen stood quietly to the side of the tinted picture window at the front of the flower shop, studying Plummer's Funeral Home with deep intent. Moments after the unmarked van from the crematorium loaded a dun-colored cardboard box from the service entrance, she made her move. Seeing the driver walk around the far side of the funeral home and out of sight, Doreen slipped into the van and drove away.

"Chief, Ethel's gone." Lew Givens hooked his thumb between his gun belt and his belly, a posture he practiced to look more authoritative.

"We know she's gone, Lew. I was out to her house with you when she died. What else is new?"

"I don't mean that kind of gone. I mean she's vanished from Plummer's. She's that kind of gone: Disappeared."

"Disappeared? Jesus on a wooden stick."

Soon, police cars surrounded Plummer's. Deputies decorated the funeral home with crime tape. Scheduled services were postponed indefinitely, causing additional grief for bereaved clients all over the county. In short order the police investigation would show that the corpse of the late Ethel Chesney had been stolen, driven away from Plummer's Funeral Home in a refrigerated service van belonging to Georgia Family Anatomical Services, Inc., out of Atlanta. Perpetrator was person or persons unknown. The driver, who was hung over from a night at a strip club along the highway, had been enjoying coffee and the tail end of a joint in the Memory Garden next to the funeral home at the time the van drove off. He was questioned by Lew, released and promptly fired by the company. The van was found northeast of town, nosed into a ravine next to a tree farm. Ethel, who had been tagged for transport to Atlanta for cremation, lay quietly warming in her packing crate. The van was towed out of the ditch, and the dismissed former driver caught a bus home.

The story led the news that night, punctuated by an interview with Emmett Chesney, who displayed understandable anger and grief, as he announced his intention to sue Plummer, Georgia Family Anatomical, and the driver. Ethel had not been intended for cremation, but for burial. She had a morbid fear of being burned, said the grieving husband. For that reason and the circumstances of her death, he had refused to allow cremation. Somebody had to pay for this.

At a press conference the next morning, the Georgia State Attorney General's Office of Consumer Protection announced the suspension of Plummer's license to operate, pending both civil and criminal investigations of the appropriate handling of human remains. Charges of fraud were added when the state confirmed that Ethel was supposed to be interred, not incinerated. Plummer himself hid from view, alleging that "dark forces" were out to get him. That left Washington and Washington as the only funeral service providers in Pincus. Every white citizen in the area hoped for a long life, so as to avoid burial preparation by the black funeral home operators. Calls to crematoria in Brunswick and Statesboro surged.

The investigation report rolled out in pieces. For some time, Plummer had been charging Pincus families for a full range of burial services, including embalming, clothing, caskets, and the like, while secreting the bodies of the beloved for shipment to Atlanta for cremation at a fraction of the cost. Plummer pocketed the difference, minus a small kickback to Georgia Anatomical, in which he had an investment. Television news interviewed many former Plummer's clients, who now claimed that he always recommended a closed casket. The evening anchors broadcast a special report from the cemetery for additional effect.

"No one knows how many empty caskets are buried here at Yamacraw," the newscaster intoned. "No one knows which of our dearly departed have gone to Atlanta on their final road trip." Of course, this script had been true before Ethel. No one knew who was in the ground and who was in the furnace, because the people charged with knowing such things had turned out to be the worst of scoundrels, betraying the bereaved by mishandling the remains of their dead. The only witnesses to the Ethel Chesney crime were those stacked in Plummer's cooler, awaiting transport. And they weren't talking.

Faris greeted the news in the company of Angeline, who was helping him clear out Turner's as part of its transformation into The Bread Basket. Their intimacy was implicit in the way they moved in harmony with each other, stopping to laugh or tell a small story when one of them found something in a box or drawer, otherwise remaining quiet. They tiptoed around the question of their relationship.

"Jesus, Faris, can you believe this stuff about Plummer? Did you ever think it was possible?"

"If you mean did I think it was possible to have a bad man in

Pincus, the answer is obvious: yes. Dad used to say that bad people are everywhere throughout the earth, and we have our share. I can't say I gave Plummer credit for this kind of complexity or imagination, though. I am shocked by the nature of what he was doing, which is shameful and nasty. He appears to have been a real ghoul.

"I knew something was sour. After the confrontation between him and Rodney, I thought I'd look into the possibility of opening a crematorium in Pincus. I made a few phone calls to Brunswick and Statesboro to get more information from the operators there. I thought Rodney might develop a business plan that would secure financing for a modest facility and take some of the new market he and Plummer had argued about. I was desperate to do something to take the pressure off the situation and help Rodney out. But strangely, everywhere I turned, the people I talked to said that Plummer would scotch any idea of a crematorium in Pincus, even if it made his business easier. They said that Plummer already had a sweet enough deal. I guess they knew about his arrangement with Georgia Anatomical Services. Maybe they have the same kind of setup themselves. I hope to God they weren't privy to the fraud and abuse of the dead. You don't think they could have known about that, do you? Could it be true that more funeral operations are as sick as this one?"

"How would I know, Faris? The only thing I know is that your attempt to front for Rodney in a crematorium venture is about as ridiculous a plan as I could imagine. Do you actually know anything about that business, or any business, or business planning? Or, were you just playing broker? What were you thinking?" Her exasperation with Faris was evident in her voice, punctuated by a sigh and a shake of her head. Her grey-shadowed hair waved at him.

"No, I guess I don't know any of those things, or much of anything else. I had the idea that I would be a sort of *Deus ex machina,* hovering around the town's tensions and insinuating myself to resolve them. You know, kind of a broker for the future. Silly, now that I think about it. I'm not much of a doer. Or a broker, for that matter."

"You're right. You're not. You need to stop living in a dream world and figure out how to live your life. Try taking it a step at a time. And stay away from the funeral business. Jesus."

Faris chuckled. "Well, the upside of all this is that Rodney's finally got all the funeral business in Pincus. I guess that's progress. Depends on your viewpoint, of course."

Across town, Doreen and Rubén ate popcorn and drank diet sodas at her apartment over the flower shop, watching the news of Plummer's arrest and celebrating her guerrilla triumph. Doreen had promised not to stand for a talk-only Curtain of Hope; she was proving herself to be a woman of action. Even she could not have expected such a dramatic outcome as this. Maybe she had a gift. Rubén, meanwhile, had become slightly afraid of her and her willingness to go to extremes. Kidnapping the dead was an act for which he felt completely unprepared. For her part, Doreen had become completely bored with Rubén, who was the intellectual equivalent of her dish drainer, but she needed him for direct actions to come. The next target was his father. She told Rubén to get dressed, all in black, and meet her at WILD ANIMAL KINGDOM after his shift at the café. He should leave his car by the ruins of The Bread Basket and walk in along the dirt road. Rubén did as he was told, in return for some intimacies he could barely have imagined.

The Curtain of Hope

Sit with us. Let it be as it was in those days

When alcohol brought our tongues the first sweet foretaste of oblivion.

Donald Justice, *Invitation to a Ghost*

CHAPTER XXII

Someone had turned Jesús' animals loose. They were all lost, at least for now. He knew it was his son. Only Rubén knew the ins and outs of the holding areas and the easiest place to come through the fence. Jesús couldn't figure out who had helped Rubén. He certainly would not have guessed it to be Doreen, because he couldn't imagine Rubén as a man, much less one who could attract such a beauty. Man or not, Rubén had to pay.

The animals had been released late at night, but before Jesús returned home from drinking. They scattered in all directions, with the exception of the snapping turtle, which was down in the pond with no reason to leave. Now, days later, the whole attraction was closed, and the feds were investigating the operation for compliance with regulations governing safety and animal well-being. Jesús doubted he'd have the opportunity to reopen. Even if he did, he couldn't stand the loss of cash flow and would go broke. Rubén had to pay, but good. Jesús wanted his son dead. He just couldn't figure out how to kill him. But he would make him suffer.

In the late afternoon gloom of a cloudy day, Jesús stood in the scrubby woods of myrtle and oak, reflecting on the sad turn of events and looking for optical yellow practice golf balls that lay in the litter. The storm that had resulted in the death of Oscar Turner had also torn through the nets at the end of the WILD ANIMAL KINGDOM golf driving range, leaving them in tatters. Busy with other matters, including the animal escape, Jesús had not noticed the damage until early that afternoon, when a snotty eighteen-year-old kid wearing chinos and a polo shirt with an upturned collar waltzed into his office.

"Hey, Jay. Where's our money?"

"What money, kid?" Jesús knew this kid and liked him about as much as he liked polo shirts and being called Jay.

"We heard that anybody who hit golf balls through the holes in the net got a dollar a ball. We've got about two buckets out there, I figure. Minimum." The two jackasses with him sniggered and fist bumped.

Jesús walked outside and looked at the hundred-yard expanse of netting that he had not yet repaired. "Who told you that?"

"Dizzy told us, man, said it was a contest. So, where's the money? And how do we figure where we placed?"

"There's no contest, no money, and you placed DFL - dead fucking last. *Man.* Get out of here before I kick your pink ass."

"Look, Jay...." Jesús stopped the argument dead in its tracks with a deadly stare, telling the kid and his buddies without a word that they were walking a ragged edge with him and shouldn't go any further. They got in their truck and pealed out of the gravel lot, shouting obscenities about Mexicans.

Jesús fumed in the woods, squat-walking with a bucket to pick up the balls, which cost him $8.00 a dozen. It was not a big deal, but the more he seethed the more it was growing into one. As his back began to ache and the early mosquitoes came out, he decided to set the task aside and wait until Rubén came home from the Sunnyside. Jesús could make Rubén pick up the balls while deciding on next steps. He did not have to wait long.

Rubén had made great progress as a line cook working for Muscadine when Ethel was away from the café. Now that Ethel was gone for good, and Muscadine was suffering what she called post-electrical stress disorder, Rubén's shift hours and responsibilities grew. Muscadine had always liked Rubén for his kind and quiet nature. She even called him by his true name. She was confused by his apparent lack of interest in her as a woman, though. Or, better yet, his interest without action. He liked her, all right. She had seen him staring and didn't mind a bit. He was a fine looking young man, after all, and did not display any of the shortcomings of her other mates. Sensing Rubén's latent desire for her and unimpressed by the barrier posed by his goodness, Muscadine tried to brush up against him whenever possible, or to lean in his direction to show her breasts. Sometimes she leaned the other way, to show proudly what she called her monster thigh gap. It was a kind of hobby, breaking men's resistance. But as the bus boy Wilson said, "Dizzy different. He got his eye on the eggs, not on the legs."

Rubén did have his eye on the job. He knew his good behavior and talent for line cooking endeared him to Emmett, who, since Ethel's demise had been short on endearments. He began to show more interest in Rubén long term. Muscadine laid off her flirting, now that she didn't seem to know where she was half the time and couldn't remember what she was up to, mid-flirt. Rubén's wages increased. He verged on being proud of himself. And as a cook, he didn't have to talk to people all the time.

The positive spell of personal accomplishment vanished at the threshold of the Santamaría household. Rubén knew that opening the door to home meant leaving his name and his pride outside. His father would make sure of it.

Jesús waited just inside the living room of the low-ceilinged ranch house, pushing with his feet to make quarter circles in his swivel chair. He had been drinking. When Rubén entered, Jesús stood from his chair as if ejected by a spring. "Dizzy, what the hell were you doing telling those boys there's a contest to knock golf balls through the net? You know how many are out there in the woods? What the fuck?"

Rubén offered no response, knowing that nothing would change his situation. His stoicism infuriated Jesús, who employed the only weapon he knew. "You retard sonofabitch, get out there and get them balls and when you come in you better have a story. And you better make up another one, while you're at it, since I know you let the animals loose." He slapped Rubén in the face with the back of his hand, not too hard, just to punctuate his sentence.

Rubén put Jesús on the floor with one blow to his throat. "Get outa my house," Jesús croaked, as he tried to regain the upper hand. He was physically overmatched and stunned by his surprising loss of psychological power over his son.

"My house, too. You don't mean shit," Rubén stuttered. The newly-liberated Rubén gathered a few things and before leaving, turned with a cryptic smile and said, "Watch it, old man." Jesús was warned.

Hours later, exhausted from a long day painting nails and listening to inanities from her customers, fingers cracked and chapped from solvents and soaks, Carmita trudged through the door into the darkened parlor. She could practically smell the anger. Jesús drunkenly told her the story of Rubén's disrespectful behavior and their fight. His story favored him and disparaged Rubén.

"Where is Rubén? I'll talk with him."

"He's gone. I told him to get out."

"You told him to get out? You told your own son to leave? You told my boy to leave his home and his mother? Ay, Dios, qué hiciste, Jesús? Qué tipo de hombre se lo haría a su propio hijo? Sinverguenza. Desobligado. Irresponsable. Ya me voy también, cabrón. Quédate solo con tus bichos, y muere pronto. Hijo de la chingada!" Carmita turned on her jellies and slammed the door. Then she reopened it to shout "y la puta qué te parió." This was absolutely the nastiest thing she'd ever said, and yet not nearly enough. She crossed herself and said a little prayer to the Blessed Virgin. Then, she left for good. She knew she could sleep at LeDonna's shop, which had an apartment over it. She would deal with the rest in due course. She felt oddly at peace.

CHAPTER XXIII

By earlier agreement, Faris drove to Ken Carstarter's office to settle Henry's affairs. He had invited Angeline to accompany him, with Ken's agreement. After all, she was the other interested party in The Dog Ear. It turned out to be a relatively brief meeting, after which they climbed a narrow stair at the back of the store to Henry's old apartment. Henry was a man alone, who lived in a way that fit his condition. His apartment, which he had occupied for most of his adult life, could have kept a team of forensic anthropologists employed for years, without coherent result. Despite the intriguing remains, there was little clue to the person who had lived his life in this small space. Piles of letters from students, old term papers from past English classes, stacks of cardboard filing boxes with notecards spilling out in every direction. A whole corner was taken up with research on Melungeons, including genealogical charts, lists of names, correspondence, photographs and testimonials. What amounted to a Melungeon habitat map covering the Carolinas, Appalachia and the Cumberland Valley of Tennessee sat on top.

An entire wall was covered with volumes of poetry, mostly anthologies. Among the thick, dated volumes lay more specific collections, favoring Russians and various Romantics: Akhmatova, of course, but also Pushkin, Pasternak and Marina Tsvetaeva. Thomas

Wyatt's complete poems sat next to a scholarly work on courtly love and Elizabethan verse. The Yale volume of Shakespeare's plays sat on the floor as big as an ottoman, completely unmanageable as a book. On a lamp table was Nadezhda Mandelstam's cripplingly sad memoir *Hope Against Hope*. One might have thought these were clues to Henry's interior, if it were not for the two dozen Everyman editions of various poets, awaiting the owner's first caress. Auden, Eliot, Hardy, Tennyson.

Aside from the general clutter, there was nothing personal, no photographs of family or of trips abroad, no plaques of recognition or memorable artifacts of life. Henry's pots and pans were generic, too; no skillets passed down for years or trivets and potholders or bric-a-brac. Then, Faris finally realized that no one ever really knew Henry at all. He was a cipher. The town had treated him like a stray dog, tolerating him from a distance and nothing more. No one cared to scratch behind his ears or take him to the vet. Henry, too, held up his side of loneliness by refusing love and friendship. He invented his friends, either by keeping up with former students or creating artifices such as the poetry group. In time, the members of Henry's little associations had thought kindly of him, had indulged him, but had never loved him. Faris and Angeline were his only claim to having true friends, and one had decamped for most of his life, while the other took the precious little space available in Pincus for a do-gooder. Well matched to Henry, Faris and Angeline thought of him mainly in relation to themselves.

In fact, the three of them had an additional attribute in common, besides their intellectual interests. They were alone. They had chosen, somehow, to abjure the normal commitments to life and to someone else, preferring to think that their lives alone were preferable to all other options presented to them. They were cold from a lifetime of being their own sole source of warmth. And they, no less than Henry, thought they could help the world in its downward slide without being fully part of it, to instruct people on good behavior and neighborliness, rather than to lead with it, to evoke the spirits of community engagement from a position of emotional and civic impoverishment, to see the world from above and to guide its actors as the ancient gods. These three had been Pincus' moral meter maids, strolling around in observation, chalking tires, waiting for someone to be out of line and deserving of kind correction, or a ticket.

He looked furtively at Angeline, to see if she might reveal her thoughts at the scene before her. She had tears in her eyes, but tears are all the same, wet and colorless, whether from regret or shame or pain or loss. He could not divine the origin of hers.

With his modest salary as a teacher, Henry had accumulated little wealth: a checking and savings account at the local bank, but nothing amounting to much. Faris worked with Ken to dispose of Henry's belongings, with Angeline's advice, sending clothes to charity, books to the public library, and the few sticks of furniture to the thrift store. They were surprised to find a small life insurance policy with double indemnity for accidental death. Faris instructed Ken to add up all the sums and to make a gift in Henry's name to the Pincus High School library for acquisitions in poetry and to award an annual Henry Jeffords prize to the outstanding senior English student at the Christian Academy for Boys, where Henry had taught. That was that. It had not taken Henry long to lead his life and little time to clean up after it. Still, his surviving friends hoped his legacy would live in the scholarships.

Ken left the keys with Angeline. She and Faris stood together in the apartment window, watching the lawyer's car depart. To the surprise of both, Faris took her shoulders and turned her for a kiss. They both felt it deeply and held a long embrace, she sobbing into his shoulder and offering her salty mouth to him over and over again. The kisses were pure tenderness, though, without eroticism or romance. They were kisses without future, the kisses of Russian sisters at a war memorial, or a mother finding her only child in the rubble of an earthquake, heavy on wet tissues and panicked emotion, without a shred of embarrassment at the intimacy.

"You asked me if there could be a future between us, Angeline. We're standing here now, looking into our future, the two of us alone, unless we figure out something that connects us to each other. I have been talking with Leo because of his yard and so on, and I realize that his greatest burden is living alone, facing the prospect of dying by himself. I don't want to live the rest of my life alone. Will you think about that? Will you think about marrying me, or being with me?"

She looked at him with the surprised, affectionate and slightly annoyed expression of a woman whose lost cat has come home, battered and weakened from adventures who knows where. "Faris, your sense of timing is the world's worst. I love you. I do. I can't help it. And I have the same fears. I want to talk about this and to think carefully about it with you. But, not now. It's not the time to think of us. I think the best thing you can do now is to go see Leo, since you mention it. He has taken the whole incident with Muscadine and Pipsy very hard, and we forget that he's an old man alone. Just call on him. It'd do you both some good. We'll take this up later."

"Okay. But let's not take too long. We need to do instead of talk. You've always said I'm a better talker than a doer, and now I'm a believer. There's a woman dressed up in that nun suit of yours, and we need to let her out. And I'd like to wake up with someone whose stories I'm tired of hearing over and over. I'd like to read the same books and fall asleep watching an old movie together. Eat leftovers, go for walks. Corny stuff. I'd like to fight over politics, or the last piece of toast. I need to belong to someone and to be bossed around. Who would be better at bossing me around than an old nun? We're getting old. Who knows? Maybe God does have an egg timer, and our eggs might be almost done. Don't put this off."

CHAPTER XXIV

In what remained of an oak hammock behind the golf driving range, down a one-lane yellow clay track, stood an unfinished cedar building with a screened wraparound porch and one large room, about the right size for a beer hall. Toilets had been added on either side of the back elevation with a simple extension of the original structure. Bracketed along the metal roofline stood an old railroad station sign, painted over to read BIG LICK. The site had long been known to attract animals from the swamp because of minerals in the upland clay and had long been a hunting ground. The advent of a nightclub ended that, keeping only the name and a few nocturnal varmints.

Friday and Saturday nights, Jesús ran a juke joint at BIG LICK, which he had sort of inherited when the original place shut down and he claimed it. The place was old enough to have preceded desegregation, and most of what had been the colored side survived: a simple corrugated tin roof sheltering picnic tables set on a hard dirt floor.

BIG LICK was a joint venture. Ed Prewitt provided barbecue, slaw and grilled corn in season, and was the Saturday night impresario. Friday nights were "Latin hot night," overseen by Jesús, and Saturdays reserved for jazz and rhythm and blues more to the black community's liking. Jesús had obtained a liquor license by bribing Sheriff Hockett. He served the cheapest rum, gin and blended whisky, as well as beer on tap. Bottles were forbidden, since they tended to become flying objects as the nights wore on.

The interior sported a few rustic round tables and walls lined with old license plates and pinup posters. Out back among the picnic tables, patrons could enjoy their food, some fresh air and moonshine, which always seemed to be around. Jesús didn't realize any profits from the 'shine, but it was part of the scene, as was the single bare bulb that ran from the back of the roadhouse to a big hickory tree. Ed called it a country chandelier.

The spirit of the joint was "rough friendly," with the evenings starting friendly and slowly getting rough. Patrons were careful in their choice of nights and times to visit. Music started at 10 p.m. and ran until 2 a.m. Usually, a party or a fight broke out after closing. The black clientele were slightly older, as Ed permitted refused to play hip-hop music. Jesús' Latino clientele were undemanding, and someone could always be found to sing Tejano music or mournful ballads from Mexico. A surprising number of women had the poor judgment to patronize BIG LICK. There was little else to do on weekends.

After his son and wife left him and his animals escaped, Jesús spent more time at the juke joint, which reduced pilferage at the till and gave him some superficial company. Still, he was drinking up the profits. His nose was now deep in the bottle, and he feared, correctly, that he was headed along his father's path of dissipation. He consoled himself with the daily dulling of his thoughts; when sober, he considered extending the roadhouse's schedule to weeknights. Or, maybe Ed would consider a opening a second barbecue house during the day. Jesús could sell liquor and beer, and the drunks could lie out back around the picnic tables. Jesús had doubts about any further collaboration, though, and he distrusted Ed because he was black.

On a cold November night, Jesús was sampling a glass of *miel de caña*, a euphemistically named rotgut rum that sold well among the Latinos. He could buy a case for twelve dollars a half gallon minus a ten percent case discount and then sell it retail at two dollars a shot for a terrific hundred dollar profit per bottle. Actually, a little less, because whoever he hired to tend bar was inevitably sloppy with the pour. Still, margins on liquor were a miracle of God. Right now, though, he was thinking about the cost of installing a wood stove in this firetrap. Crowds thinned out in the winter chill, and skinny as he was, he was almost always cold.

As he pondered these great questions, Bobby Lee staggered in, already drunk at dusk. The few regulars who had come early for the evening called out to him. "Hey, Bobby, I hear Leo sparked up your wife and your dog. Whatchagonna do about it, have another drink?" Someone else hooted, "I hear Leo's better than you at making Muscadine hot." And another: "I'll bet that little dog don't shit for a week." General laughter followed, as Bobby reddened. He motioned Jesús outside, where they sat down at an old tipped over cable spool serving as a picnic table next to a fire pit grey with ash. He stared seriously at Jesús, red-eyed with drink and malice.

"Them guys don't never get enough. People need to know when is enough." Bobby was a spitter, and he hawked on the bare ground for punctuation.

Jesús looked at Bobby like he was the ambassador from not knowing what was enough.

"What the hell did you expect when you walked in here? Are you here to whine, or have you got something to say to me?"

"I seen your monkey."

"I'm listening."

"You said you'd pay a thousand dollar reward." Bobby Lee wiped his nose upward with the dirty bottom of his palm and lit a cigarette. He exhaled and spat again, chasing it with a drink.

"Only if I get the monkey back."

"How do I know you're good for it? You could just steal my story and the monkey and then tell me to fuck off." Bobby Lee was a self-pitying slob of a drunk, a wasted young man no different than any other who has given up on life prematurely. He found himself among the permanently aggrieved, feeling he had been denied his proper station in life by nameless forces – the system, the man, whoever was in charge. His poorly formed conceit allowed him to justify a complete lack of morals or social compunction, in favor of grasping at any opportunity that didn't involve work.

"Either tell me the story or fuck off, Bobby. I'm not coming up with front money, if that's what you're asking. And if you got such a big story, maybe we should just talk to the sheriff. Somebody has it out for me, and I'm going to find them. Or maybe you let my animals out, which I'm beginning to think is a real possibility."

Bobby Lee drank slow and deep from a half pint of sloe gin he had in his coat. He was a true drunk, drowning in a true drunk's choice. He deftly untwisted the cap with thumb and forefinger of the same hand that held the pint, flawlessly poured cheap, sweet liquor down his throat, and exhaled smoke-nasty breath, flicking the ash of his cigarette with the pinky of his free hand. He spat at the ash as it tumbled to the ground. He was a most experienced lush. "Neither of us wants that," he responded with a sighing belch. "And I didn't do nothing. So, I'm going to tell you what I saw, and then expect you to make it good. If you don't, I'm coming after you, get it?"

"Well, get on with it, then. And I'm real scared about you coming after me. I might die laughing." Jesús knew Bobby to be a desperate man, and he wanted the monkey, so he indulged the melodrama. He wasn't worried about Bobby.

"So, here's the deal. I'm out at night, out on the other side of the cypress bottom behind your place, hunting pigs. Not your pet pigs, wild pigs that have been tearing up that little bit of land I got over there and sucking eggs. Don't need no license, pigs is free meat all year long. Sometimes I can sell the meat. I sit out on a tree stand with night goggles and bait a little corn and just wait for them."

"I know how to kill pigs. What does this have to do with the Admiral?"

"Easy, Jay. I'm coming to it. Just remember that I'm just trying to help you out. Anyway, it's about midnight or a little after, cold as bear shit, no moon, spitting rain. I'm blowing into my hands, sipping a little gin and freezing my balls off. I can tell you I wished I hadn't come out."

"Skip the weather report." Jesús had a suspicious nature and a mean face, and he showed both. He hated drunks and knew he was becoming one, so looking into the mirror across the table from him didn't do his mood any good. Bobby smelled like Jesús' old man the day he got fired from his last job after the Air Force, as a janitor for a Buick showroom. He had found a gift decanter in the shape of a vintage 1967 Riviera, commemorating the dealership's record sales that year. The decanter was full of port; he emptied it, passed out on the showroom floor and was swept out with the trash when the owner came in. Never trust a drunk.

"Well, then, I seen movement, which I naturally think is pigs.

But it ain't pigs. It's two people down on their hands and knees in that old storm ditch alongside your property, the one that used to be for irrigating rice. Remember, when a few years back some of them university boys found an old wood irrigation trunk there that regulated the flow. That's how they know it was a rice ditch. It was in the papers."

"I don't give a shit about the ditch. What about the monkey?"

"So, I start to watch them, them two people I told you about, and what do they do but cut the damn fence and go right into your property. One of them either has a key or knows how to pick a lock, or maybe you just don't keep it locked, I don't know. But pretty soon there they go into the barn, or whatever you call it, you know, where you keep the critters." Bobby lit another cigarette from the butt of his last, pausing to inhale for what he thought was dramatic effect, and then to spit. "I guess I should say kept, since they're gone." He was warming up to his story. He lazily swatted the smoke away from his eyes. "After about two or three minutes, there's a whoop and cry, and, whoa, Billy, here comes pigs, white chickens, mink, otters, a donkey and who knows what else. Raising hell the whole way, with them two flapping their arms and chasing them. Then I seen it was a boy and a girl. Coming up the rear is that damn monkey, the one you call the Admiral. He's running like his ass is caught fire, with them two barely in front and losing ground. I couldn't do nothin' but laugh, it was so crazy. I shoulda been pissed, since they had ruined any chance I had of shooting a pig that night, unless I'd shot that one you keep. But it was like going to the movies, it was so funny. Shoulda been there, I'm telling you." He gave out a sigh of self-satisfied amusement and shook his head. "Whooey."

"So, where's the monkey? And stop spitting all over the damn place. You're about to make me sick."

"Well, like I was saying, all hell had broke loose, and it looked like the animals was going to run till Sunday. I can't say for sure exactly why, but I stood right up in the stand and yelled out at the two of them. Just shouted 'Hey!' real loud, like, what in the hell do you think you're up to? Scared a fart out of both of them, running along in the night and then all of a sudden me yelling out of a tree, them blind in the dark. They split one to each side and went into the bottom, down in the cypress hole, but the monkey kept going straight down to the creek. That's where I lost him."

"What do you mean you lost him? What good is this horseshit story if you can't tell me where the monkey is? I'm not going to give you nothing for *seeing* the monkey. That don't do me no good. You could have made all that up, for all I know, since everybody in town knows somebody let out all my animals. You want a reward, produce the Admiral. Otherwise, go crawl back into the bottle."

"Ok, then. I think I can do that."

"Which, the monkey or the bottle? Don't be thinking nothing. You got him or you don't. If you got him, produce him tomorrow right here. You pick a time. I'll have the money, and you produce the monkey. You don't show, and I'm going to the sheriff, because I'll be thinking you set the whole thing up to play me. You want me to pay you, do something to earn it. In the meantime, quit wasting my time." Jesús got up from the picnic table and left in his car without looking back. Bobby tipped up the last of the gin, spat and threw the bottle on the ground next to the trashcan.

The truth was only slightly different from the account Bobby Lee told Jesús, but the difference was everything. In fact, the Admiral had run down to the creek, splashing his way to escape, only to find himself exhausted and frightened, trapped in a freezing current too strong for his little arms. When Bobby found him, The Admiral was barely hanging onto a branch that dangled from a narrow sand bar in the middle of a stream swollen by rain, too weak to pull himself up. Drunk as he was, Bobby Lee managed to throw a game sack over the shivering monkey, fortunate to have brought several along to haul pig meat home. He shoved the terrified animal in his pickup toolbox, which was barely big enough to hold a sack lunch and a few wrenches. He drove slowly home, as drunks do, with his right two wheels on the shoulder of the road, weaving as he pulled into his garage, still buzzed and already spending his reward in his mind. He texted Jesús that they could meet at noon. The monkey would be fine until then. High noon at BIG LICK. It sounded good. He smoked the last of his cigarette, stomped the butt on the garage floor and went into the house to pester Muscadine for sex. For once, it felt good to be Bobby Lee.

The next morning, Bobby Lee awoke in a bad mood. He had gotten too little from Muscadine and too much from the hangover banging in his head. He vowed to stop buying sloe gin; his dad had warned him that the sugar wasn't good for him. Meanwhile, he lit a cigarette and hurried outside to his truck. It was after ten. He had slept in and did not want to miss his appointment with Jesús at BIG LICK.

He pulled off at a turnaround near WILD ANIMAL KINGDOM to retrieve the monkey from his toolbox. Just as the key turned the lock, The Admiral came flying out at Bobby like a mad dervish, whirling and tearing at his abuser's face and eyes, biting the fingers that were trying to protect his captor from certain mutilation. Bobby was being bitten to ribbons. The monkey, horrified by a night in a box, must have flashed back to his tortured life with the organ grinder. In his frenzy, he moved as a single, manic muscle with intent to kill. He bit like a piranha. In a panic, Bobby grabbed the little monkey tightly, and while suffering even more bites in the process, smashed his charge against the truck trailer hitch. The little guy went limp. Intending merely to stun The Admiral, Bobby had killed him instead, just like Anthony Quinn killed Richard Basehart. Bleeding from head wounds and punctures all over his arms and hands, a mangled septum and a severed forefinger tip, Bobby ran to the irrigation ditch and buried The Admiral in a shallow, covering him with leaf litter and pine straw. The poor little capuchin finally found an end to his tortures.

Doreen had been watching Bobby, as she had for some days. She knew his type and suspected he was up to something she could use against him. She had been feeding Rebel and Tarbaby treats of crushed pistachios and brown sugar at the liquor store when she heard Bobby Lee yapping about coming into money, which was a clear tipoff. Who would give this worthless clod-kicking drunk anything? She was enraged by his murder of the tiny monkey. What a pig Muscadine had married.

Now, Bobby was in a panic, and Doreen took advantage. Waiting until he sped off in his beat-up truck, Doreen retrieved the Admiral's corpse and laid it gently in a cloth laundry bag, which she later put in the back of the flower shop's cooler for further consideration.

Bobby, in the meantime, failed to show up for his rendezvous with Jesús, who promptly called Lorne to report his suspicion that Bobby was the defiler of WILD ANIMAL KINGDOM and kidnapper of The Admiral. Jesús did not believe his own accusation for a moment, knowing that if Bobby had told the truth about a young couple involved in the invasion of his menagerie, that couple could only be Doreen and Dizzy Pickles. Now that Bobby was out of the way, Jesús had to plan. His revenge would be private. First, he had to sober up. And he needed to find The Admiral.

CHAPTER XXV

L eo and Strother had bonded, not as friends, exactly, but as senior fellows of the academy of misanthropy. They spent a lot of time together, working on the yard and removing debris. Leo groused about the neighbors and the dogs and the teenagers; Strother listened as long as Leo cared to talk. You couldn't find many better companions, their compatibility accented by mutual disinterest in the other's conversation. Finally, after several sessions, Strother got Leo's attention by saying that the black-headed girl, meaning Doreen, had hexed Bobby Lee, Leo's principal source of complaint. To his own surprise, Leo asked how Strother knew such a thing. Strother explained his long association with hexes and offered to add one for a twarter. Leo gave Strother a quarter and forgot the whole thing. He didn't believe in hexes, but he was beginning to like Strother and thought this would show him respect. Strother promised that he would hex Bobby Lee down.

Early on a too-warm January evening, Faris stood with Leo as they surveyed the damage to his lawn and reputation. Strother was wandering around somewhere behind the house. Leo was mortified by the turn of events with Muscadine and Pipsy. "I never meant to kill the damn little thing," Leo said by way of private apology, not knowing that Emmett had killed the damn little thing by euthanizing it. Leo did know that he had turned his loneliness into bile, and the result was a little dog dead in his yard. Faris felt a share of the guilt, since he had suggested what had turned out to be yet another terrible idea. He had come to call on Leo at Angeline's encouragement, but it just made him more miserable. At least, he thought, this would help him move closer to Angeline. He and Leo were deep in conversation about the unfortunate bordergrass incident and failed to hear Bobby Lee approach.

"You rotten sonofabitch," Bobby Lee growled drunkenly at Leo. He had come straight from the ditch where he had left The Admiral, in pain and losing blood, thoroughly jacked up on cheap gin and reminded of the teasing about Leo, Muscadine and Pipsy at Jesús' dive. "You nearly killed my wife and burnt the shit out of her dog. I'm done with your crap for good. Get ready to get shot, Leo. I'm gonna shoot your ass and watch the blood drain out of the hole I make."

Leo stood in shock, which made him seem less afraid than he was. "You never gave two shits about that dog, and you know it. The last time you paid it any attention was when you tripped over it drunk and threw it through the screen door of that dumpster you call home. As for your wife, I feel sorry for her. Being married to you is like walking around town with shit on your shoes. Get back on your side of the yard, you trashy little bastard. And sober up for a change, just to see what it feels like. What happened to your face, anyway? Was it Muscadine or one of the cats at House of Mao?"

His eye bloody and inflamed by his confrontation with the late Admiral, nose running snot and blood, spirits riled by liquor and pain, Bobby pulled a pistol and waved it at Leo. The old man ducked behind Faris, from instinct more than fear. Faris stepped with his hand outstretched as if to offer a candy to Bobby Lee. Before Faris had a chance to speak, Bobby drunkenly stumbled forward and discharged his pistol with a menacingly loud crack. Faris caught the bullet in his thigh and tipped as his leg went out from under him. Bobby fell to the ground, exhausted by the exertions of the moment. He lay face down in the grass half-conscious, while Leo spryly wrested the gun away and began to hit him on the back with the butt. Faris began to laugh at the absurdity of an old man beating up a drunk with his own gun, but soon grew lightheaded with shock. He looked at his pants leg, which pulsed with dark blood, beating to the rhythm of Leo's drubbing and Bobby Lee's wailing. He shut his eyes against the setting sun, grateful for the lack of pain and reminded of the oddly combined humiliation and peace of a colonoscopy, just as they put the sedative in and count you backward into unconsciousness. Not so bad. He rested. He imagined the Great Ruth and smiled, as his blood wet the grass. As he always did in his endless reveries, Faris called up the spirits of his mother and father, who in death had left him alone, except in these quiet pockets of peace. A kind of sleep veiled him, shutting out the sounds of sirens and the scuffle of police, tackling Leo, hauling Bobby away, shouting at onlookers. Two guys he didn't recognize were lifting him onto a gurney, bouncing him roughly into an ambulance. It was too hot inside, and stuffy, too noisy. He had a hard time focusing his thoughts or even recognizing the blood pressure cuff, the IV or the radio chatter in the ambulance. He resisted the oxygen mask, then relented. He struggled to catch his breath. As he surrendered, all he could see was a path beginning the long walk backward into unknowing, the journey to join his parents and the innumerable host on the other side, the forgotten dead. He couldn't remember all the questions he wanted to ask them, he was so tired. He wished he tried to remember the names of those on the gravestones in the cemetery in case he met them. He wondered if Angeline would be with him at the hospital, and whether she might love him someday. His last thought, though he didn't know it to be the last, was remorse for what he had caused, calling forth a line from a favorite novella by

Theodor Storm, a smallish exit phrase he taught in his course in short fiction: "[A]ll that ought to be seemly has now become sin." Faris always had a good line at hand. And then, nothing.

Later that day, after Faris had been declared dead from loss of blood and Bobby Lee had been treated for a broken scapula, he was arrested and charged with second-degree murder and various lesser charges. He was remanded to the county jail.

The Curtain of Hope

"Bring out your dead," I cry,

And how this must be done

You can, I cannot know.

Instead, I lie here feasting

On your habitual dust

Of sunlight. Slowly I bend

   And sit upright like a man.

    James Dickey, *Lazarus to the Assembled*

CHAPTER XXVI

The day of Faris Turner's funeral, Doreen failed to show up for work. The flower shop was closed, and Rubén professed to have no idea where she had gone. Her car was nowhere to be found, but her clothes were hanging in the closet. No evidence suggested anything suspicious. She would have an explanation. Faris' funeral went forward without flowers, as no one but Doreen had keys to the cooler.

The next day, the ordinarily exuberant mood of the Mt. St. Helen's Homecoming Parade was muted, owing to the murder of Faris Turner and the somber funeral that had carried the whole town along in a stream of grief. Faris' demise seemed to be the final crippling blow to Pincus, at least in spirit. Ethel and Henry were dead. The Dog Ear was closed, as were Turner's Hardware and Plummer's Funeral Home. Emmett Chesney walked around in a daze, leaving the Sunnyside Café in the care of his seriously nutty daughter. Only the deep feeling of togetherness felt by the townspeople at Faris' service reminded them of his hopes for the town, now seemingly in disarray. Their community felt precarious in competition with their individual woes.

Life went on. Parades in Pincus were a big deal. Preparations for the Mt. St. Helen's parade took an entire year, with floats and bands and flowers and bike stands turned into parade route curb barriers. Town leaders wondered whether to postpone the parade but never considered canceling it. Marlon Hockett reminded everyone that the NFL played two days after the Kennedy assassination, which had exactly nothing to do with anything. Still, Mt. St. Helen's was an institution in Pincus, a Catholic bastion in a Protestant town; perennially the best Class A football team in the region; a safe house for white refugees from the public school system; and, thanks to its tuition, an annuity for the diocese. Besides, Marlon had his best float ever for 301 Liquors, a tilted martini glass with a pretty high school girl sitting spraddle-legged on an olive. He bragged about finding an eighteen-year-old who looked sixteen, dancing at a titty bar. He wasn't willing to forgo that, no matter how many people died. The world is for the living, he always said.

The parade itself was a civic event that embraced the whole town. This year was different in many ways, beginning with the much-lamented absence of The Admiral, who always led the parade dressed in a Lord Nelson-style short double-breasted jacket with brass buttons and epaulets. Sporting a vintage bicorne felt hat with a black silk ribbon, The Admiral marched chest out with a little riding crop in on one side and proud salute on the other. The Mt. St. Helen's marching band always played the 1980 single "Funky Town," and the townspeople would cry out a chorus of "Monkey Town," in honor of the little guy. Now, with The Admiral having been left dead in a shallow grave near Pincus Creek, the parade began more conventionally. Tiny children, who lived for The Admiral's appearance each year, whined and cried and asked unanswerable questions.

The event began with the scarlet and gold Pincus High School Band, strutting its way through Parliament's classic song, "Give Up the Funk (Tear the Roof off the Sucker)" with extra brass and percussion.

"You've got a real type of thing, going down, gettin' down.

There's a whole lot of rhythm going round."

Pincus High always showed up the more staid Catholic band in style and color. Then came the veterans, including Jerry Hardcastle, the last surviving Pincan from the Korean War, slumped sideways in a motorized wheelchair.

"You've got a real type of thing, going down, gettin' down.

There's a whole lot of rhythm going round."

A series of clubs and lodges sponsored simple floats, as did LeDonna, who every year dragged out more or less the same float, with hairstyle models and a big hand with painted nails. This year Carmita rode the float, too, though it was hard to see her holding the big hand.

"Ow, we want the funk,

Give up the funk.

Ow, we want the funk,

Give up the funk."

The percussion rattled store windows and vibrated in the chests of children. Pincus Chevrolet always produced a red Corvette for the Grand Marshal, which this year rode empty in tribute to Faris. Most years, a Shetland pony from WILD KINGDOM walked in the parade with a little kid on it; this year did without the pony, which for all anyone knew had been eaten by coyotes in the swamp after its escape.

A new county ambulance van, handsomely fitted with strobe flashers and a European emergency siren, added to the parade. Slowly motoring up the street, it showed off its high gloss finish, flashing lights and occasionally a burp of the siren to startle the crowd, adding to the dazzle of the parade.

With the Funk diminishing into background as it crossed West Street, the Mt. St. Helen's float appeared: a two-story volcano, made out of fresh flowers and crepe paper, mounted on a flatbed truck. The Homecoming Queen's court decorated the lava field, supported by six-foot rebar stations for the girls to hold onto as the float lurched through the street.

The float was Doreen's crowning achievement each year, though she loathed the whole idea. As the town's leading florist, she played a role as other civic notables did. This year the ratio of crepe paper to flowers was higher than usual, as the school budget was tight. Still, Doreen had done a magical job with color, interspersing ashy blue hydrangeas among the white carnations, Black-eyed Susans and marigolds, as if snow and flame and ash were pouring down the volcano's side. She had been seen late on the eve of the parade, adding finishing touches. The sides of the flatbed trailer supporting the volcano were draped with Independence Day bunting, creating the image of a true American volcano.

Traditionally, at the midpoint of the parade, the float stopped and the Homecoming Queen erupted from the volcano's innards on a lift, to great oohing and aahing. Tinsel streamers dangled from the mouth of the cone, sparkling as stringy hot coals illuminated in the sun.

This year, of course, was different.

Earlier, Emmy Jean James, the prettiest girl at Mt. St. Helen's and reigning Homecoming Queen, ascended the stamped aluminum step stool at the rear of the float to enter the small half door to the interior. As she closed the hatch behind her, she fainted dead away without a sound. She had been shocked unconscious by the vision of The Admiral strapped to the lift as if he were Homecoming Queen. Intact and lifelike, his arms held out as if in supplication to the living, The Admiral was ready for the parade, in death as in life.

On cue, Mt. St. Helen's trundled downtown to assume its rightful place on the parade route. Mr. Green from the fertilizer store drove the tractor he had lent to the parade, the high point of his year. As the float arrived at its appointed spot in the middle of town, and the two high school bands joined in a poorly rendered but brassy version of Jackie Wilson's "Your Love Keeps Lifting Me Higher and Higher," upward on the lift rose the dead Admiral, arms outstretched to his fans, stiff as a board, with an odd blush of decay-induced verdigris. A little boy in a cowboy outfit cried out, "Look, Mommy, a zombie!," whereupon he was jerked up by the arm and away to the parking lot. Riding in The Bread Basket food wagon float, Angeline stared into the bright sun silhouetting The Admiral and whispered, "Sweet Jesus, will this poor town's affliction never end?"

After the parade, Marlon returned to 301 Liquors, ready to tell Amy about his float and the weird scene with the dead monkey. He found her crying. Rebel and Tarbaby were dead. Doreen had stopped by the day before and asked Amy to feed them their treats while she went on a weekend out of town. Amy was afraid that she had fed them wrong, somehow causing their death. Without a veterinary pathologist, it would be impossible to tell that the treats were laced with a pesticide used to kill starlings in crop fields. The sheriff was devastated, but consoled himself by embracing Amy.

CHAPTER XXVII

Henry and Faris were dead. Angeline stood alone, shackled between loss and self-abnegation. Personal loss, by its nature, is incommensurable. Angeline had to suffer alone. She had known these men as boys and as lifelong friends. Now, they were gone. She knew she wouldn't have time in life to replicate such deep devotion. She was forever a nun, forever alone. Her service to The Bread Basket was her only remaining comfort.

With Henry's death, The Dog Ear's life as a bookstore ended, too, since no one else in Pincus had the genuine devotion required to ply the waters of a difficult small business. Besides, Henry's death voided his lease with Oscar Turner's estate, meaning that Angeline had an additional property on her hands, consisting of the bookstore space and an apartment above it. It enabled her to execute her vision of a broader set of services for the poor and to integrate those in need with their wealthier brethren in what she called "human fellowship." The vehicle was The Dizzy Pickle.

The reception after Henry's funeral had revealed the bookstore to be a surprisingly adaptable space. With minor renovations it could work as the restaurant annex of The Bread Basket. In a few short months, Angeline received the permits to transform The Dog Ear into a café, which she proposed to open as a "pay what you can" buffet. Using the endowment Oscar had left, she added a modest kitchen, consisting of a range, hood, oven, grill and coolers. She consciously avoided competing with the Sunnyside, which had dropped its buffet in light of Ethel's death and Muscadine's infirmity. She did offer to hire Rubén, their best line cook. In a private meeting with him, she made the pitch. He responded by saying cryptically that his mom could keep books. Angeline saw this as a condition of acceptance. She loved Rubén's protective pride and agreed. He accepted the job for both of them, immediately.

"There's one more thing, Rubén. I'd like to open the café as The Dizzy Pickle."

He recoiled, then lowered his eyes, unable to meet her look. "Then, I don't think so."

"Hear me out. Practically everybody in this town knows you and likes you, but you've had to carry this name around for what, fifteen years? Up to now, it has been a way to tease and bully you. Reverse all that by opening your own place with your nickname on the marquee. No one will ever be able to use dizzy pickle in the wrong way again. This is going to be a quality operation. Your friends will understand, and whoever else is out there will either be ignorant of dizzy pickle's origin or undone by the fact that you've made it your signature on the most generous business model around. You should think about it. I have a lot of confidence in you."

"I have to think."

"I can't offer a lot of money, but The Breadbasket is well-financed, and I'll throw in the apartment upstairs rent-free. There's room for your mother, if you like. Your own place, your own business: What have you got to lose?"

"I have to think." Rubén left Angeline wondering why he would have to think.

Two days later, LeDonna came to see Angeline. She was not happy, and when LeDonna was vexed, most people found it wise to take a step back. Angeline smiled her most welcoming smile, which was not returned.

"Miss Angeline, may I ask just what the hell you are doing with Carmita's boy? She came to me yesterday before the shop opened – you know she's been staying there because that pig of a husband of hers threw her boy out. Anyway, she told me you wanted him to open a restaurant named Dizzy Pickle. Is that right? Could that actually be right? Or did I misunderstand Carmita, because sometimes she's a little confusing with the *inglés*."

"No, that's right. I offered Rubén a job as principal cook at the new café I want to open in the old Dog Ear space. I know he's interested. I also told him we could name it The Dizzy Pickle, to neutralize all the harassment he's suffered over the years. You know, he could own it, so no one could use it against him."

"Well, dear, I always did think you were a daffy old thing, but I admit I had no idea. I don't know whether it's because you've been alone all your life or just don't have any sense at all, but I can't think of how you could put him in a worse spot. You've turned something he'd like into something he'd hate, and you've made him an offer that he's liable to take just for his mother's sake. So, nice going. Is that your version of a favor? What would punishment look like? If you were hiring Stevie Wonder, would you call the place The Blind Guy? Jesus!"

"No, you don't understand, LeDonna." Angeline was surprised and embarrassed at LeDonna's chastisement. "I thought…"

"Honey, I can't believe you thought at all. If this is what you came up with, you have got to get a new thinker. Rubén has suffered all his life over that name, and you think you can make all that disappear by putting it up on a sign? He's had his guts turned upside down, has been bullied and treated like a dog, and now you want to tattoo it on his forehead. He'd do anything for his mama, so he'll want to take the job for the apartment. And he sincerely would die to take this job for himself, too, so you've taken something sweet and curdled it with your damn do-gooder silliness. What in the world? Do you live in a cocoon?"

"Ok, ok. I get it. I'm sorry. What should I do?"

"Well, first pull your head out of them nun drawers and start thinking about other people instead of yourself. And, second, if you do manage that, rethink what you're doing. Rubén is a good boy, and he deserves better. If you want him to work for you, treat him like a human being, not a damn social studies project.

"Oh, and, just so you know, if you cause them to move off and I lose Carmita, I am going to come back here and make you real sad, with a punch in your nose. I am a church-going woman, but I know God will forgive me."

"LeDonna, if you see either Carmita or Rubén, just tell them I'd like them to work with me, and to forget the whole Dizzy Pickle idea. Tell them to come see me. We'll think of something else. Thank you, LeDonna. I really didn't want to do the wrong thing, quite the opposite."

"Well, damn, you got a talent for it, sweetheart. Mother of pearl." LeDonna shook her head and left. Angeline, bruised from LeDonna's scolding, lost herself in polishing the brass doorplate.

CHAPTER XXVIII

In small, shallow lakes, ordinary winds create extraordinary turbidity. Nutrients and toxins flow into the lake and find rest on the bottom, only to rise with the current into the water column, muddying and often poisoning the water. Changes around the lake alter the benthic sediments in ways often imperceptible.

Pincus was that way. To those passing through, the little town seemed impervious to change. Visitors no more knew that The Dog Ear was gone than they could find the turn where the old smokehouse had been. Plummer's and the flower shop were hardly noticeable by their absence, except when those in need had no place to go. In short order, Doreen was forgotten, even by young boys, whose fantasies turned elsewhere in her absence. A few even questioned whether she had been real. But not Rubén.

Pincus was changed. With Faris gone, the string continued to unravel, now without the annoyance of someone who hoped the future might be brighter. Henry had tried to marshal support for continuing the assemblies, or as he called them, "the great call to public dialogue." But Henry had died in public disgrace. Emeritus had only been interested as long as meetings added to his sense of self-importance and provided a stage for his bitter antediluvian posturing. Leo, in shock from his part in Faris' shooting, returned to his seclusion, emerging from the great yellow house on the corner of Hemlock and Landing only to throw small stones weakly at dog walkers allowing their pets to shit in his yard. Plummer was in jail on charges of mishandling human remains and improper operation of a mortuary. Jesús continued the slow, miserable process of fitting a miniature of himself into a bottle.

The Bread Basket expanded into its pay-as-you-can café, minus the offensive name. It was called, moralistically, COMMONGOOD. But it failed, when people realized they could actually eat for free and did so in great numbers. Young people, particularly, liked the free lunch and spread the word through social networks. High schoolers packed the place and left nothing. Often, those in need were unable to find a table. After depleting the funds Oscar had left her, Angeline closed it. The original Bread Basket lived up to Henry's prediction: a slightly down-at-the-heel food bank with an odd placement in the middle of Broadway. Angeline's vision had been private, lacking practicality or custom.

Carmita still had a full time job at LeDonna,'s, where she retreated into her art. Rubén took a job with Animal Control; he and the animals communed, while they awaited adoption or euthanasia. He had a gift for wordlessly talking people into adopting pets, and he visited them afterwards to ensure the animals' safety. Angeline was too embarrassed to ask Rubén to leave the apartment above the former Dog Ear. In time, the parties worked out a reasonable rent.

When Strother died, quietly, while pulling his wagon on a side street, the last dimly lighted path to the spirit world went dark. In short order, no one knew a thing of The Other Side. Trees stopped singing, and no one had an ear to notice the silence. Only Leo was lonelier without Strother, his boon companion and oracle. The spirits were happier, unmoored from the troubles of the living.

Old Ridley finally found his vocational voice at Faris' funeral, invoking the spirit of Oscar Turner, whom he hardly knew, and acknowledging what everyone felt in their souls about Faris. Angeline had given a handwritten passage to Ridley after finding it in Faris' effects.

"And now he sees

All his son's good deeds and confesses that

They are greater than his own, and he rejoices

To be surpassed by him.

And though the son forbids

His own deeds to be ranked above his father's,

Fame, free and obedient to no one's command,

Puts him forward, only in this opposing his will."

(Ovid, Metamorphoses,15.954–60)

With the death of Rebel and Tar Baby, two more symbols of racial division passed from the scene. Marlon refused to blame Doreen, who after all, was an animal rights person and a sweet, flirtatious girl he'd always liked. Instead, Emeritus blamed Rodney, who hated the birds. But Rodney was long gone, resettled in Macon as a grief counselor for a funeral home there. He remained popular with widows.

Hope is the beautiful whore

Whom I followed down the dark track;

I knew her from years before

And she asked me why I came back.

You promised to save me, I said.

She admitted to no such thing;

Save you from what? From life?

From the void death is sure to bring.

After she had me, she left,

Hips waving goodbye with a smile.

I looked down to wipe dirt from my shoe tips

And walked on alone for a while.

Faris Turner, *Fragments of Pincus* (unpublished ms.)

ABOUT THE AUTHOR

Steven Sanderson has lived in the South off and on since the 1960s. He currently resides on an island near Savannah, Georgia with his wife Rosalie, and Spud, the dog of a lifetime

Made in the USA
San Bernardino, CA
12 March 2019